THREE KINDS OF NORTH

BOOK ONE OF THE SHATTERED MOON

JON SPARKS

For Bernie
First, last, and best beta-reader, and a whole lot more.

CONTENTS

1. Jerya   1

Part One: The Way Things Are

2. Jerya   9

3. Rodal   18

4. Jerya   26

5. Rodal   37

6. Jerya   50

7. Jerya   58

Part Two: At the Heart of Things

8. Rodal   77

9. Jerya   86

10. Jerya   96

11. Rodal   103

12. Jerya   108

13. Jerya   118

14. Rodal   123

15. Jerya   131

16. Jerya   141

17. Jerya   149

18. Jerya   158

19. Rodal   171

20. Jerya   176

21. Jerya   180

22. Jerya   190

23. Jerya   199

24. Jerya   211

25. Jerya   224

26. Rodal   229
    Part Three: The Edge of The World

27. Jerya   240

28. Rodal   250

29. Jerya   256

30. Rodal   262

                                             269

                                             270

CHAPTER 1

JERYA

PART ONE: THE WAY THINGS ARE

Jerya moved quickly, climbing the steps almost at a run, hurrying beneath the Dawnsinger's tor. There was nothing to be seen above but rippled and bulging stone, but every time she passed there she felt as if the rocks themselves were watching her.

Just beyond, by two lesser pillars of rock, the path split; but one was forbidden, the Singer's private path to... who knew what? Curiosity burned within her, as always, but there were some rules even she dare not break. She kept to the main path, moderating her pace now, calming her breathing. Above, the moons were pale ghosts of themselves in the bright sky.

The day had begun cool, the stonecourt still in shade, yet Jerya had felt the promise of heat in the air. She bent to her work with extra speed, attending to the ebb and flow of gossip even less than usual. As the heat and glare grew, the women began gathering their things and grumbling their way inside. When no one was looking, Jerya had simply stepped back between two of the great boulders and waited for the court to empty.

At the next fork, both ways were open to her, but today's destination was already settled in her mind. Today the forest called, and she spared only a fleeting glance for the other path rising to the right, towards the moor.

She had climbed that way times beyond counting. On top of the moor her small world became great. Above all she went to gaze on the mountains, watching the day's light shift slowly across their scarred and seamed faces, revealing new ridges or hinting at what lay in the depths of the gullies. Ever and again she had tried to imagine what it would be like to be there.

She knew rock, lived within it, slept in a cell carved from it. She knew all Delven's steepest, narrowest ways, had often hitched up her skirts to climb over boulders and through crevices. Sometimes it seemed that the mountains might be just be the same, only a thousand times higher. If that were all, it would surely be possible to climb them; but something in her heart felt that there was more to the mountains than that.

Whatever the truth might be, she would never know. She could not reach even the base of the mountains and return before night—no one could, not even the fleetest of the men—and the mountains were beyond the reach of Dawnsong. As for what lay beyond the mountains... folk rarely even spoke of that.

Once she had lingered overlong, transfixed as the moons rose over the skyline, the Three preceding the One, chips of light climbing above the sunset-painted peaks. Then she had had to race back to Delven, scurrying frantically down the rough path and through the darkness of the forest. Her aunts had been furious, but behind their ire she sensed a deep fear. To be caught out by night was alarming; to be caught out by night in an Unsung place was the darkest of terrors.

It was midday when she reached her tarn. Jerya needed no Dawnsinger to tell her so; it was written in the light on the surface of the water. Only when the sun stood at its highest could its beams reach down through the canopy of the great trees.

The water was still, but stirrings in the trees high above made the light dance. It had looked just the same the first time she'd seen it: another day like this, heat simmering in the stonecourt. Then, too, the call of green shade had been irresistible. A glimpse of the sparkle on the water had lured her from the path, skirting brambles, twisting between rocks and under a final shielding wing of foliage before that moment of revelation.

The water nipped at her feet, icy after the warmth of the air. But she had learned. She slid full length into the tarn, came up gasping. She wanted to scream, to laugh, but honoured the silence.

Once she could breathe again, she began to swim.

Other women did not swim. Many, she thought, might never have seen water wide enough or deep enough. Some might not even know what swimming was. But Jerya, who read books—who had read every book in Delven's meagre stock—had encountered the word, and deduced its meaning. Having discovered the tarn, she tried it herself. She could put a foot to the bottom almost everywhere, so it seemed safe enough, but it had taken more than one season to find a method that felt right. Now, though, she swam easily, barely splashing. Her hair trailed behind her, lightly caressing her back. She felt weightless in the water, light as a soaring hawk.

She swam for a while, feeling the alternation of sun and shadow, warmth and cool in the water. Then she floated where it was warmest, and tried to think of nothing. But her mind, being *her* mind, immediately threw up the question, *if you think of nothing, are you thinking at all?* And then, *What is nothing anyway?*

She laughed silently. *Questions*, she thought, *always questions*. It was a common plaint of her aunts: "Jerya, why do you ask so many questions?" Once she'd replied, to Aunt Vilina, "I don't know, aunt, but that's a question too!" She'd barely escaped a slap for that.

She looked at a floating leaf, a patch of yellow pasted to the water's surface, and thought, not for the first time: *why do things float?*

It began, years ago, with one simple question: why do sticks float and stones sink? She'd asked Sarria this time, but Sarria only said, "What sort of question is that, girl? It's the way things are." They often said that, an answer that wasn't really an answer at all.

Later she had overheard Sarria retelling it; heard her own name, in all-too-familiar tones (half-amused, half-exasperated), and listened though she knew she shouldn't. "...What she asked me this time? Why do stones float and sticks sink?" Jerya had jammed a fist in her mouth to stay silent. Sarria had mixed them up—and none of the others had noticed! They'd only chuckled, as they often did. Well, chuckles were better than the alternatives. Once she'd asked Hyadelle something and, receiving the usual answer, retorted, "The Dawnsinger would know." Hyadelle grabbed her arm, hard: there'd been a bruise. "None o'that, girl! Never even think it, hear? You don't go near the Dawnsinger, understand? An' if she comes by, you step aside and let her pass. Understand?" Hyadelle shook her fiercely. "You understand?"

"I understand, aunt." But she didn't, not really.

Eventually she'd concluded there was no point in asking her aunts—or the other girls—anything. Not anything... interesting. And she couldn't ask the Dawnsinger, so who was left? Only herself.

Why do sticks float and stones sink? Well, she'd thought, early on: *is it always so?* She'd discovered that, if you were careful, you could take a tiny pebble, the merest sliver of stone, slide it off your finger, and make it float. Looking as close as she could, she'd seen it made a tiny dimple on the surface of the water. But it floated, if you were very careful.

So some stones floated. Later, diving in the deepest place, she found some sticks on the bottom. She collected one, brought it to the shore, noticed its slimy, queasy, feel. It seemed to stay damp even after it had lain a long time on the sand. A word came to mind: *waterlogged*. Another she must have read.

She'd taken a dry stick, one which floated easily, and held it under the water; observed bubbles of air forming on it, breaking clear and rising to the surface. In a small, slow, way they looked just like the bubbles she could make by blowing out a breath under water.

And she'd thought: *water belongs below, air belongs above*. It wasn't right, she knew; 'belongs' wasn't the right word. But perhaps it was a groping reach toward something true.

What else could she do? How else could she... she found, or formed, another phrase in her mind: question-test. What question-tests could she do? A few days later she'd filched one of the lightest bowls from the kitchen-chamber, tucked it into a pocket, and brought it here.

Floating it in the tarn, she'd dripped water into it, seen how it dipped deeper but continued to float, dripped again. The bowl had been half full before it finally tilted to one side and slipped beneath the water. She'd had to dive to retrieve it, laughing at herself, but knowing that if it was lost or broken it would be missed and she would have to own up.

Playing some more—*question-testing*—she discovered that with great care she could place the bowl upside down on the surface of the water and it would float there, sticking right up, only its rim immersed. With even greater care, after several attempts, she managed to keep it there while she dipped her head under and saw the air inside. Its surface, bulging a little, looked silvery, almost like metal; yet when she, with infinite gentleness, poked a finger at it, it felt... well, it felt like nothing at all.

And how did any of this get her closer to answering the original question: why do sticks (mostly) float and stones (mostly) sink? It wasn't that stones were heavier than sticks. A large stick was heavier than a small stone, yet the stick floated and the stone sank. She, herself, floated, yet she was heavier than any stone she could lift. What about a stick and a stone of similar size...? Surely, then, the stone would be heavier than the stick.

Maybe that was the next test. She began to swim towards the shore.

And then... A far-off crashing, loud in the great hush of the forest; a wood-pigeon, perhaps, shouldering through the foliage. Jerya drifted, listening for its crooning call. Instead she heard the crashing again, and then again. It took the rhythm of a stride, someone tramping along the path, not trying to be quiet. Wearing boots, so a man. She floated silently, treading water gently to keep her face in the air, waiting for him to pass.

But the stride stopped; she heard what could only be someone pushing aside the brambles. A sudden cold sick feeling twisted her guts. Two strokes took her into the cold water under the overhanging rock, but what was the use? Her clothes were lying on the sand.

The footsteps halted. Jerya was sure he had not passed the final barrier of foliage. She held her breath and willed him to turn away. "Jerya?" The voice was uncertain. It sounded like Rodal, but his tone was strange.

He called her name again, and slow certainty gripped her: something was amiss. "I'm here," she called quietly. "Wait there."

"Very well." It *was* Rodal; she was sure now.

Standing on the soft dry sand, she squeezed water from her hair, towelled herself with her apron, shook a few questing ants from her garments, her headcloth. Dressed, she turned; some premonition demanded she absorb that image of water dark under sun-strewings, vast green-pillared shade beyond.

Rodal was waiting where she'd thought. He began to speak, then stopped with his mouth open. A long breath leaked from him.

"What is it?" demanded Jerya. Then she realised her hands were full. The blue of her headcloth—washed so many times it was almost beyond blue—was the answer he had not voiced. Looking up again, she saw his eyes trace the fall of her hair.

This, she understood, and it gave her something to do. She wrung out her hair a second time. Then, with the unthinking deftness of a lifetime's practice, she folded the cloth around her hair, wrapped the whole tightly on her head, drew the tail across beneath her chin and tucked it in securely.

Rodal's broad face visibly relaxed. "Come," he said, turning away.

Her skirt snagged once on the brambles. It didn't usually; haste, or something, had made her clumsy. When she reached the main path, Rodal was some paces ahead. "Wait..." she called. He stopped, half turned. "Tell me... what's happening?"

"I don't know."

"You must know *something*."

"Little enough, besure. Holdren wanted you. When he found you weren't with the other women he set us all to searching, the women in the courts and caves, the men afield. And...I've seen you come this way many times."

And found my tarn; my place... "You... Did you...?"

"No!" he protested hotly, so that her suspicions shamed her. "But you've made yourself a path, clear enough to a tracker's eye. You must have come many times."

"I never thought anyone else would..."

"I like to walk in the forest also... Beyond the ridge, on the sunset slope."

That he could share one of her secret loves, feel somewhat as she did, was as unexpected as a miscounted step in back-cave gloom; literally, for she stumbled on the level path, saved herself from falling only by catching his arm.

"I thought I was the only one," she said, quickly releasing her grip.

"The only woman, perhaps," he said, looking straight ahead.

She wanted to grab his arm again, to make him look at her. "And among the men?"

"We all go into the forest, of course. And I don't think the others feel nothing for it. But I think I'm the only one who wanders for no reason."

"No reason? You don't mean that, surely?"

He smiled; he almost glanced at her. "Well... None that I could speak of."

"You could speak of it..." She broke off, not wishing to appear forward, but Rodal seemed to catch the unspoken words: *with me.* He stared bleakly at her, sweeping a hand over his coppery hair.

"Rodal, you *do* know something."

"No. Only a notion... summat in the way Holdren spoke."

"What?"

"Somehow... as if you were going away."

"*Away?* But women don't..."

He said nothing, only glanced at her, level... they were almost the same height, she realised.

A memory surfaced: sitting in the shade with the women, watching the half-naked men wrestling in the sunglow. She had liked best to watch Rodal—but that was usual, most of the women did. Even ones who scarcely glanced up from their needles when their Own-men wrestled could be seen stealing glances at Rodal. Young as he was, he'd gone close to three years undefeated in wrestling and throwing. He had triumphed with the heavy stones too, last time.

She felt her thoughts gathering impetus, like running down a steepening downhill path. What Rodal said about her 'going away'.... how could that be? But whatever was afoot, it was surely better to know than get mazed among unnamed fears.

She stepped on again. The great trees withdrew behind. A band of lighter wood, rowan and larch and sunny tangles of man-high undergrowth, screened the deep forest. Then they came into full sun, day-bleached colours and sudden heat. A butterfly tumbled away, bright as a candle-flame. They crossed flower-deep meadow, passed a row of beehives, skirted threadbare ground where goats were tethered. A stone path, a dodge under the leaning thorn-tree at the gate-like nick in the rocks beneath the tor, and she looked down into the stonecourt of Delven.

The whole village seemed to be gathered, men as well as women. All eyes seemed to follow her as she started down the steps, but it was the silence that made her shiver, in spite of the heat. Now she grasped Rodal's fear.

She halted at the foot of the steps. Rodal darted a look over his shoulder, then stepped aside. Holdren faced her, tall and thin, space around him though the throng pressed behind.

"Come," he said, no more, but Jerya trembled. Behind his headman's gravity she sensed unease. She followed him, back up the steps she had just descended. At the top, just as Jerya was wondering where Holdren could possibly be leading her, he turned sharply to the right, onto the other steps, the one flight in all of Delven she had never climbed.

The breath fled Jerya's body. Holdren was halfway up before she could gather her wits and her skirt-hem and scramble after him.

CHAPTER 2

JERYA

No degree of awe could entirely suppress Jerya's curiosity; she had often wondered what the Dawnsinger's chambers might be like. She knew of old how the topmost rocks spiked up like men standing in a ring, and how the great slab of the songstead rested between them, but the room or rooms below had always been forbidden, mysterious.

Now at last... but her eyes at first saw only gloom, and one splash of light where the sun fell through a hole in the slab. There was no light to speak of from the entrance, where Holdren had closed the wooden door. Doors were a rarity in Delven, entrances usually being closed with heavy curtains of felted goatswool.

Slowly her eyes adjusted. The chamber was about seven paces across; at the far side, sunlight spilled down a rough wooden ladder, which must lead to the songstead. The rest was almost bare: a table, a single chair, a large wooden chest, a single shelf of books above. She wanted to count them—were there more here than the twenty-three she knew so well?—but knew she should take in the rest first.

The stones of the wall were mostly concealed by hangings worked in intricate designs. Jerya saw nothing she understood, but somehow she felt there was more to those patterns than mere decoration. Circles overlapped and interlocked, picked out in gold on blue that was almost black. Here and there were tiny bright disks and stylised stars, the stitching minute and exquisite. And there was one... a larger disk superimposed on a star... what could it be meant for if not the sun? There was meaning in those designs, she was convinced; she could almost grasp it, but she lacked the words to make sense of it.

Holdren, standing by one of the hangings, cleared his throat. "Dawnsinger," he said quietly. "I've brought the girl."

Fingers, bony and crooked, appeared around the end of the hanging, tugging feebly at it. Holdren jumped forward to assist and draw back the heavy drape. There, wrapped in bleached homespun on a low bed, reclined the Dawnsinger.

Jerya stared, forgetting entirely that she should avert her eyes. She had never dreamed that the Dawnsinger was *old*. It seemed impossible that this withered form could be the same one who stood so proudly on the songstead to chant in the days and the seasons and the years—white-robed, erect, apparently unchanging come sun or rain, gale or blizzard.

"Come closer, Jerya," said the old woman. Her voice was low, firm enough, but the world away from the pure sweet voice of morning.

She gestured; Holdren bowed and retreated. Jerya heard the rasp of his boots on the sandstone as he descended, feet whispering to greet him, low, anxious voices.

The Dawnsinger smiled. Her brown face was worn and lined, the hairless scalp mottled, but her teeth were white and sound and her eyes seemed clear. "The people are concerned, then. Perhaps they think that you have been summoned with some secret forest herb to heal me."

Jerya had to swallow hard before she could speak. "Are you... sick, Dawnsinger?"

"Sick? Maybe. But herbs... herbs may help, but that is not why you are here. I believe it is the sickness of age, though 'tis true it has come upon me with a rush, a strange and sudden weakness. These past days I have consumed all my strength in the Dawnsong. I rest for the remainder of the day; all I can do is eat and doze and shit."

Jerya swayed. She almost felt as if the tor itself were tottering, like a great tree about to fall. The Singer smiled. "I suppose you thought a Dawnsinger was above such things? I suppose you thought I would not even know such a word?" She could only nod.

"You'll learn, girl. Once I was like you. I knew those words you won't admit to knowing, whispered them with my friends in corners. I grumbled at my work and wished to escape from it. In a way that wish came true. These hands have not sewn a garment or cooked a meal for more than forty years. A Dawnsinger is permitted only useless work." She waved a hand, vaguely, but Jerya caught the intent: the darkly dazzling tapestries were her own work. *Useless?* she thought. *Hardly useless.* And she also thought: *but there's no loom.* There must be another chamber, concealed behind one of the bright hangings.

"No more, however," the Singer continued. "My eyes are not so keen, nor my hands so nimble. I cannot see you as clearly as I would wish... Go a moment, stand where the sun falls. Take off your headcloth."

Jerya complied. Her hair, still damp, snarled from its hasty wrapping, slumped over her shoulders. Without the sun to kindle its ruby highlights, it looked dully black.

On a normal day, no one saw her hair. She kept it clean because it felt better that way, not for vanity. Its unruliness might have irked her, but she could hide it under the headcloth.

The Singer eyed her with a sad kind of smile. "You have been in water this morning?"

"There is a tarn in the forest."

"Well, my girl, I dare say you may continue to go there. I have my secret places too."

Jerya snatched for a breath, felt only hollowness, as if her lungs were collapsing. There was an awful silence where her heartbeat should have been. The room darkened as if night had come early.

She was on her knees, her hands pressed to her face. Short jagged breaths whistled through her fingers. She stared at the Dawnsinger, who still wore the sad half-smile.

"*Me...?*" whispered Jerya.

"It must be so... Holdren sent word to Carwerid— you doubtless call it simply The City—some days ago, when I first felt these intimations. There is a certain obligation... Delven pays little enough in tithes, and I doubt any can recall when a girl from here was last Chosen. Something must be done."

Jerya did not understand half of this, and indeed it seemed almost as if the Dawnsinger was talking mainly to herself, but she grasped the essence. She started to form a question, then swallowed it. Take away those already wed... and surely a Dawnsinger must be able to read? Who else was there?

"Delven must have a Dawnsinger," she said in a voice unlike her own. "But..."

And she shuffled forward, caring nothing for her knees on the hard sandstone scarcely softened by rush-matting, to hide her tears in the Dawnsinger's blanket. A hand began to stroke her hair, gently sorting its tangles.

"I did not wish it this way, Jerya," the quiet voice said. "I should have had my strength for many years more; I have too long neglected to look for a girl-child to send as a Postulant, but there should have been time to rectify matters. You are older; you surely had your own dreams. It grieves me to shatter them like this. A Dawnsinger in a place like this must be lonely."

Through the haze of tears, Jerya seemed to see in the Dawnsinger's face an understanding she'd never met before. "I don't want to go away. I want to know you."

"Perhaps you will. I may live longer than now seems likely. But you will know me in time, just as I know you somewhat already. You will be what I have been.

"But you cannot stay with me now. I must save my strength to sing in the Dawn for the days that are left to me... even talking to you now tires me. You must go, today, to begin your training. I fear you will have little enough time..."

"Go..." whispered Jerya, forgetting all her contempt for the women who barely strayed beyond the sheltering rocks of home. The faraway prospect filled her with unformed dread, as if she had never read the books that told of places faraway, never felt the longing to see them for herself. *Easy to dream when you've never believed it could come true.*

"It's not so bad, believe me. I made that journey to the City when I was much younger than you are. They told me fifty thousand people dwell there, and I could not even grasp what a number that was."

Neither do I, thought Jerya. How could you count that far? How long would it take?

"Are your eyes keen, child?" She nodded, though the question puzzled her. "Then... if you leave Delven on a dark night, the clearest of winter frosty midnights, away from all man-made lights, wait for a... wait until your eyes grow more sensitive yet... still you will not see fifty thousand stars. Perhaps, with sharp young eyes like yours, a tenth of that number."

Jerya shook her head.

She had done just as the Dawnsinger described—did the old one know all her secret doings? There was no need to go far, after all. She had lain back in a hollow in the rock and watched the vast night wheel overhead until, though she still felt the winter stone chill and hard beneath her, she seemed to be falling *upward*. But she could not hold all the sky in her mind, could not hold the number of its stars; how then could she imagine an even greater number—and of people, too? In all her life she had never seen more than a few hundred gathered together, and that only when the men of Burnslack came to Delven for a wedding. Even that number of strangers had turned her shy, blushing, girlish. *Fifty thousand...* she tried to picture that gathering multiplied a hundred times. Her head swam. "It frightens me."

"It's good that you admit your fear, though in truth there is no hard reason for it. No one would harm a dedicated Postulant, as you will be. And Holdren will send an escort with you, in case of wild beasts and suchlike, though that risk is nowhere greater than in your own forests, and you have never feared to walk there, Jerya, have you...? No, it is not a perilous journey. But you have an active imagination, I think, and your imagination conjures terrors to fill the spaces beyond what you know."

Jerya bowed her head, unsure whether she had been rebuked or praised.

"Come now," said the Dawnsinger. "Help me to stand. We must proceed with your dedication, if you are to have time to reach Thrushgill this night before dark. It's fortunate that it's nearly midsummer, but even so, there is little enough time."

Jerya hoisted the old one easily from her bed. She seemed to weigh almost nothing. Once up, she moved stiffly but unaided across the small room. Stopping by the wooden chest, she made a small bow. Jerya thought it was perhaps an obeisance, but then the Singer straightened again. "I cannot bend so easily. Help me, child... child! In half an hour you will be a child no more, if indeed you are one now."

Jerya wondered what, or where, this 'half an hour' might be; but the answer must wait. The Singer stepped back, giving her access to the chest. It was massively made; it must have taken several strong men to carry it up the steps. Its wood was dark, close-grained, and the metal bindings were purplish-black, like no iron she had ever seen.

The Singer indicated a white-wrapped bundle, bidding Jerya carry it to the table. "Now sit."

She placed a chair squarely before the table and sat. The old woman took a stance behind her, resting her hands on Jerya's shoulders.

"Now, Jerya, you do not know the names of your parents?"

"Forgive me, Dawnsinger, I do not."

"Forgive?" The grip on her shoulders tightened sharply. "It is for you to forgive, not me."

There was silence, brief but weighty. Then, with a sigh, the old woman said: "Repeat these words:

"I, Jerya, daughter of Delven;

"Do solemnly bind myself and undertake to serve;

"The most perfect and immaculate Guild of Dawnsingers;

"The ancient and secret Knowledge of time and space;

"And this my community of Delven;

"Accepting no other loyalty to the end of my days."

Jerya repeated the words dutifully, but each line seemed more burden-some, more confining, than the last. It was all she could do not to falter at 'the end of my days'.

"Now unwrap the bundle."

The cloth held a collection of objects, mostly of metal: some seemed to be pieces of jewellery; the others made no sense at all. The Dawnsinger called for one of these, a kind of knife with a squared-off blade and a bone handle. She bade Jerya fill a basin from a tall jug that stood on another chest, then: "Take that basin and hold it in your lap."

The basin, too, was of metal, something Jerya had never seen before. Metal was rare in Delven, saved for sewing-needles, cutting-edges, arrow-heads, and other uses for which nothing else would serve. Wood, stone, and clay were the mainstays. She found herself wishing it was earthenware; the cold of the water seemed to leak straight through the thin metal into her thighs and her stomach as she clutched it to herself.

The Singer wetted the blade in the water, muttered something incom-prehensible, then grasped a hank of Jerya's hair and sliced it away at the roots. Jerya went rigid, then trembled violently. "Be still, child. It's a shame to lose your lovely hair, but it must be so. I do not want to spill your blood at the same time."

Jerya tried to relax, but could only attain a quivering paralysis. At least the Dawnsinger's hand was steady. She shaved away Jerya's hair with regular strokes, wetting the blade constantly. The shorn locks fell to the floor, lifeless, blacker than ever. When there was nothing left but stubble, she took more water, and something from a pot, and made a lather; spread it all over Jerya's head then plied the blade again, shaving her down to the skin. Not another word was spoken until the task was complete.

"Now," said the Dawnsinger, "Wash yourself. Use the cloth there."

Jerya took up the cloth which had wrapped the bundle and carefully washed her face and her newly denuded scalp. This gave her a feeling so strange it might equally have been horror or delight. To her fingers it was merely peculiar; cool skin as elsewhere, but with no softening of flesh beneath, only the curve of bone. To her scalp, however, the touch of fingers was utterly new and alien. A tremor ran up her body and over her head. She felt sick.

"You will grow accustomed," said the Dawnsinger. For a moment Jerya had forgotten her, forgotten everything but the all-consuming strangeness of her new state. "I had fine curly hair once. I grieved for it too." Jerya heard her numbly. "It's different, that's all," the old woman said. "Not better, not worse, just different... Look at me."

Jerya looked. She remembered, now, that she had always been taught to drop her gaze when the Dawnsinger passed... but things were different now. She, herself, was different, even if she could not say how. The Dawnsinger was old, but she had dignity; and now she was up, her movements had a slow, careful, grace. On her, the lack of hair looked not strange but entirely natural. Jerya could not imagine her any other way.

I am like that now, she thought, or tried to think: it was beyond her.

"There is a robe in the chest," the Dawnsinger said after another interval. Jerya located it, slipped off her old outer garments, wriggled into the robe. The white wool was soft—lambswool, perhaps, from lower pastures, not the more familiar goats' wool—and it was exactly the right length, which seemed odd, for the Dawnsinger was some inches shorter than herself. But if you allowed for the slight stoop, and for the shrinkage of age... it was possible that the old one had once been as tall as herself—'tall as a man', as some of the women said, not meaning it kindly.

The Dawnsinger, too, seemed to approve of the fit; she was smiling softly as she looked at Jerya, and nodding slowly.

"Now... step up to the songstead. Face the sun."

Jerya climbed the ladder, distantly aware of the old woman following with no apparent difficulty. She stepped onto the slab and faced the South, but the sun's hard gaze made her lower her eyes.

No-one had left the court, she thought; and every face was turned up to her. She felt their stares as physically as a gust of wind. Her hand twitched; if she had still been wearing her headcloth she would have settled it more closely around her face and thought no more about it, but now she wondered why. Shame was proper to a woman, or so it was said, but she had always considered herself differently. Only now did she realise how often she had stooped to disguise her height, how closely she had always wrapped up her headcloth... if not for shame, then why?

There was no answer now, but there was no shame either. She stood tall and straight in the sun and looked squarely down at the throng.

Rodal was not where she had left him, near the foot of the steps; he had moved to one side, a little apart. His eyes stared, his fists clenched and unclenched. She wanted to give him some sign, some token of the things she felt, but she could not smile. Her face was locked in impassivity as if it no longer belonged to her.

The old Dawnsinger stood beside her. Now in her voice, though she was not singing, Jerya could hear the sweet power of the Dawnsong.

"People of Delven... I give you Jerya, Postulant of the Dawnsong. Salute her."

They filled the air with an exultant blur of sound, its colour slowly changing as the women's voices drifted in after those of the men, as the children joined in, perhaps not knowing what was being hailed. In all the court, that she could see, only one was silent.

Chapter 3

Rodal

Rodal started violently at Holdren's voice calling his name. He wanted only to be alone, but there was no refusing a summons from the headman.

Folk made way for him, but still it took a little time to thread his way through the crowd. When he reached Holdren's side, a white-robed figure was descending the steps of the tor. He would not look at her. He knew it was not the old Dawnsinger. He kept his eyes downcast as she approached.

Beneath the new robe, she wore her old sandals. A strange medallion hung on a thin chain around her neck. He concentrated on this because he could not, would not, look at her face. Beneath a low dome of some clear crystal, symbols were spaced around its edge; two black needles sprang from its centre.

"Blessings on you, Postulant," said Holdren. Rodal wondered; had he seen a shudder in the body under the white robe? She said nothing. Holdren continued. "All is prepared for your journey. Rodal shall be your escort."

Shocked, he looked up. It was a mistake; he did not want to see how she closed her eyes; he did not want to see the pain flit across her face. It was just too cruel... not intentionally, of course. To anyone else it would make perfect sense, besure.

"I thank you," she said; Jerya's voice, but with a gravity that was unlike Jerya. "I thank you for my escort and... I thank all the people of Delven."

For what? he wondered; wondering too if the words were her own or had been given to her; and then Holdren was close, handing him a packed haversack, and he must attend to his talk about what was therein. Where to go, what to do, who to seek out when they reached the city.

❋

At first they went in silence, the sound of their feet lost among the murmur of the woods. It was a sound as constant as breathing, and Rodal usually paid it no more mind. Now, on his way to new places, he listened with a new ear to the sounds of home, sounds that changed as they went. The soft sighing of larch and pine filled the first woods; on a more exposed descent juniper grew where it could, huddled and dark, all but silent in the light breeze. Here and there a rowan or a dwarf oak gave louder greeting, a faint clatter of stiff leaves.

Below, the trail ran straighter, in one place lifted on a rubble causeway across a green and reed-thronged tarn. A stretch through chest-high bracken, its green still fresh, preceded the lower forest, of oak and ash. Here sometimes the trees closed overhead, with clear dry ground beneath; the air was still, shielded from the wind, but still there were insect musings and the stirring of the treetops.

A couple of becks were crossed on log-bridges—split pine from the high forest, rather than the crook-backed oak that grew nearby—and Rodal found himself beyond the limit of his previous roaming. When you marched steadily it did not take a great part of a day to reach new lands.

He realised then that he had been walking fast—faster than truly needful—simply to keep himself ahead of... of the Postulant. The title was strange, but then she was a stranger, now. She had been a few paces behind him all the way, never making the small effort required to draw alongside even where the path was broad. He was thankful for that. They walked on further, and he did not slacken his stride. There was nothing new in this new country: oak-trees, grass, moss, a faint trail littered with acorn-cups and twigs and last year's mouldering leaves, just like the oak-lands he had explored before.

Time, however, brought them to a dividing of the trail. The left branch swung into descent; the right continued nearly level. Rodal did not know which to follow. He stopped, and the Postulant's white shift and the still-shocking paleness of her head arrived in the margin of his vision. Paler than her face, anyway, and paler far than the hair he'd glimpsed this morning; but Jerya's skin was darker than usual for Delvenfolk, a deep gold like the honey that came from the hives bordering the heather moors.

She was rooting in a leather satchel; he had not noticed, before, that she was carrying anything. She pulled out a paper, studied it a moment. Then, in an ordinary voice—*Jerya's* voice—she said, "Rodal, help me be sure I understand this map."

He had to move closer, to see, but held himself stiffly, to be sure of not touching her. Still, he was aware of her, warm and solid, breathing a little fast. It did not seem right that a Dawnsinger—a Postulant, whatever that meant—should be any of these things.

Jerya—*the Postulant*—spoke slowly, thinking out aloud. "There's Delven—see the name, such tiny writing; a clear hand someone had. There's the steep rocky place, an inch or so beyond. We've come as far again twice, I'd say. This must be the forking of the trail."

She pointed to a branching of brown lines, then traced one of them along to where a cluster of tiny squares was irregularly arrayed under the word 'Thrushgill'. "Thrushgill is our halt for the night," she continued, "So this is our trail. Left is our way, don't you agree?"

He nodded, drawing a sharp look from her. She frowned a little, said nothing, began to fold the map, made a mistake somewhere. He moved to assist. Somehow, accidentally, their hands touched. He felt it like a splash of cold water, jumped back. He swung away from her eyes, but it was too late to conceal the heat that flared in his cheeks.

"Oh, Rodal..." she said softly. "Please... there's no harm done." He did not reply. "Rodal, don't be like this. Talk to me, at least a little."

He remained still, unspeaking, back to her.

"There's no law says you can't speak to me. Holdren talked—talks—to the Dawnsinger." She fell silent then, and this time it did not seem as if she was waiting for an answer. Rather it seemed as if she was thinking over some part of what she had said. Then she resumed, so suddenly that Rodal started, felt his heart race. "Rodal... I know what you're thinking. I'm no longer Jerya, whom you played with when we were both little. I'm a Postulant of the Guild of Dawnsingers. True?" He nodded stiffly. "Well, that I am, so it seems. But I am still Jerya, too. I am not—I don't *feel* changed, not really. I... I know I look different...

"Rodal, please... don't make this journey any harder than it must be. At least have the courtesy... the *kindness*... to answer a direct question."

Rodal turned slowly. Facing her, though he knew it was wrong, he suddenly could not stop himself gazing on her face. The strangest thing was, it was just the same face. Seeing his eyes on her at last, she smiled, the same smile he had seen a hundred times.

But the face he had known had always been framed by a close-wrapped headcloth. And just the once, this morning, he had been startled and shamed and confusingly delighted by the sight of her glossy-wet hair, deep brown burnished by the green-gold forest light. Perhaps all women looked like that, but other women did not strip off their headcloths outside their private chambers, let alone forget to put them on again. Even Jerya was not usually so careless...

Well, all that was gone by. She gave him time, let his thoughts run on. The smile lingered in her face. But he knew that she still wanted, required, an answer. Then, as if guessing where his thoughts had led, she asked again, "Why won't you speak to me?"

He felt commanded to answer, but the words would not come. It was as if she had asked, "Why is winter colder than summer?" It was in the nature of things. How could he answer such questions? How could she even ask?

But to her, he saw, it was clearly not a foolish question. His failure to reply was hurtful; her lip quivered. He was angry then, though he did not know where to direct his ire. How could a Postulant of the Guild of Dawnsingers act like any weepy girl? How could *he* have brought her to it? But, anger or no, he felt her tears almost as he would feel his own, knew he must do something to relieve her pain.

In desperation he fumbled out an answer. "Holdren is headman. He has business with the Dawnsinger. What has a plain man like me to say to a P—postulant of the Guild?"

She blinked. "Rodal, you sweet fool, you've been charged to escort me; you have business with me. Besides, you're no more a plain man than you were before. We're both of us the same people."

He looked again at her and shook his head. "I should not presume to correct you," he began. To his bewilderment, Jerya laughed. It was the same open laugh he'd heard many times; she'd never been one for giggling behind her hand, or a corner of her headcloth, like other women. Gossan, it hurt—but she *was* the same.

She was the same, yet all was changed. Then he saw that the change was as much in him as in her.

Still chuckling, as if she cared nothing for dignity, she said, "How can you win this dispute now? If you can't presume to correct me, then if I say you may speak to me, it must be all right... Or else, I *am* in need of correction, which would seem to suggest that I have not changed so much." She smiled again.

He was too perplexed to answer, but there was some unspoken agreement. They started to walk again, their pace more measured now, and side-by-side.

The oaks that flanked the trail were greater now. The shade grew deeper. The light flickered on and off their faces as they walked, feet silent on the loam. In the shifting light he saw clearly, for the first time, how, though her skin was that golden hue, her scalp was still paler than her face. Her skin, though darker than most in Delven, was not too dark to take a tan.

Presently, seeing that he still had nothing to say, she went on, "It seems to me... I haven't changed: I don't know anything new, no secrets or mysteries.

That's why we're going to the City, to Carwerid, so I can learn such things. Then I suppose I shall change. But not yet."

He thought for the first time how new and strange it must be for her, how sudden. It had all been such a shock to him, such a shattering of hopes and prospects that had barely begun to take shape. How much more shattering, then, must it have been for Jerya? He was suddenly ashamed of himself. "Besure, I'm a fool... To think that we... before this, because we both liked to wander in the forest, to think that we might be a little alike, that we might understand each other... I was a fool then, too. I did not know you at all."

"The other women always said, if I did not mend my ways, I would never be wed—or that at best I might find a husband who would make me change. They never saw that, if that was the only choice, I might prefer to be alone. But you... suddenly I saw it might not be quite the only choice."

"Are you so sure?" If—" It was too late to leave it unsaid, however much it hurt— "If we had been wed, maybe I still would have made you change."

"You might have tried!" She laughed, grew serious again. "Besure, we would have changed. Both of us would. I would not have given the other men cause to mock you. I would not neglect my duties; I never have. And when troubles came, we could have talked... just as I need to talk now. If you will talk with me, then I will be glad Holdren chose you as my escort. If you will not, then no choice could have been more cruel."

There were many things in this speech which Rodal wished to answer, and he did not know why he picked the one he did. "Do you call it trouble, then, your being Chosen?"

She frowned. "Perhaps 'trouble' is the wrong word. But it is not a soft thing, this. So strange, so sudden... I am proud to be Chosen... but who else was there? Yet she—the Dawnsinger—seemed pleased with me. I cannot believe she erred—but it is hard to believe I am truly worthy. And... it's too much, too soon." She darted a glance at Rodal then, quick and shy and half-downcast, as if not wishing him to know that she looked at him.

"Postulant—"

"—Rodal, please! My name is still Jerya. Use it, please, at least while it's just us two. When others are about, then, of course, say... Postulant. But let's grow used to all this by little steps. Like... finding a shallow place to learn to swim, so we can put our feet on the bottom if we need. Don't throw me straight into the deep water."

He gaped. "You can swim?"

"Besure I can."

"But... but how did you learn?"

"I went to my tarn and tried different ways until one seemed right."

"I suppose there's no law says women may not swim. They just never want to."

"This one did!" Then her thoughts must have leapt ahead; before he could speak, she asked, "Rodal, what will you do in the City? Or will you return at once?"

"No, I am to wait, until your training is complete, or until... until we are summoned home."

"I am glad. For myself, anyroad. The City will not be so strange to me if I know you are there."

"But we may never see each other."

"I suppose not. But it will comfort me just to think of you nearby. But you... how will you pass the days? How will you live?"

"I have coin," he said. "You know what that is?"

"Rodal, I haven't spent all my days wandering or swimming. When I'm sitting at my work, I see everything that happens in the court. I have seen strangers come with metal-goods or messenger-birds, and I have seen Holdren give them coin. I may not know the worth of the pieces... but I know what coin is."

"You know much..."

"Oh, I think not. I think I know hardly anything. But I am going to learn..."

There was sense in what she said. She had not changed, but she would. She must. All that learning would change her. And then she would be a Dawnsinger, not a Postulant.

Postulant, he thought. He'd never heard the word before today, and no-one had told him what it meant. What it seemed to mean was someone who looked like a Dawnsinger but still spoke and acted like Jerya.

And who, one day, it seemed, would be Delven's Dawnsinger. Even if he one day rose to headman—it had crossed his mind more than once, and why not?—they would never speak of anything but the needs of the village and the business of the seasons. She would not then call him friend. It was his task to guard and guide her—and, he accepted now, to listen to her, to offer what comfort he could—on a journey that would set them apart forever.

On the way home, when that time came, they would indeed walk apart, and speak of nothing but the necessities. How else could it be?

CHAPTER 4

JERYA

T hey came to Thrushgill in the golden part of the evening, came on it suddenly as they topped a little rise, halted as one and looked on it in wonder.

Neither of them had ever seen dwellings that weren't delved into the earth but raised above it, made of stone that—she saw—must have been quarried some distance away. The village had a green at its centre, a heart-shaped space many times wider than the great court of Delven, level and smooth. The fields lay beyond the river: wide flats, thorn-fenced, quite unlike Delven's scattered plots worked into folds and dimples among the rocks.

"I'll walk ahead of you," said Rodal quietly, not looking at her. "Shall I speak for you?"

She thought briefly. "To start with, aye. If the headman addresses me directly I shall reply, of course." *Though what will I say?*

They walked on down the bare rutted trail and between two of the strange stone houses (*cottages*, she thought, plucking a book-word from memory) into the heart of the village. A crowd came spilling out, men and women and children. The men were mostly bareheaded in the cool of the evening; the women wore light caps, only half-hiding their hair, and instead of shifts they wore skirts and smocks, often in contrasting colours.

In the centre of the green space they halted. One man faced them, lithe and tanned but silver-haired. He was not over-tall, but carried himself as if he were. Jerya did not need to be told that this was the headman.

"Greetings," he said, smiling politely. She resisted the urge to smile back. "Welcome to Thrushgill."

"We thank you," answered Rodal. Jerya managed to conceal her surprise at his sudden gravity. "We seek your hospitality for the night, as we travel to the City. I escort Postulant Jerya."

"You do honour to our humble village," the man said. "All will be made ready. Doubtless the Postulant wishes to pay her respects to our Dawnsinger; may I conduct her thither while you see that the accommodation is to your satisfaction?"

Rodal half-turned, seeking Jerya's approval. She nodded.

"Very well," said the headman. He clapped his hands sharply. "Jasto! Show the Postulant's escort to the Guesting-house. See that suitable food is prepared... Postulant, if you will kindly follow me?"

She nodded again. Just as she'd feared, she didn't know the right words, she didn't have the right voice... but, more than that, she was in the grip of what she had become: a white robe, a shaven head. It was the robe and the shaven head to which the headman spoke, and the robe and the shaven head which walked after him now. Suddenly she understood more clearly how Rodal must have been feeling.

She bore the marks of a Dawnsinger, but she did not know how to *be* a Dawnsinger.

She followed the headman along a side-trail, between two houses then alongside the great river, which must have been twenty yards wide. It was utterly unlike the bright, turbulent becks around Delven. Its slow, dark, splashless, rolling made her think of the flex of muscles in a man's back as he strained to lift a competition stone.

Soon, the river swung away and their way rose. Before them on a knoll stood another stone house, this time two storeys high, with a flat roof or none that she could see. She knew it at once, a crafted reflection of the Dawnsinger's tor in Delven.

The headman halted at a wooden door, rapped twice with his knuckles.

"Enter!" came a voice. The headman pushed the door, stood aside.

"Dawnsinger," he said quietly, as Jerya halted a pace inside. "I bring you a guest."

"Greetings." The voice came from above. There were wooden stairs; there was a floor of wood above her head. Another new sight. Sandalled feet were descending the stairs, then the red-trimmed hem of a white robe.

The Dawnsinger of Thrushgill was a tall woman, taller than the headman, taller than Jerya. She seemed neither young nor old. She had unlined skin like a girl, but her movements were unhurried, certain, like one long past the awkwardness of the years of growth. And Jerya saw that she had been mistaken, for the Singer wore not a robe but a long skirt and a sashed tunic, both of white with narrow edgings of lustrous thread red as rowan berries. Her sleeves were cropped above the wrists, and both arms wore coloured bangles, clattering softly as she moved. On a gold chain about her neck she wore a medallion, much like the one Jerya had been given. She wished the Dawnsinger had explained it, wished she had felt able to ask for an explanation.

The strange Dawnsinger halted at the foot of the stairs. "Thank you, headman." He bowed and left, closing the door quietly. "Welcome, young one. Who are you?"

"Jerya of Delven, Dawnsinger. Newly made Postulant. I travel to the City."

"You're new indeed". The Singer bent to an odd globed lamp on a small table. She made some adjustment at its base and its soft glow waxed brighter. "Look at you! You're quite skewbald. How new?"

"This very day, Dawnsinger."

"Hmm, it would be, I suppose. Delven's not so far, is it? Only at the ends of the earth... But don't stand on ceremony, girl. You're Jerya and I'm Marit. I don't hear my name spoken very often. Give me that pleasure for the few minutes you're here."

"You're very kind... Marit," she said, wondering what 'minutes' were. The word had occurred a few times in the books of Delven, and had always puzzled her.

"Kind? Faugh. I'm just an ordinary Dawnsinger who gets the chance of conversation once in a blue moons... Sit yourself... the other one, that one wobbles. Will you have a drink? They make a passable cyder here... not vintage, not to match what you'll get in the City, but it goes down easy enough... Delven, eh? You'll have been walking a fair few hours, then. Must be thirsty."

"That I am," said Jerya gladly, since she understood that and almost nothing else. Well, she thought to herself, *watch, listen, learn*. It was a motto she'd followed before.

As she settled into the chair, the Singer fetched wooden mugs and a flask from a corner cupboard. The drink she called 'cyder' was a green-gold colour, almost like a pale honey, but it poured as freely as water. Its aroma suggested some fruit Jerya could not name. She sipped cautiously, gasped. The fruity sweetness overlay something half-bitter and half-fiery.

Marit laughed. "Not used to it, eh? Better not over-indulge, then. It wouldn't do to have a drunken Postulant wandering around, would it?"

"I beg your pardon?" asked Jerya in polite bafflement.

"Bless me, your Delven must be even more of a backland hole than I thought. You don't have alcohol there?"

"Oh..." She glanced down at the innocent-looking mug in her hands. "Aye, there's mead, but it's mostly only for the men."

"Oh, horrors! Never do for me."

Jerya sipped again. If the Dawnsinger—Marit—thought it was all right to drink, it must be. It was not unpleasant; perhaps she could grow to like it in time. As she sipped again, it seemed to warm her.

Still, this was not quite like her misty vision of the meeting of Dawnsingers. Even before the shattering events of the morning, it had occurred to her that Delven's Dawnsinger could not be the only one. But she had imagined something altogether more... elevated. White-robed figures moving silently; low, melodious, voices speaking of mysterious matters.

Marit drained her mug and refilled it. "I drink too much of this. Makes it hard to rise in the mornings, and my head rings sometimes when I sing.

But it's my only companion, most days. I used to keep a cat, but one day he didn't come back. Must have met something nasty in the woods." She tossed back half her mug-full.

With every sentence—almost with every word—Jerya was reminded of her own ignorance. It seemed strange that a Dawnsinger, of all people, should find it hard to rise in the morning. She herself—with no such vital duty—was usually wide awake before the first echo of the Song crept into the caves. And how did you 'keep' a cat? The only cats she knew were wild, shy, beasts of the forest. Many of the women in Delven would never have seen one; she herself had enjoyed only a scant handful of clear sightings.

"You haven't much to say for yourself," Marit commented.

"I'm sorry." Jerya felt the rebuke keenly. "That's ever my failing; to talk when I shouldn't and be silent when I should talk... and now no one expects me to talk at all."

"*I* expect it. I hardly care what you speak about. Just to have a conversation."

Before Jerya could speak, however, Marit went on, "It must be eighteen months now since I had a proper conversation. It's all right down in the plains; you'll see a troika of Peripatetics every couple of years at least, occasionally one of the Masters on a Progress. But here... you've only one trail in this valley, and they don't care for it, having to leave the same way they came. Makes them feel they're paying double for the trip, and the tithes are hardly worth the effort—oh, aye, I don't kid myself they come just for the good of my soul. And as for your, what do you call the place, Delven... you can't have had a proper Visitation since... well, I doubt you'd be old enough to remember. Maybe before you were born." She looked at Jerya; really looked at her, it seemed, for the first time since their meeting. "You poor child. How could you let yourself get dragged into this life?"

Jerya did not like the sound of this, any more than she liked being called 'child', but all she could do was answer what seemed to be the question. "There was no one else to send. I was Chosen by default—but she who chose me seemed satisfied enough."

"Oh, you'll do well enough, I'm sure. I dare say it's better than anything else you could have expected... wedded to a loom all day, wedded by night to some unwashed yokel who can't keep his filthy hands off you." She shuddered, emptied her cup, refilled it. "More cyder? No, you've plenty left. Sensible girl... aye, you'll do very well. The unimaginative ones always do."

Inwardly, Jerya bristled. She had always lived half in her imagination. Her aunts had despaired of her 'dreaminess'. And the Dawnsinger—Delven's Dawnsinger—had recognised it. 'Unimaginative', in Jerya's mind, was a term of withering scorn. She had often applied it to others, to those women whose minds could encompass nothing outside their own caves and stonecourts. The stars were nothing to them; they never wondered what lay beyond the forest; they would never creep with a candle to the chest where Delven kept its few handfuls of books, never lose themselves for half the night in a struggle to comprehend those tales.

Marit had misjudged her; had barely seen her, if the truth be told. But she did not know how to protest. Marit was a Dawnsinger; she must be far wiser, know far more of the wide world than she did. Perhaps one who was eccentric and fanciful by the standards of Delven might seem dull and *unimaginative* elsewhere. How could she know...? No doubt the world was not only stranger than she knew, but stranger than she could ever have dreamed. Thrushgill was only half a day's journey, yet already everything was different, in greater or lesser ways. And they had barely even begin their journey.

Marit was still speaking. "I was much younger than you, of course, when I was Chosen; half your age, I'd think; what are you, twenty?"

"Nineteen, I think."

"Ten years and a half, I was, and so proud. Proud when they shaved off my hair. Proud when they took my toys away, and my pretty clothes, and dressed me in plain white for the rest of my life... At ten you don't know there *is* a rest of your life. But *you* must know. Maybe it still makes you proud—even happy."

"I want to learn," she managed.

"Ah, but you'll hardly have time. So much to learn, and perhaps only a few months to do it in... and then, just when you're growing used to that life, you'll be plucked away again..."

She looked up suddenly. Her hand tightened as if to crush the frail turned wood of the cup; knuckles showed white.

"Don't think I'm not a good Singer, girl—Jerya? I am and I still love it. Once I've dragged myself up to the songstead I'm fine. Fine for an hour or two, usually. It's the emptiness of the rest of the days, that's all..."

She banged her mug down on the sturdy low table. "Forget all I've said, please, Jerya. I drink too much in the evenings and it makes me... Mornings are the good time. Make sure you're awake to hear me. That's what I'd like you to remember. You'd better go now."

Jerya rose; bemused, unsettled, but obedient. There were so many questions she wanted to ask, but she could not gainsay a Dawnsinger. Perhaps this was how it was for Rodal, she thought. The same contradictions.

"Thank you for your welcome," she said at the door: she would not forget her manners. "You have been most gracious."

Marit made a low sound that might have been a bitter laugh. "Me? You shame me, child. You're the gracious one."

"You flatter me."

"No, that I do not." Marit grasped Jerya's shoulders, pulled her closer, then planted a kiss on her scalp, a sensation so strange that for a moment she was aware of nothing else. "I almost wish I were you," she said in a confidential whisper. "Ah, but... go quickly. Listen for me in the morning."

She held the door open, almost thrust Jerya out into the cooling night, and closed it at once. Jerya's scalp prickled suddenly in the new chill.

The headman came towards her from the river's edge, where he had been gazing into the dying reflections of the evening sky. "Your pardon, Postulant. There is little enough light. New moons. I was a fool not to bring a lantern. But my feet know the path, and if you follow me close all will be well."

Darkness is no hindrance to me, she almost cried, *Don't you know I've lived all my life in and out of caves?* But his deferential tone had set the cloak of apartness about her again, and she could only dip her head in mute, remote acknowledgement.

Coming back into the village, she saw again the strangeness of Thrushgill. Lights surrounded her: squares of yellow warmth in the walls of the cottages, making a necklace round the dark centre, banishing the evening stars and making the vault of the night as black as the vault of a high cavern beyond lamp-reach.

The headman, sure-footed in the dark, led her straight across the central space, halting before a house which sat with its back to the last embers of sunset. In the opposite direction, the Three were rising (*so not quite new*, she thought), creamy flecks in the indigo night.

"Your Guesting-house, honoured one," he said. "Your escort awaits—and your meal."

"I thank you," she replied, and then doubted if she had done right to speak, but he only bowed slightly. He opened the door for her, bowed again, and withdrew into the night. In the yellow lamplight, Rodal scrambled to his feet.

"Oh, sit down," she begged as soon as the door was closed. "I've been honoured enough for one night. I'm weary of it."

He retook his seat more slowly. "I hope the food will suit you," he said. "I've kept it warm, best as I can, by the fire."

"Thank you." She took a seat while he filled a deep plate with food. It was a kind of stew with fish and mushrooms and various green vegetables, none of which she could immediately name. Its taste was strange, pleasantly pungent, but she could not summon much appetite.

Rodal watched her listless eating. "You must have more," he urged, when she set the plate aside half-finished. "We'll have a long march tomorrow."

"I've no appetite. I'll make a good breakfast."

His eyes searched her face. *Well*, she thought, *at least he's looking at me.* "Are you quite well?"

"I'm all right. There are things on my mind, that's all—how could there not be? It's hardly been an ordinary day, has it?" She was disappointed he did not at least smile. "Ah, well... where do we sleep?"

He pointed to a second door. "There's a bed in there for you."

"And you?"

He glanced down; she saw a couple of folded blankets on the floor, frowned. "No matter," he said stoutly. "I could sleep on less than that."

And so could I, she thought. But she knew that it was no use arguing with him.

"I'll go to my bed, then," she said. It was no good trying to talk: he was too much aware of other folk around, even at a distance, in the other cottages. Anything she wanted to say would have to wait for the morrow, the privacy of the trail. And she was tired; not from the walking; half a day, most of it downhill, was nothing to her. It was all the rest that left her ready for her bed.

She bade him good night and went through into the side-room. No lamps burned here, so she left the door open an inch; that admitted more than enough light for one raised in Delven. The bed was a low, wooden, construction, scarcely less solid than the stone shelf she was used to, but its raised edge surrounded a mattress of—to Jerya—incredible softness.

She sat down, sinking further than she expected, the edge of the bed-frame hooking under her knees. There was nothing else to be done. She removed the medallion and pulled her robe over her head, then her undershift.

The blankets were of softest wool—lambswool, she thought dreamily—lovely on her skin. She wriggled down deep and worked the blankets close around herself. Warmth, and a softness she had never known, enveloped her.

❋

Later, she shifted in the bed. Sleep had come, but not, she thought, for long. The mattress seemed to have collapsed in the centre where her weight rested, forming a kind of valley around her. And it had grown cold. She realised that these upraised houses were like the shallowest of caves. In the deeper places, where Delven's folk slept, it was never either cold or hot, but near the surface, cool and warm came and went with the days and the seasons.

There were no more blankets; she could only try to wrap herself more snugly in those she already had. It was not enough. Cold gnawed at her fingers and toes. She would shiver, wriggle a little, feel warm again for a moment; then the chill would creep back once more.

Of a sudden she found she was crying.

Jerya had cried in the night before, though she could hardly remember what she had found to cry about. In the darkness of those nights it had been her habit to take a strand of her hair into her mouth, draw the rest across her face; there was a kind of comfort in that. Now she had not even that. She felt naked, the stone walls a flimsy barrier against the night.

The cold bit deeper, like her fate; that too had her in a grip that brooked no resistance.

Action seemed to happen to her, rather than springing from her will. She climbed laboriously from the bed, wrapped one blanket around her, trailed the second behind. She pulled the door open with her foot and padded through into the other chamber. The lamps were all out, but there was a dim red glow from the embers of the fire—strange to one accustomed to the utter darkness of the caves. Rodal was a dark bundle, his face a blur of paler grey. He was sleeping easily, breathing with a slow soft rhythm.

Without debate, the part of her that scrupled perhaps asleep already, she laid herself on the blankets between him and the embers of the fire. There was enough room to avoid touching or disturbing him, but she was close enough to sense his easy repose. She pulled her blanket closer, became still, filled her thoughts with the sound and the presence of his breathing, until her own fell easily into time with him, and in warmth and comfort she drifted into sleep.

CHAPTER 5

RODAL

In the half-light, Jerya slept quietly, a faint smile on her lips, calm in her face, one arm thrown across her brow. Rodal sleepily returned her unconscious smile. *It's good to see her at peace*, he thought, and nothing else. He felt not the least desire to move.

But Jerya stirred and rolled onto her back and the shielding arm fell from her face. He saw the nude skin of her scalp; the shock was like a slap in the face. Suddenly, horribly, wide awake, he rolled away. As he did so, Jerya stirred, blinked, and looked straight at him. Her tentative smile crumbled as she saw the look on his face.

Just then, however, the first notes of the Dawnsong came drifting in with the grey light through the cracks of the door. She cocked her head, then stood, wrapping herself carefully in her blanket, opened the door and stood there listening. Rodal sat up to watch, stirred by something, hearing the Song as if for the first time, knowing that it was beautiful.

Mostly, Rodal slept clean through Dawnsong; he could never hear it in his own chamber, but there were days, especially in winter, when the men were up beforehand, preparing to head out to hunt. Still, never had he heard it clear as this. There were other reasons why the Song sounded fresh. Thrushgill's Singer had power in her voice. *Does that make a difference to the Sun?*

Dawn came in a new way, too. On Delven dawns, he had watched the shadows creep down the walls of the stonecourt, day pressing night slowly back into the earth. Here, the light was flung all at once across the level green, throwing long shadows and gilding the spaces between.

The light flew in at the door, making a silhouette of Jerya. Her body was shapeless in the blankets, but her head, half-turned, was outlined in a fine unbroken trace of light. He could not help but see beauty in the smooth curve described by that radiance. It was like seeing her for the first time.

He knew, though, that his delight was wrong; he felt sick at himself. How could a simple, slightly irregular, arc of light have such power, make his breathing falter, make his head spin, make him forget what was right and wrong?

She looked entirely a Dawnsinger, he thought, fixing at once on that observation. Perhaps, on their return journey, she would join her voice to the one he heard now, sing as finely as she looked, sing a Dawnsong to elevate the soul. She would be utterly beyond him then. That would be simpler.

The last notes fell away, but he felt that if his ears were only sharper, the sound would still be audible. Jerya turned slowly, and her face slipped from golden profile into shadow. She came towards him, a dark shape haloed in sun-glow, until she stepped aside, out of the beam, and was Jerya again. But he could not forget; awe lingered in him as he gazed at her.

There was awe in her face also as she knelt near him. But he could not speak, and as they looked into each other's eyes her expression changed. She dropped her gaze, looking into her lap where her hands stirred under the blanket.

"You're angry with me," she said in a small voice.

Rodal was baffled. "Never. How could I be angry with you?"

"You looked angry when I woke."

He remembered then, with a cold, sick, tremor. It seemed a double crime, now that he had seen her in the exalting light. "I was only angry with myself," he lied feebly.

"Oh, Rodal, don't be a fool." The impatience he heard was the old Jerya, pure and simple. "You were fast asleep; I came to you. If any wrong was done it was my fault."

"I don't know. I hardly know what's right any more, besure."

"Maybe I can tell you that. I have taken a Vow, by which I am bound; that is right. You are taking me to Carwerid, to learn what that Vow means; that is right. If we hold to those purposes, the rest is of little import, is it not?"

Her words heartened him, though doubts lingered. Before he could pursue them, however, some flicker in the light made him look up, through the open door.

"Someone's coming," he said, urgent and low. She nodded once, retreated into the other room, closed the door.

A woman halted at the step, bowed slightly. She wore the skirt and smock and curious cap affected by all the women here. "A fine morning. I am Annivel, Headman's Own. He bids me greet you. Doubtless you wish to be starting soon. I bring breakfast for the Postulant and yourself, if you're ready."

"Thank you kindly."

Jerya emerged again, in her white robe, to find their breakfast laid out on the table. There was a pitcher of milk, sweeter than that of Delven's goats; hot, crusty, soft-hearted wheaten bread; golden butter; and a sharp-sweet fruit preserve. They set to, and Rodal was pleased to see that Jerya ate heartily.

"And now we must resume our journey," Rodal said to Annivel, who had waited on the step.

"You're wise to start soon," she said, glancing at Jerya. "Today you enter the Scorched Plains, and it's bad to travel there in the heat of the afternoon. There is no shade but what you carry for yourselves." She looked again at Jerya, who stood ready to leave.

"Has the Postulant no hat?" she demanded. "Surely you cannot mean her to go bare-headed into the Scorched Plains? I fear the sun strikes as hard on a Dawnsinger as on the rest of us. Fiercer, perhaps, when you think..."

Rodal held his own wide-brimmed hat in his hands, turning it around and around. Surely Jerya could not go forth in a man's hat? Yet they had nothing else, and she would need something. Women were more vulnerable to the sun, though Jerya's darker skin might make her stronger than most.

"There was no need, yesterday, on shady ways," said Jerya herself suddenly. Both Annivel and Rodal started. A quiver of Jerya's lips, a faint tremor in her voice, suggested suppressed laughter. "Have you a cloth, perhaps as long as I am tall, and... about so wide? A white one, if possible."

"I am sure such can be found," said Annivel, and bustled away. Jerya glanced at him once, with a strange little smile, then they waited in silence for Annivel to return, the headman with her now. She presented Rodal with a folded white cloth, and he handed it on to Jerya. She wound the cloth about her head in what—he supposed—was the only way she knew; Delven-fashion. Rodal's heart stumbled. Save that the cloth was white rather than long-faded blue—not so great a difference—he saw her again as he had always known her.

With that, and a few formal courtesies, they turned to the road again. Rodal went ahead of her, up a little slope and back into oakwoods. As soon as they were out of sight of the village, Jerya quickened her pace to come alongside him. She released a great gust of a sigh.

"Choss!" she said. "There's so much to keep in mind... Never daring to laugh, barely even to smile, keeping silent nearly all the time, having to say the right things when I do speak... I hope I'm not faring too badly?"

"Nigh on perfectly," he said.

"Ah, thank you! But you didn't see me with Marit. I was plain, ignorant, Jerya again. I didn't know what to—no, I won't speak of that. Let's have a look at the map."

They stopped, bent over the map. "Look," said Jerya, "The way we came yesterday is about the length of my longest finger, and—here—the width of my smallest fingernail... then we pass the last woods and come into the Scorched Plains. Think you we shall reach this place, this Stainscomb, tonight?"

"I see no reason why not." The distance was little more than twice that from Delven to Thrushgill, and near halfway there was a scatter of black dots, the marking of a settlement, though it bore no name. Doubtless they could find food and water and a midday rest there.

Soon the oaks grew thinner, and one or two were dead. There were other trees, too, strange to them, taller and straighter than the oaks—and then, in the space of no more than a hundred strides, they thinned and ended. Ahead there was only the trail, a dusty scar, winding and dipping its grey-white way across a faded rolling land that bore the merest hint of green.

Jerya stepped closer, pressing the map into his hand. Their fingers touched for an instant. "Keep close watch on any branching of the trail. I can see no other way to find our direction in this."

They walked on into the plain. There were ruts in places, as if the trail was sometimes muddy, but few other signs of use. They saw no one, nor any creature save one distant herd of horses. Rodal had seen horses before, once, and was able to tell Jerya what they were, and that men in some places rode astride their backs. But there were no men with the beasts here, and he thought they must be wild.

"It seems a shame," she commented, watching the horses run lazily, disappearing over a crest into hidden immensity. "They look so fine like that, wild and free." A shame to ride them, he supposed she meant.

The sun climbed. The trail wandered on, never the same, yet never really changing. From occasional slight rises they could see only a featureless sweep in every direction. The horses had vanished; there was only emptiness, and a pressing silence.

At one such crest, after they had drunk a little water from Rodal's flask—which was running low—Jerya suddenly clasped his hand as they walked on again. "This place—this *unplace*—frightens me," she said. She had hardly spoken since entering the Plains.

Rodal looked down at their joined hands. He was unnerved also, and was glad she had had the bravery to admit her fear. So long as no one saw them, he was glad to hold her hand. It made him feel stronger. "We must come to that midway settlement soon, besure," he said. "We seem to have been walking a long time."

Jerya glanced up, then winced away from the sun. "It's short of midday yet," she said. "It just seems longer. There's nothing to judge distance by in this land."

"Still, we should see that place afore long. Perhaps just beyond that next rise."

Walking on perhaps another thousand paces, they came over the rise and saw a brown stream and trees and stone houses below them, not ordered as at Thrushgill, but sheltering wherever the trees grew.

"Not much of a place," said Rodal, releasing her hand.

Jerya smiled, and he saw her thought; how many places had he seen, to judge? But she only said, "Still, a welcome sight."

He started down ahead of her. They had stopped on the skyline, would have been visible from the village, but no one came out to look at them. Nothing moved at all. An awful suspicion began to gnaw at him.

As the ground levelled, and they neared the first buildings, Jerya moved up alongside him once more. "Now we know why this place has no name on the map." Her plain acceptance left him abashed. He had been close to hollering out, running from house to house in rootless hope of finding someone. Jerya had gone straight to it, faced it: the place was dead.

They went on, hands clasped again, into the centre of the empty village and the welcome shade of the trees, though their leaves were faded and brittle. Where the doors had fallen or rotted, interiors had become choked with rank vegetation like pale dry brambles. Other doors still stood, equally uninviting. The clay blocks that made up the walls were beginning to crumble, revealing paper-dry straw that had once helped bind the clay.

They sat together in the shade with their backs to a tree and drank the last mouthfuls of their water. "There may be a well," said Rodal. "If not, we'll have no choice but to drink from the beck. It looks vile, but we surely cannot go on as far again in this heat without something."

"Then let's search," said Jerya, hauling on him to get to her feet. "Now, before it gets too easy just to sit here on and on."

They separated to search more efficiently, Rodal heading away from the river. At the foot of a little slope, close to the road, he found a well under some trees which leaned in around it. There was a bucket, too, but the attached rope was bleached and rotten, a few strands crumbling at his touch.

It might bear the weight of a lighter vessel if we had one, he thought. *Or I might climb down and up again. It's not so far.*

Then he heard a cry. Jerya came running up. She had stripped off her headcloth to improvise a sort of bag in which something weighty was slung. On her bare head a faint sheen of sweat glistened in the sun, dulled as she came into the shade.

"We won't starve, at least," she crowed, panting lightly, flushed with exertion or excitement. "Look..." She held open the cloth to show him the heavy golden fruit; round, blushing. "There are some berries too. I didn't pick any, I thought they'd just be crushed if I carried them with these, and make a mess of—"

Then she saw his face and stopped, biting off the happy flow of chatter. "Choss!" she swore. "I forgot... for a little time I actually forgot. And I had to show you this and remind you."

Rodal had nothing to say. He turned again to inspect the well.

He heard Jerya lay her bundle on the ground and come up beside him. Her hand crept shyly into the crook of his arm. "Please, Rodal. There's no one to see... That's why... It's more lonely here, where folk once lived, than out in the middle of nothingness. I realised we could die here, without food and water, lie down and die and no one would know. What does it mean then to be Postulants or Escorts or whatever?"

She wrapped her hand more firmly around his arm. Rodal did not move, did not pull away or push her off, but he tried to feel nothing. This closeness was everything he most wanted and everything he most dreaded.

Too soon, and yet not soon enough, she released his arm. With renewed, perhaps forced, briskness she said, "I've found food and you seem to have found water. Things could be worse."

"Then again, they could be better." He explained the problem of the rope. The only other vessel was Rodal's flask, and a moment's thought showed that it would just float uselessly, its mouth above the water. "There's only one thing for it."

So he began to climb down, back against one wall, feet planted in opposition. Someone—it might have been Holdren—had shown him this way of climbing, as a way to reach certain birds' nests. The bucket swung from a loop of rope, doubled and doubled again in hopes it would be strong enough, about his thighs. Descending was easy—he'd done much worse on the rocks behind Delven—but on the return, the swinging weight of the bucket, even barely half-full, made each move both more strenuous and more precarious. The crumbling mortar held the stones of the well-shaft only poorly; many shifted as his weight came onto them. He tried to reason that the pressure he applied would push them more firmly into their sockets, but his heart was in his mouth every moment. Jerya hovered above, waiting, no doubt hating the helplessness of her part; as soon as he came close she was leaning perilously over the parapet to take the weight off the rope.

He sprawled backwards over the wall, knocking a stone from its crest, and sat heavily on the ground, panting. Jerya knelt before him, took his hands briefly in her dry grasp. This time he was whole-heartedly glad of her touch.

In a moment she handed him the flask, full of well-water. It was a little stale, but fresher than the last dregs of the flask had been, and his need made it as sweet as any drink he had ever tasted.

"Ah, thanks," he said, breathing more easily, sitting up straighter.

"Thank *you*," she said, amused. "Yours was the hard part."

"Who found the fruit...? I'll try some now, if you think it's safe."

"It has to be. Who'd let poison trees grow in the middle of a village? Anyroad, I tasted one as soon as I found the tree. It's fine. It tastes like the *cyder* I had, back in Thrushgill."

They ate a couple of the fruit each, packed half-a-dozen more into her satchel and his pack for the journey. On the way out they picked handfuls of the berries she had mentioned; they were a little like blackberries to look at, but rosy-red, juicier, and sweeter.

The water of the beck was opaque as a broth, and there were pale crusts on the stones alongside; he cautiously dipped a finger, and then his hand, before deciding it would be safe to wade. They forded with care, holding on to each other, but happy to soak their clothes above the knee. Jerya doused her headcloth before winding it on once more.

As they started up the slope beyond, between the last of the trees, Rodal glanced back. "I wonder how this place came to die. I suppose..."

He broke off, but she was too sharp. "You suppose their Dawnsinger must have failed them?"

He nodded dumbly. The image of Delven dead and empty like this was one he would prefer to keep to himself, and to his relief Jerya did not seem to catch on to it. "And yet," she said. "The sun shines here—and strongly, too, though we're far from anywhere with a Dawnsinger. Almost as if it were too much sun which killed this place, not too little. You'd scarce think of that in Delven, would you? Never dream there could be such a thing as too much sun."

Then she was silent, fallen into thought, and they walked on up an easy slope that felt steeper in the heat. The half-dead trees and the wholly-dead village slipped out of sight. The afternoon of the Plains grew like a great colourless flame around them.

Time dragged. They hardly spoke save, briefly, when they took more water or another fruit, savouring them more for juice than for flesh. Nothing seemed to change, except the slow descending arc of the place at which they could not look, a blazing white wound in the sky, as if the sun were swollen far beyond its normal size.

"I know now what you meant by 'too much sun'," said Rodal once; he had just taken a sip of water, and his voice came almost naturally.

Jerya's, however, was husky, barely recognisable. "Why's it so cruel? I go to serve the sun, to learn her mysteries... But how can I...?" She glanced up, flung an arm hastily across her eyes. "Rodal, do you think... it doesn't want me? It's telling me to go back?"

"I don't know," he said. Thought came slow and clotted. "I can't read it; it's not for me to say. And you... your Vow."

"Aye... my Vow." That was all she said, perhaps all she could say, but he sensed it was a burden to her. He had no comforting words, could only offer the debatable comfort of a squeeze on her hand.

They had stopped, and he hadn't even realised. He looked around. There was scarcely an undulation in the ground now to relieve the uniformity. The world had no edges, merely fading at some unfathomable distance into a haze which blended earth and sky. There was nothing in any direction but a single dead tree, a white skeleton. He couldn't tell if it was small and close or large and far-off.

Suddenly he no longer knew which way they had been walking. Panic nibbled at his balance; he swayed, staring wildly at Jerya.

"It doesn't do to stop," she said, and walked on.

He stumbled to catch her, grab her hand, fall back into the plodding rhythm. In a moment he forgot his doubts. Delven, Thrushgill, the far-off City called Carwerid; perhaps they were walking away from them all. It didn't matter. They were no longer real.

Reality... reality was a litany of discomforts. His feet pulsed with heat, as if he were sitting too close to a fire. Blisters, he supposed, but as time wore on the pain seemed to spread but also to grow duller. It seemed impossible to speed up or slow down, and he knew that Jerya had been right; it did not do to stop. Next time, they might not start again.

The yellow fruit hung uneasily in his guts, but he felt as if he had drawn no sustenance from it. His mouth burned with thirst. His hands and forearms, uncovered, were near as red as if he'd stumbled among nettles.

He looked at Jerya. Her darker skin perhaps gave some protection, but still there was a flush in her face, where the headcloth gave no cover. He saw now that a hat like his own would have been a better choice. Some things were surely more important than decency.

He forced himself to speak. "You should cover your face. The sun's burning you."

She glanced at him, nodded, released his hand to re-wrap the cloth, winding it across her face, pulling it low on her brow, leaving only a narrow slit to see through. After that they spoke no more. Rodal's thoughts drifted back to the hills and rocks and forests of home. He was walking with Jerya, hand-in-hand (he could feel her grip, so it must be true), down to the tarn in the soaring shade. She was pulling off her headcloth, shaking out the tumbled loveliness of her hair, a sunbeam waking garnet glints in the black. Then he dived and cool water cried welcome all over his body. Again and again he felt it close over his head, felt it slide all down his body.

When next he saw his true surroundings, their shadows had doubled their length. Slowly he realised that what had dragged him back to reality was a sharp tightening of Jerya's grip. She turned to face him. The cloth had slipped down her face a little; from the shadows her eyes drew his fiercely.

She tried to speak but could not, pointed along the trail instead. Not far off, scarcely softened by the distance-haze, rose a line of low hills, a fringe of trees at their feet. He pulled the map from his pocket, but at first could see nothing but a jittery muddle of colours. Then he had to take a drink, a trickle from the near-empty flask, before he could speak. "Those are the hills behind Stainscomb, if I can still read this. We're almost there."

She took a drink in her turn, enough to moisten her lips. Then she put a hand on Rodal's neck, drew down the cloth covering her face, pulled him close and kissed his cheek. He felt as if the settlement, as yet unseen in the trees, must be watching, but he had no strength left to resist.

They walked on. Freed from his dreaming daze, Rodal knew now how tired he was. That last short distance was the hardest of all. When they drew near enough to see houses under the trees, they separated without a word. He went first, Jerya followed.

They came into shade. A dog barked. A half-naked child playing at the foot of a tree looked up, startled, ran off yelling. As at Thrushgill, a crowd gathered in no time. The people here were more subdued, doubtless wearied by the heat, though the tree-shade felt deliciously cool to him. Their clothes were similar, but more worn, sometimes patched. The women wore headcloths, but often they were draped carelessly, revealing much of their hair. They milled and stared and no one came forward to take charge and welcome them.

As he came among them, Rodal felt the stubborn strength that had carried him across the Plains dissipate like smoke in a breeze. He stumbled; hands reached out to catch him. He sagged into their grasp, heard Jerya's anxious voice. She was there. Then there was nothing.

❋

He was lying on something soft, someone mopping his brow with a damp cloth. He wanted them to continue forever.

He opened his eyes more from duty than desire to do so. Jerya was bending over him. Her face was stained a rusty red, sharp contrast to the honey-hue of her scalp. "Don't try to sit up," she said. "They said to make you do everything slower than you want to. Here... drink a little."

He sipped cool water. It was impossibly good. She pulled the cup away before he was ready, stifling his protest with soft fingers. "A little at a time, they said. More soon."

He struggled again to sit, and this time she helped him, rearranging cushions behind him. His head creaked at every movement. He was glad the light was dim. Looking around, he saw a small chamber, with but one door, closed. A small window was the only source of light. Outside it seemed to be still day.

"How long have I...?"

"Four days," she said, then laughed in quiet delight as she watched his face. "No, teasing; it's the same day."

"And you? You're well?"

"Just tired. Oh, aye, very tired... but they say the sun is kinder to women. It's not what we say in Delven, but these folk see more of it than we do, besure. And... well, why *are* Dawnsingers women?

"Anyroad, I've had a little food. I didn't want much. I'll have some more, if I can, with you, when you're ready. It's plain fare. They don't have much here, I reckon; I wouldn't ask for more than they could give."

Suddenly he laughed. There was ease in his limbs at last, which seemed reason enough for laughter. "Escort? What use am I to you if you end up looking after me? What kind of an escort is that?"

"Only the best," she said, pressing his hand firmly. "You never faltered, not till your task was done. I could not have crossed those plains alone, besure."

"Choss!" he said with a yawn. "No more could I, I reckon."

"But you would not have had to, if not for me," she said with a smile. "Yet... I'm glad to have shared this journey with you, Rodal."

She smiled, but her eyes strayed away from his, and he guessed her thought: *This, if nothing else.* It would soon be over; once he had delivered her to the City, there would be no more sharing of any kind.

He knew it was wrong—and perverse, for who could wish to endure such a day again?—yet he found himself wishing the journey could go on and on.

"I doubt I'll be fit for much tomorrow," he ventured aloud, almost in hope.

"No need," said Jerya. "From here there is a cart-road—you know what that means? They say there should be one—a cart—passing tomorrow. No more walking for us, Rodal; tomorrow we ride!"

CHAPTER 6

JERYA

T wice already that day, Rodal had leaned forward eagerly and asked, "Is that the City?"

Each time, Jerya had held still and kept silent, yet had felt a quickening of the heart and wrenching emptiness of the stomach at the distant appearance of towers and walls and roofs more numerous than geese overhead in autumn.

And each time the driver of the great creaking cart had laughed negligently and said, "Just a little town, my lad. When you see the City, you'll know," and Rodal had subsided back beside her on the load of bales of wool, flushed and sullen and slow to be cheered by the secret comfort of her hand on his.

Now the great horses—they were the largest creatures Jerya had ever seen, tree-solid, with great shaggy feet and gentle eyes—now they strained a little as the cart rumbled up a white road slanting across a line of green smooth hills that had swallowed all view ahead.

On the slope above them rode the shape of a great white horse, taller than any tree. Jerya and Rodal had stared at it, then at each other, unbelieving, until they came close to the horse's hindmost foot and saw that it was simply the bare white stony earth of the hillside stripped of its turf. An answer—and a different mystery.

The gradient began to ease as the road neared a notch in the long ridge. All at once the land opened and their eyes fell into sudden distance, a great valley, a bright haze beyond.

"That's the City," said Rodal, certain this time. "That's Carwerid."

"Aye, lad," said the driver, not looking back, beginning to guide the cart down the slope. "And a fine sight it is, from here."

Jerya hardly heard their exchange. All her thoughts flew with her gaze across the distance into the pale golden uncertainty of distance. The City of Carwerid stood astride a silver thread that must be a great river. In its outer reaches it was simply a dark stain on the haze-paled land, but in its centre it took on height and solidity, thrusting up towers and spires that seemed like craggy outcrops, too vast to be the work of human hands.

She had ample time to absorb the picture as the cart crept down the slope, no faster than they had climbed. The driver kept one red, massive, arm on a lever—the 'brake', he called it—which forced iron-bound blocks against the wheels to slow their progress. The horses shuffled patiently in slack traces.

Then they came into low lands again and the view was lost; the City almost disappeared. Only now and then, when no trees intervened, could they glimpse the tallest of the towers, like stains on the sky, like distant thunderclouds in everything but the regularity of their outlines. The cart rumbled on and those outlines seemed scarcely to swell or draw nearer. That could only mean, thought Jerya, that they were still more huge and more distant than she had first guessed, almost indeed as tall as thunderclouds. It was hard to believe that such things could be, harder still to sit in decorous silence, as if such things were commonplace.

She itched to talk with Rodal, share her feelings at these new sights. Indeed, to say almost anything might help ease the tension that was growing in her, but they could not chatter in the carter's presence. Perhaps it wouldn't have been possible anyway; even walking down the wide, now-level, road they might never have felt sufficiently alone. If there was no one on the road itself there was someone driving a waggon down a side-way or tending some strange crop in the endless fields. Even when there was no one in sight, there were constant reminders of people; tethered animals cropping the grass of the verges, rough wooden fences, trees with half their branches lopped, boards on posts by the roadside proclaiming that eggs or fruit were for sale.

Before the City, they passed through a band of woodland, oakwoods reminding her of the first stage of their journey, though the ground was level and the trees were fat-trunked and far-spreading. There was no distance here, only trees and broken sky and shade, until a sense of something looming over them grew undeniable, and Jerya thought of thunderclouds again and expected the sky to turn dark.

Then the trees ended, and hooves and cartwheels made a sudden booming racket on a wooden bridge flung across a wide straight water, still and green as grass. At the far end of the bridge twin towers leaned over them. Perhaps they were not truly as high as the clouds, but surely they were taller than the tallest pines. Rodal craned back his head and stared up at hanging stone, but Jerya knew she must act now like one who has seen all things before. She sat erect, but still she looked about her, as best she could while barely turning her head.

In the shadows of the gateway, one to each side, stood men fierce-featured and beardless, seeming to stare at each other even through the opacity of the great cart. Their clothes were the strangest Jerya had yet seen, fashioned of metal as if it were cheaper than wool. Their domed and spiked hats were of shining steel and over leather coats they wore linked plates of the same bright metal. Each held a wooden staff with a metal end-plate somewhat like a vastly oversized knife-blade. Only their eyes revealed that they were living men.

The cart rolled into light again. The Postulant sat unmoving, as if her white robe had turned stiff as the metal suits, but the Delven-girl within her wanted to shrink and cry out and clutch at Rodal as a storm broke around her: a storm of sights and sounds and smells: the City.

The cobbled street was little wider than the main court of Delven, but crowded into it were more people than Jerya had seen in all her life together. She recalled the Dawnsinger's figure of fifty thousand. It seemed as if most of them were here. It was like nothing, she thought, so much as a broken ants' nest. People were hurrying—or trying to hurry—in every direction, pulling and pushing, squeezing and shoving. It was hard to see how anyone could make any kind of progress through the seething chaos, let alone how the space could appear for their broad cart to push through, but the driver chewed casually, as he had throughout, and kept tickling the horses forward. The crowds parted so late that to Jerya's bewildered eyes it seemed as if people simply disappeared under the feet of the horses. She glanced back—she could not help it—to see if there was any trace of their passage, but the load behind her was too high. And then she sensed Rodal stiffening beside here, and knew that she had forgotten herself. More truly, perhaps, she had remembered herself and forgotten the Postulant.

She fixed her gaze forward again. Under the guise of impassivity she studied as many of the people as she could, but she could form no general idea of them. There were too many, they were too various. It had not been so at Thrushgill, nor at Stainscomb nor—so far as she could tell—in any of the villages or towns they had passed through on the days they had ridden on one carter's waggon or the next. In each, the people had their own look, their own typical colouring and cast of feature and their own ways of dressing. Here in the City, however, no two seemed to be alike. No one looked ordinary to her, but some caught her eye more than others. At some it was hard indeed not to stare.

All her life, she had been the darkest in the village. It was, perhaps, another thing that made her stand apart, but no one made great play of it. There were other things to task her with; inattention at her work, asking impertinent questions, 'wandering off', staying out past nightfall to gaze at the stars.

She had never really grasped, until she saw her close, that the Dawnsinger was also darker than the rest of the Delven-folk. On the days of their various rides, the nights in villages and towns, she had seen people darker still, all the way to the colour of roasted chestnuts. Now, in the teeming streets of Carwerid, she saw a man who might accurately be called black. But it was his size that truly seized her attention, scarcely less tall than their horses.

Even at a distance his head stood out above the mass, so that when they drew close it was almost a shock to see that he had a body and limbs like other men, only impossibly elongated.

She recalled how they had burned in the Scorched Plains, the mark that, though fading slowly, still stained her own face. Was it simply that some people had taken too much sun? Had the people fled the dead village because they were turning black?

But it could hardly be that there was too much sun here, in the City of the Dawnsingers. There must be some other explanation... Then again, she told herself, the variations in colour might have no significance at all.

As she looked, and wondered, she heard a chime ring out from somewhere unseen. *Bells*, she thought. There were no bells in Delven, but she had heard them in the towns of the last two nights. In a private moment she had spoken to Rodal, and when he got his chance he had asked the name, and that was one more word from a book made real. She had learned a few things that way, learned many more by following her own precept: *watch, listen, learn.*

The bell sounded again, and again. She counted; five chimes in all. Something about the sound told her the bell must be large, but it didn't come loud to her ears. Its source was not close.

The last chime died away, and the sounds of the City filled the space. She could pick individual faces from the mass, but not voices; there was only a roar of sound, like a waterfall. In the same way, the smells of the City were blended; man-sweat and the sweat of the horses; filth and flowers; boiling greens and frying fish.

Then, squatting at a corner, in a space marked out as clearly as if walled by the avoiding steps of the crowd was a man—she thought—a figure at whom she was glad not to look twice. One glimpse had shown her legs twisted like old oak boughs, and an empty eye-socket. Between those distorted legs a bowl held a few small coins.

The cart ground up a little twisting rise and stopped. Jerya found herself gazing across a wide space like a vast stonecourt, walled in by many-windowed buildings with stepped or pointed gables. The square was full of gaudy canopies; from her high seat she could not see what was beneath them. Then Rodal said something, and helped her down, and the City surrounded her, and she could see only a few yards.

Suddenly the people, so strange and so motley, were all around, close enough to touch, though none did; perhaps her shaven head and white robe won her a little extra space. Still, it was all she could do to stand quietly, hands clasped in front of her, and resist the urge to fend them off.

But Rodal was speaking to her, she realised, waking with a little start. "I have been told which way to go," he said, or repeated. "If you will follow me."

His face had been a formal mask, no more revealing than his broad back, which she now followed into a tight lane between two lines of canopied stalls. She realised quickly that they were places for trading; she had seen things of this kind several times in the past few days, but never more than a handful together. Here, she thought, there must be hundreds, and they bore goods of every description. Voices, their words indistinguishable, argued furiously over price, quality, whatever it was men argued about when trading. And then she saw, with only a small shock—her capacity for shock was almost exhausted—that there were women too, both buying and selling.

On her right were bolts of bright cloth, lustrous as the sheen of a magpie's wing, in every colour of the rainbow and more besides. Then, on her left, on beds of ice dripping steadily onto the cobbles, lay familiar fish and strange ones, and creatures like crayfish but as long as her forearm. A little further on, another stall was draped in dark green fabric to set off its array of brilliant metal ornaments. Before it, on the ground, were baskets full of objects she could not identify; some were large as a dog's head, others no bigger than a larch-cone, but all were shaped in folds and convolutions, sometimes smoothed like river-worn stones and shiny as such pebbles were when still wet; others were spiny as a hedgehog or dark and gnarled like hawthorn bark. She could not fathom their origin or possible use, but as they stood before the stall, halted by some random knotting of the crowd, a barefoot boy, perhaps eight or nine, plucked one from its basket and held it to his ear. A rapturous look settled on his face. She ached to know what it was he heard.

They moved on along the cramped and jostling lane, where light and shade alternately flickered like a wood-path at home—the only similarity—until at last they emerged into relative calm on the far side of the great court. Here for a moment Rodal looked uncertain, glancing one way and the other, but then made off sharply to the left. Jerya understood, somehow, that she was not supposed to run, but neither should she call out, so it was with relief that she saw him recall her, glance back, slow his pace.

Shortly they turned out of the square and into a narrow way between high blank walls, shady and cool and blessedly quiet. Almost at once it began to rise, but hesitantly, in an irregular succession of steps and inclines.

The walls were as high or higher than the Dawnsinger's tor in Delven. A few small windows looked into darkness or blankly mirrored the sky. Doors or gates were few and far between. In odd places there were little corners left by some misalignment of the walls, and here there might be a patch of grass, a few straggling flowers, even once a tree clinging to the last of its blossom.

Finally they halted. The lane levelled out for a short way, and on their right was a break in the walls, revealing a view back over the lower City, the river curving around it, the field-chequered lowlands. To their left, beyond a low wall topped by an iron fence, wide lawns rose. Between them a long flight of wide, shallow steps climbed to a white building on the hilltop. At one end, slightly apart, was a stone tower, and in an aperture below its summit she saw a great bell. *The one she had heard?* She could not know, but it seemed likely.

"This is your place," said Rodal in an odd, hushed, voice. "I can take you no further."

Jerya gazed up, through the iron foliage of the gate, to the unpeopled steps and inscrutable walls above. She knew not what to say.

"I'll take my leave, then," he continued stiffly. "I'll send word when I am lodged, so that you may summon me when we must return to Delven." With that he began to turn away, but then swung back. "I should give you this." It was the white cloak she'd been given, which he'd carried in his haversack all the way from Delven, Jerya's satchel being too small.

"Wait!" cried Jerya. He turned back, but his face was set, in disapproval or embarrassment. "A few words won't hurt, besure. We can't part so... Rodal, it may be useless, but so much of me wishes it had been otherways. How can I say, now or ever, all that I feel?"

"There's no need." He mumbled, as if terrified of being overheard, though there was no one in sight. (That was strange in itself, when the streets below were so thronged.) "I think I know. Feelings... good in themselves, but they don't mix. Like the wrong foods in the same dish."

"I can't say it better than that. All you leave me to say is... thank you, Rodal."

"Choss, for what?" he asked, amused in spite of everything.

"I doubt I know. Perhaps... perhaps just for being who you are."

He stared, then. It was only an instant before he turned away, but the moment seemed long to Jerya.

Head high, he went back down the way they had come. Jerya watched him through shadows and narrows of sunlight until the twist of the lane concealed him. Then she grasped the gate, pushed it open with a grating squeal, and started up the steps.

CHAPTER 7

JERYA

PART TWO: AT THE HEART OF THINGS

Jerya went slowly up the length of the stairway between the green lawns. Of course it would not do to arrive flustered or out of breath, but, more simply, her feet dragged because she was afraid. She was too honest to pretend otherways.

It was all beyond her. She was just an ignorant girl from Delven at the end of the world. The simple life of a Delven-woman, which had always seemed so confined and insufficient, appealed as never before. If she had been offered the chance to return home, put on a headcloth, to plight her troth with Rodal, bear his children, never travel again... would she take that chance, turn her back on all this grandeur? What was she doing here, Jerya of Delven, who had barely known how to behave even by the customs of her own folk? Who could be less fit to walk alone into a place such as this?

But no one was offering her that choice. The Dawnsinger had chosen... but the Dawnsinger had seen something in her. The Dawnsinger had said she had courage. It was the Dawnsinger's faith, not her own, that kept her feet moving, kept her back straight and her eyes fixed on the gateway ahead of her.

She went in, under the arch, where two great wooden doors stood back against the walls. The entry-way opened into a broad grassed court, stone paths lining the edges and crossing at the centre where a fountain played. At first she saw no one, and was flummoxed all over again, but then she noticed a low door standing open in one of the walls under the arch. She hesitated a moment, then went in, stooping slightly.

A woman sat in the small room, behind a table. She was dressed in grey, with a pointed cap tied with strings under her chin. In her hands, still as soon as Jerya entered, lay some knitting. She was not a Dawnsinger, presumably, but some kind of servant. Jerya was relieved; easier to speak to such a one than to be faced right away with a high personage of the Guild. Still, she mustered her politest manner., speaking as people did in the books. "I am Jerya of Delven. I hope you have had word of my coming."

The woman laughed. "I hope so too, my dear. 'Twould ne'er do for you to catch us on th' hop, now would it?"

Jerya was taken aback. Not since she had donned the white robe had anyone spoken to her in so easy a manner. Not even Rodal, not really. Perhaps it should have relaxed her, but it left her bemused.

She glanced about her as the woman searched through papers on her desk. The smooth walls were painted a creamy hue. Around window and door, the stonework was left exposed, revealing the thickness of the masonry, and giving her a homely sense of stone all around. Not everything was wholly unfamiliar.

"Ah, here it is," the woman said, more to herself than to Jerya. She read the paper, muttering some words out loud. "Bird received... Delven... Singer Sharess... health... You're late to be made Postulant, aren't you, dear?"

"The others were too young," Jerya tried to explain, "Or else already wed, or—"

"Your Singer Sharess knows her business, I don't doubt. Well, come now, and I'll take you to Senior Tutor Perriad. She'll just have time to see you before dinner." As she spoke, she glanced up at the wall behind Jerya, who turned and was startled to see a round plaque, like a much larger replica of the medallion the old Singer had given her. Sharess: she knew her name now.

As she looked at the plaque, one of the needles—the longer, thinner, one—moved a little, with a jerk, so quick she could almost believe she had imagined it. She glanced down, but the medallion hanging round her own neck was as inert as ever.

The woman rose. Jerya's first thought was that her skirt was rather short. Then she was truly shocked; the woman was wearing trousers. They were cut very loose, so that most of the time they appeared to be just a short skirt—shorter than any woman in Delven would wear, exposing half of her calves—but still...

They went out, under the arch, into the wide court, turning right on the wide path that bordered the immaculate lawn. Two Dawnsingers were approaching; Jerya's immediate impulse was to halt and cast down her eyes, but the serving-woman kept walking ahead of her, greeting the two Singers only with a nod and a quiet "Good afternoon." Jerya did not know what to say, so passed in silence, merely stepping aside to keep out of the way. As they passed, she saw that the Singers were girls perhaps two or three years younger than herself. Arm-in-arm, intent on soft conversation, they seemed not to have noticed her at all.

She followed her guide round one quarter of the court and through a narrow arched passage into a smaller quadrangle, shaded by trees, with a still dark pool at its centre. She thought back to her own tarn in the forest, and wondered how long it might be before she could swim again. Or if, indeed, Dawnsingers indulged in such pursuits.

A corner entrance gave onto a tightly wound stone stair. At the first landing her guide knocked on a dark, polished, wooden door. A voice, deep enough to be a man's, called, "Enter!"

"A new arrival, Senior Tutor," the woman said to... to an empty room. "Jerya of Delven, lately made Postulant by Singer Sharess."

"I recall, thank you, Muna," came the voice again. It did not quite sound like a Dawnsong voice, Jerya thought. And where was the speaker?

The serving-woman, Muna, gave Jerya a quick little smile, then left, closing the door almost silently. Jerya stood, nervously, just inside.

"So, Jerya of Delven, you have arrived." Now she traced the voice to a second doorway, open, showing a segment of a second chamber. At its end she saw books, hundreds of them, ranged on shelves from floor to ceiling. She wondered if she should advance, but uncertainty paralysed her.

"It's a pity you weren't half an hour earlier. Still, I'm sure you can't be held culpable. But I can only give you a few minutes before dinner... would you care for some ale?"

"Thank you," she responded hoarsely.

Finally, Senior Tutor Perriad entered. She was a tall woman, perhaps no taller than Jerya to the shoulder but with a long neck and a high-domed head. Her sleeves were trimmed with silver thread, and in her hands she bore two mugs. Those hands were angular but elegant, with extraordinarily long nails; how could one sew a seam or embroider a yoke with nails like that? Before she had even completed the thought, Jerya saw its stupidity; why should a high Dawnsinger like Perriad need to do such work?

She handed a mug—fashioned of grey metal—to Jerya, sipped at her own, then settled back, half-leaning, half-sitting, against a heavy desk strewn with papers. Her posture struck Jerya as less casual than it appeared. No, she felt sure, there was nothing casual about Senior Tutor Perriad.

Perriad's eyes, a deep blue that was almost indigo, were fixed on Jerya, who felt almost transparent, as if all her secrets were being held up for examination.

"Well, Jerya of Delven, what are we to do with you?" said Perriad, after a brief time that had seemed long.

Jerya wasn't sure whether the question even required an answer. All she could say was, "I beg your pardon, S—Senior Tutor?"

"I see no need for *you* to seek exculpation, Jerya." She hardly understood this, but Perriad left her no time to even puzzle over it. "No, the question which comes to me—comes forcibly, now I see you—is... what was *Sharess* thinking of?"

Again Jerya could not see how she was supposed to answer this. This time she merely waited, head submissively bowed.

"You must know," said Perriad, "That girls are normally Chosen at ten or eleven... How old are you?"

"Nineteen, I believe, Senior Tutor."

The Senior Tutor sighed. "At that age, you should be in your final year as a Novice, if not already Ordained. I suppose Singer Sharess saw something in you, but why she couldn't... Was there no Visitation when you were closer to the usual age?"

"I beg your pardon, Senior Tutor?" Jerya knew she was repeating herself, but did not know what else to say.

Perriad tutted impatiently. "Visitation? You don't know what that means? When was the last time you saw Dawnsingers in your village? Apart from Sharess, I mean."

"I don't recall ever seeing other Dawnsingers, Senior Tutor."

"I am aware of my title, Jerya. You do not need to remind me of it every single time you speak... But what are you telling me? You haven't seen other Singers in all the years you can remember?"

"I never saw any Dawnsinger but our own until I left Delven six days ago." A memory came to her. "Singer Marit, in Thrushgill; she was the first. And she said something about it." She closed her eyes a moment, recalling. "'*It must be eighteen months since I had a proper conversation.*' That's what she said. And something about Singers in the plains seeing others more often..."

Perriad *hmm*ed. "I see I'll need to have a word with the Master of Peripatetics..." She turned to her desk, scratched a few words on a sheet of paper. "But that is not the immediate issue. The question remains, as I said, what are we to do with you...? What education have you had, Jerya?"

Education? It was not a word in common use in Delven. It occurred in some of the books Jerya had read, enough to give her a sense of its meaning. It seemed, suddenly, as if an honest answer might be dangerous, but to respond in any other way went against her nature. "I suppose I must say... none, Senior Tutor."

Perriad narrowed her eyes. "If true... Really, more than ever, I have to ask: *what* was Sharess thinking? But is it true? At least tell me you can read..."

"I can, Senior Tutor."

"We must be thankful for small mercies. In truth, if Sharess had sent me some illiterate girl, I should begin to fear she had utterly lost her reason. But if you can read, then you *have* had some education, have you not? Someone must have taught you?"

"No one taught me." Recalling Perriad's *you do not need to remind me every single time*, she managed to refrain from adding 'Senior Tutor.'

"Surely you mean you do not remember being taught."

"No, not so. I stood at the feet of the headman and followed his finger as he read."

"And it all just came clear to you after that?"

Perriad's tone was sceptical and Jerya felt a surge of indignation. "It took some time, besure, but that is what happened."

"Well, *if* that's true, you may just be more interesting than I supposed. But still, what are we supposed to do? What did Sharess expect? Start you at the beginning and give you eight years training like every other Postulant who arrives?"

"I don't believe that is what the Dawns—Singer Sharess—was thinking." Sharess; she had a name, though she had always been simply 'the Dawnsinger'.

"No, indeed, or why send you now when we are two thirds of the way through the year?" Perriad, frowning, scratched in front of one ear.

"No, Senior Tutor, I believe she thought the matter was much more urgent. Her own health..."

"Aye, and of course it's very much to be regretted if she is sick. That must be looked into also. We cannot leave any community, however insignificant, without a Dawnsinger." Turning again to make another note, she fortunately missed Jerya's reaction. *Insignificant?* Delven had been her whole world till just a few days ago, the village, its forests and moors, its mountains and its unfathomable skies.

Quickly she composed her face before Perriad turned back toward her. The Senior Tutor glanced at her left wrist. Jerya saw another ornament like the one around her own neck, but mounted on a leather bracelet. "Well, you're here now. And she took your Vow, I suppose?"

"Aye, Senior Tutor."

"Took your Vow, shaved your head, put you in white. All well and good, but it's one thing to look like a Singer, quite another to *be* one." Perriad sipped at her ale, then sighed. "Ah, well, we may as well at least take a proper look at you. Though if you truly are as uneducated as you say I really cannot imagine what use we shall find for you. Well, we shall see. I shall speak to some of the other tutors tonight. You'd best come and see me again in the morning... about ten, let's say. For now, let's settle the immediate practicalities. You'll have to sleep with the other Postulants initially, there's space in the dorms. Maybe when those nearer your own age get to know you, someone will be prepared to share a set... So, maybe, it would be best for you to take your meals with the senior Novices. For as long or short a time as you're here...

"I'll take you down to Refec now," added Perriad, straightening. "No, bring your ale, you can finish it while you eat. Come..."

She swept past Jerya, then held the door open for her. It felt strange to receive such a courtesy from one so exalted.

❄

Perriad gave an impression of unhurried grace, but she had a long stride, and Jerya found herself stepping a little faster than was comfortable. All the way, with every stride, the Senior Tutor's words rang in Jerya's mind: *For as long or short a time as you're here.* Was it really possible that she would find herself sent back, perhaps in just a few days? How would the folk of Delven, who'd seemed to rejoice at her Choosing, receive her then? How could she face them, even with a headcloth to cover the shame of a bald head of which she would manifestly have proved unworthy? Hair would grow back in time, she supposed, but shame lingered.

She tried to fix her thoughts instead on another of Perriad's remarks: *Well, we may as well at least take a proper look at you.* That seemed to say that there was some kind of chance. But what she would have to do to prove herself fit to be a Dawnsinger... as to that, she had not the first idea.

Eight days ago, she had never dreamed that she, Jerya of Delven, might find herself here, in this great and terrifying place. She had never dreamed of being a Dawnsinger, never considered it a possibility; the question of whether she *wanted* it had therefore never arisen. Now, however, she found... not so much that she wanted it; that was still too deep. She did know, at least, that she did not want to fail, to be disgraced, to be sent away with her tail between her legs.

Whatever I have to do, she resolved then. *Whatever they ask of me...*

With these turbulent thoughts, and the brisk pace, she gleaned only a blurred impression of yet more courts and passages; stone walls, lanterns, warm glows in curtained windows. She came to Refec, as it was called, a little out of breath. Perriad held the door for her again, and she passed through and then stopped, unprepared for what she saw.

It was a great hall, greater than the hearth-chamber of Delven, with a dim, barely-seen ceiling above, low pools of light below, where countless candles shone. The scent of beeswax was in the air, and its familiarity made her inhale deeply. Those pools of light held more people than the entire population of Delven; several times more, for the great hall was full in a way that the hearth-chamber never was. And every one of them was a woman or a girl with a shaven head and dressed in white. Every one of them was a Dawnsinger.

But I am the same, she told herself. *At least I look the same.* But it all seemed unreal, like a dream, so she wanted to pinch herself, or feel with a hand to test that her own head was truly hairless, that she was, at least in that way, like all the rest of them. It was too much, overwhelming, so that as she followed Perriad between the long tables she was dizzy and dazed and stumbled on the smooth wooden floor; and when they halted she did not take in what Perriad said, or the names that were given. She only stood, swaying slightly, tongue-tied and helpless, only half-aware that Perriad had moved away.

It took her a moment to realise that another voice was addressing her, and with a kindness that the Senior Tutor had not shown. "...must be all in, you certainly look it. Come and sit down here... Move up, you two, make room."

After five days doing little but sit on one cart or another, she had no right to be tired, but she was glad to slide onto the end of a wooden bench. Grateful, she managed to smile at the girl opposite, the one who had spoken. Was she a Postulant or a Novice? Could she ask? What was the difference anyway?

"I'm Railu," the girl said, in the same cheerful voice. She appeared stocky, round-headed, with wide dark eyes. Her skin was no darker than Jerya's own but had a reddish tint, like copper. "We've been expecting you for a few days. Was it a terrible journey?"

"I don't know," replied Jerya, finding her voice at last. Railu's bald head and white garments might say 'Dawnsinger', but the smile and easy manner just said 'friend'. "I've never made a real journey before... It was hard in the Scorched Plains, the heat, but after that we rode on a cart. It might have been quicker to walk, almost, but..." She stopped. Why say that she would have struggled to walk any distance, the day after Stainscomb—and Rodal had been perhaps even more exhausted?

Railu smiled, as if she understood. "How many days altogether?"

"An afternoon, a long day in the Plains, then five days by cart."

"A long way. In fact, there can't be much that's further East."

"Nothing," said Jerya. "Only the mountains, and beyond them the Blistered Lands..."

Railu nodded, but before she could speak again, a gong sounded. Everyone rose; a voice at the head of the hall intoned something. Jerya tried unsuccessfully to make out the words. As they resumed their seats, grey-clad women began to bustle in with trays.

"We were told, of course," Railu continued as bowls of soup were served, and extra cutlery for Jerya. "Though I might have guessed anyway, that you've come from the East. You've obviously worn a... what do you call it?" One hand sketched an oval around her face.

"A headcloth."

"Well, the name makes sense, at least. But why did you wear it?"

"Did the men make you?" said another girl. "Would they beat you if you didn't?"

It was a strange question, but she tried to answer plainly. "No man ever raised a hand to me. Not for that or anything else. It was the women... my Aunts, I called them." She dipped her spoon and took a quick mouthful; she *was* hungry, besure to that; and it gave her a moment to think. "I do remember, when I was little, sometimes my headcloth would come loose, and always someone, one of my Aunts or an older cousin, would hasten to put it right. And in turn, as I grew, I would do the same for the smaller girls. I never questioned it, until... but, you see, the men had nothing to do with it. I learned from women."

"Of course you did," said the girl alongside Railu. She was very pale, perhaps the palest person Jerya had ever seen. Only by contrast with her robe could you see that her skin was not truly white. Her eyebrows and lashes were so fine and blond they were all but invisible. Only her eyes had real colour, and that was startling, blue as a clear winter sky after snow.

Jerya smiled politely, and the pale girl continued, "It's only natural, isn't it? A girl will model herself on women, and a boy-child will model himself on men."

"I don't know about *natural*, Freilyn," said Railu. Jerya marked another name. "But I think it was the same when I was a child. I don't remember very clearly, but I didn't learn from men, I'm sure. I did have a father, of course." She sounded surprised, as if she had forgotten. "But I remember so little. He seemed enormous, all black beard... I imagined he had black hair all over, but I never saw him without his clothes. He was often away; he sailed with a merchant ship, I think, down the Long Shore. I think whenever he came home he'd give me a gift, pick me up and swing me through the air, and then forget me and take my mother off where I knew I was forbidden to disturb them. Other men, mostly, I had even less to do with, or I've forgotten."

Jerya thought about this. She'd always supposed that Dawnsingers knew everything, but here was Railu cheerfully admitting that she'd forgotten much. "How old were you...?" she asked, hesitating.

"When I was Chosen? Not yet eleven."

The others chimed in; all had first arrived at ten or eleven. 'Nearly twelve' seemed to be the oldest.

Railu looked at Jerya. "You're as old as we are, I guess...?" She left the obvious question hanging in the air.

"I've nineteen summers."

"Older than me, then," said Railu. "I'm still eighteen; most of us are. We've been here since we were ten, and I haven't spoken to a man, or had one speak to me, in all that time... I remember little about them and understand less."

"A thing I've often wondered," said the girl on Jerya's right, who was as dark as anyone Jerya had seen on her journey. "How is it, they'd never dream of asking a woman's advice about *anything* until she becomes a Dawnsinger—and then, *suddenly*..."

"How do I answer that? I'm not a man." That drew a burst of laughter, but the dark girl didn't join in; she looked, Jerya thought, disappointed. She hastened to make amends. "I do understand what you say... not that anyone asked my advice, but the way they looked at me, spoke to me... well, mostly they didn't speak to me. But, aye, it all changed. Nothing changed in me, I didn't feel different, it was only how I looked—but all at once to them I was someone new." She said 'them', but she was thinking 'him'; but that was not a subject she cared to discuss. There was a momentary silence at their end of the table, while talk flowed on in the rest of the hall. *How many voices? A hundred, two hundred, five hundred?* She knew she could reckon the number at this table, the number of tables, multiply... but she was aware of the local silence.

She thought a little more. "I think it's true, what you say about a man asking a woman for advice. I don't recall seeing it... but I think mostly that's because their lives, their work, were separate anyway. A woman wouldn't ask a man how to hunt because women didn't hunt. A man wouldn't ask a woman how to care for the beehives, because that was the women's province. It didn't mean they thought us stupid."

Dry-mouthed, she took a swift gulp of ale. "Not in Delven, anyroad. I don't think they'd have dared. They'd recall too well what befell Oakat, when he berated his Own, Tulis, for slow work and slow wits. She goaded him into boasting that he could do any of her tasks with ease, then made him fulfil his boast in front of everyone. I have never seen anyone so red-faced—but, to his credit, he saw the funny side in the end, saw how cunning she had been. Now, I think, he might say that a woman is not less clever than a man, but clever in a different way."

"Did you think *yourself* clever in a different way, then?" asked Railu. "Did you never want to do those things that were *reserved* for men?"

Jerya hesitated. How freely could she speak? With Railu alone, she might have felt at ease, but there were others listening, still strangers, nameless, Dawnsingers. She began cautiously. "It never felt quite like that; we didn't speak of things being reserved or forbidden. Usually the question just didn't arise. Myself, I... well, some said I was too much like a man. Because I was too tall, and too skinny—"

"I'd hardly call you 'skinny'," said Railu.

Jerya wondered if that was a compliment; she said, "Thank you," anyway. "But they say in Delven a woman should look—" She almost said, 'more like you,' but that was too much, too soon. Railu seemed friendly, but she did not know her, and still less did she know what was acceptable among Dawnsingers. "—Should have some flesh on her," she said instead. "And I... erred in other ways, too. Because I did not pretend to be too weak to carry a handloom by myself out to the stonecourts. Because I did my work and then went off alone into the forests... But these things were not *forbidden*. I was teased, even ridiculed—but by the women, not by the men."

"Thank you," said the dark girl in her soft low voice. "This is fascinating... but it's unfair of us, you've hardly touched your soup, and I'm sure you need it more than we do. If you don't finish it quickly, the servitors'll have your plate away anyway. It may be different in your Delven, but dinner-time's a regular race here; they all want to get off home as soon as they can."

"Back to their *men*," said someone, earning a general laugh. Jerya, not grasping the joke, just got busy finishing the now-lukewarm soup.

There was bustle around them as soup-plates were cleared (Jerya got a knowing smile from her neighbour, and smiled back gratefully). Dishes of vegetables were placed at intervals down the table. The talk went on as if the servitors were not there.

"I'm sure it's true," said Railu. "That men and women, in the world beyond these walls, lead separate lives. I mean that they have different roles, different tasks."

"It's true in Delven," said Jerya. "I know nothing of how it may be elsewhere."

"It fits with what we do know, what we may remember. But here, within, we—or the servitors—practise all sorts of crafts and arts which are *men's* business outside." Jerya recalled Perriad saying 'we brew the ale', and thought it unlikely that the Senior Tutor brewed with her own hands.

Plates, already laden with meat, began to arrive, and Railu pushed the vegetable dish directly in front of Jerya. "You first, I'm sure you're hungriest."

That might be true, but Jerya did not want to look greedy on this first meeting. There was one dish for each six girls at the long table, she saw, but her late arrival meant seven had to share this one. She helped herself to a carefully judged portion of each kind (carrots, potatoes, and something green she did not recognise). Railu was continuing, "Joinery, metal-working, whatever you care to mention. And the servitors stoke the boilers, they cut down that tree that was becoming unsafe last winter—I remember them climbing it, working up in the crown, must have been fifteen metres up." Jerya wondered about 'metres', but had no chance to ask. "If there's building to be done, they do it. Anything that requires to be done within these Precincts is done by women, and done well... which surely rebuts any idea that it's unnatural for women to do such things—and yet, outside, they don't. That's true isn't it?" she appealed to Jerya.

"Aye, all the things you mention, in Delven would be done by men. Except 'stoke the boilers', I don't know what that is."

"How did you keep warm, then?" asked the dark girl on her right.

"In the caves, below the first level, winter and summer make no difference. There is always warmth."

"You lived in caves?" another voice asked incredulously.

"Not entirely. We sleep in them; in summer we live and work outside much of the time."

For a while, then, she let herself be quizzed about life in Delven. Presently she found herself listing the tasks which fell to the women, which was easy but took some time. There was weaving, for example, but before that came the spinning, and before that the fleece had to be picked clean, washed, and carded. And if you mentioned tending the beehives, that too was not just one task but several.

She was less clear about what the men actually did. She could say 'hunting', for example, but what exactly did that involve? Was that, too, really an assembly of many tasks and skills? She had watched their sports, of course, but she had seen much less of the rest of their lives... And how little she had realised it, before.

But it was becoming clear that there were many things she had never thought of before. She had never known talk like this, never had such companions. Mostly her companions had been a handful of books, and her own thoughts. Books were all very well, she thought—wonderful, in fact—but they did not talk back.

The dark girl, whose name she had gathered was Analind, broke into her brief reverie. "From what you say, the women never really went out of the village?"

"That's not quite so. We'd go to the gardens, to the nearer fields, the bee-hives. Some would venture into the fringes of the forest to gather herbs and berries, but some were reluctant... in truth, I think they were frightened. I'm sure I was the only one who ever went in deeper, especially alone."

"And you were the one Chosen, of course," said Freilyn. "Do you really think, Rai, that someone who never looked further than her cabbage-patch could make a Dawnsinger?"

Railu started to answer, but Freilyn stopped her with an upraised hand. She turned back to Jerya. "I'm sorry. Rai and I have had this argument a hundred times."

"Perhaps," said Jerya, "But I have not heard it. If you must apologise, I think you must apologise to the others, not to me."

This brought laughter. It felt good to make them laugh, these bright girls.

"I apologise, I apologise!" said Freilyn, laughing with the rest. Then, to Jerya again, "But let me warn you about Railu. She's a sweet thing, but she has dangerous notions. She's even been heard to suggest that we should share the Knowledge with all women."

Jerya had never had cause before to wonder why Dawnsingers were separate, why their Knowledge was secret. It was, as her Aunts always said, the way things are. And now—or very soon—she would, presumably, be admitted to the secrets herself. She wasn't sure she liked the idea of sharing so widely. If all women partook of the Knowledge, where did that leave Jerya? Would she once again be nothing more than an unruly and unregarded girl?

"Only women?" she said. "Not men also?"

Everyone laughed again. They seemed to think she had made an excellent joke, and at Railu's expense. Jerya was relieved to see her laughing with the rest.

"I'm trying to imagine it," said Freilyn, as the merriment subsided. "It's well-known that men can't sing. I'd sooner hear the Song played on... on a broken fiddle, than crushed into the bass."

"It would sound strange, to be sure," said Jerya. "But, you know, not every man has a bass voice, and some of them sound very fine in their own songs. It's not true that all men cannot sing—nor that all women can."

Freilyn looked at her strangely, as if she did not quite believe her, but she did not challenge what Jerya had said. *This*, she thought, *is something I'd never have believed even yesterday. I contradicted a Dawnsinger to her face—and she's accepted it.*

And something more... Something to set against Perriad's *For as long or short a time as you're here.* These girls, or young women, were Dawnsingers. They were called Novices, but they had been through more than seven years of training; they were very close to the end. By autumn, some of them at least would be sent out to serve in villages and towns. But there were things they didn't know, that she, Jerya, did.

Perhaps there was hope, after all.

Indeed, Freilyn now turned Jerya's comment to her own use. "There you are, Rai: more reasons why all women cannot be Dawnsingers."

Railu gave an airy wave, perilous with a laden fork. "You know very well I've never suggested anything of the kind." She smiled at Jerya. "Don't believe everything you hear about me. I just ask awkward questions now and then." Jerya smiled. She had been guilty of that herself, and not just occasionally. Railu continued, "Enough of that; Frei's already had to apologise, and once is enough. I want to hear more about where you come from, about Delven. Does every woman have to *marry?*"

Another strange question, thought Jerya, but she tried to answer clearly. "I don't know quite what you mean by 'have to'. No one's forced to wed; at least, I never saw it so. I don't think a man would want an unwilling wife... Sometimes there aren't enough men or women of the right age. A man who can find no wife in Delven might look for one in Burnslack, or even Thrushgill. For the women, it's harder. A young spinster may become second wife to an older man who has been widowed. Failing that; well, she who is a mother to no child is an Aunt to all; her life is not empty. Still, she is sometimes pitied. I don't think—in Delven, which is what I know—any woman desires that. All wish to wed."

"Did you?" asked Railu, leaning forward avidly.

The question cut sharper than Railu could know; without thinking, when she had said 'all', Jerya had not counted herself. She would never wed now, of course, but before...

"I don't know... No one ever offered, you see, and I... I was in no hurry, you might say. Others around my age were already wed and most of them had children, but the question never quite arose for me."

"Why?"

Still, it was hard to answer. The days of the journey had stirred emotions that had lain deep-hid. There were wounds that needed to be left to heal. And what could she say, without laying herself open to yet more unwelcome inquiry? "There... could have been someone," she said, her voice so neutral that she almost stopped to admire her own self-control. "But it is fortunate—I see now—that we did not... come together, or Delven would have had no one to send when the need arose."

"Fortunate for whom?" asked Railu. "If you'd married your man already... would Delven have had anyone else to Choose?"

Jerya thought about it, as she had before, and again she could think of no one. Who else, old enough to make the journey, yet still unwed, unbetrothed... who else among that small number could even read? She shook her head.

"So the Masters'd have to find a new Singer anyway. And... I don't want to disrespect your Delven; I also came from a small place a long way away. But the Singers who are sent to such places... they don't tend to be the ones who've excelled here. Sometimes they're the ones who've blotted their copybook."

"I'm not sure what that means," said Jerya, because she didn't know the phrase, but also because she hoped the conversation might turn a different way.

"My *academic* record is, I dare say, more than adequate," said Railu. "My voice and my practical skills will at least suffice. I may, however, be adjudged not to be of satisfactory character. It may be felt that I've asked just a few too many *awkward* questions."

She laughed again, though her cheeriness seemed altogether misplaced. "Just think, even if you'd married your man, you might have found yourself saddled with my company anyway."

"I don't think so," said Jerya. "If it fell out that way, we'd never have spoken."

"You may think so. *I* think I would do the job differently."

"Differently?"

"Aye. I've looked into this somewhat, being *awkward*, and the Principle of Detachment leaves significant room for interpretation. The only part that is truly clear is the prohibition on sharing Knowledge."

"I don't know about that. It may be so—I suppose, if you say so, it must be—but in Delven... do you know, *I* am learning things about Delven tonight...? In Delven, everything is done a certain way. No one sees that it might be different—and that is why nothing has to be enforced with whips or sticks. A woman doesn't *have* to marry; it just never crosses her mind that she could choose not to. It never, really, crossed mine... but I did, sometimes, think I could see better ways of doing certain tasks, and I would say, 'Why don't we do it so?', and all it earned me was trouble." She smiled at Railu. "You see, I too know what it is to ask awkward questions.

"But I'm wandering from what I meant to say; in Delven, you would find it harder than you imagine to bring in new ways. I was always taught to stay well away from the Dawnsinger."

Railu frowned. "All right, you're not supposed to talk to her but what if she... imagine this. Imagine you weren't Chosen, you're still there, in

Delven. Imagine that it is me they send. Imagine that one day I catch you alone and I say, 'hello'?"

Jerya applied her imagination as Railu directed. It wasn't hard. "I might suddenly become deaf, stare at the ground and turn myself to stone. Other women would, I think. Being me, more likely I would run away."

Railu looked appalled. Jerya thought she understood. She need only picture herself, but herself as Dawnsinger, trying to speak to the women who had been her childhood companions... Those companions were already lost to her; that she knew. Yet here, even in this short time, she had tasted companionship of a new kind, a richer kind. And clearly Railu thrived on such companionship, rooted in talk and argument. Jerya thought of Marit, brooding over her cyder; had she, too, once loved to talk and argue like this, face fervent in the candlelight?

Well, she thought, *someone* must go to Delven. *Someone* must take on that solitary life. And she, Jerya, had already lived a solitary life—*mostly* solitary, she amended; mostly solitary, and that very largely by her own choice. And returning to Delven was what she had sworn to do.

It must be so, she thought, in conscious echo of the old Dawnsinger. *It must be so... but for now, I am here. However short my time may be, I must make all I can of it.*

CHAPTER 8

RODAL

Rodal retraced his steps from the quiet hill-top into the teeming heart of the City, noticing his surroundings only as much as he needed to avoid a wrong turning. In his mind he was fretting over the parting that had just taken place. It had all been necessary, and he could not see how any of it could have been done differently, but that did not make it all right. It was, he thought, a little like the emergency doctoring a man might have to do for himself after a solitary hunting mishap; rough binding or splinting. It had to be done quickly, it could only be done clumsily, and it was always painful. Such wounds healed slowly, and not often cleanly.

His face turned grimmer yet. This one *must* be healed cleanly, and it had better be done before their return to Delven. There must be no brooding, no festering; he must fill his days and occupy his energies. And, he reminded himself, glancing up at strange crags of dressed stone, he was in Carwerid. It was a chance he had never expected, and exceeding unlikely to come his way again. There must be countless new things to see and do. That was how he must think of it.

It was a fine resolve, but he had no idea how it might be achieved. All he had was a small pouch of coins, mostly bronze with a few small silvers, and Holdren's advice that Garam of Old Tanpits Lane kept an honest house. Before anything else, he should find that house.

Holdren had talked, sometimes, of his own visit to the city. He had brought back books too, and sometimes in the winter evenings would read from one. A picture in his mind, Holdren's face bent over a book, other faces watching, listening, in the lamplight, Jerya's always among them.

Book-tales, and tales from real life: both had warned of banditry in the streets. For the first time, now that Jerya was off his hands, he thought about possible danger to himself. As he came back into the whirl of colour and sound that was the great market-court, he kept his left hand firmly on the coin-pouch in his pocket, while his right rehearsed fists and chopping-edges.

He was wary, but he was not seriously afraid of being attacked in broad daylight. Thus far, he had seen few men in the City who looked capable of giving him a serious fight. He had not been beaten at wrestling since he was sixteen; winning had lost much of its shine, had almost become the performance of a duty. Perhaps here he might find worthier opponents. It was an idea worth keeping in mind.

Asking repeatedly for directions, he drew slowly closer to Old Tanpits Lane. Some folk seemed deaf, or too absorbed in their own thoughts to answer his enquiry. Others were better-mannered, but some said, with or without apology, that they didn't know. A few in their staccato City voices gave advice, but of such complexity that Rodal could not hold all of it. He was accustomed to a geography of three dimensions; the City was not built on flat land, but its natives seemed to believe that it was, for they spoke solely of lefts and rights. Rodal would follow a handful of these, then ask again. It was slow work. As he went, he tried to memorise the way back to the market-square, but he was doubtful it would work. He could hardly tell what would serve best for landmarks. Too many of the tall buildings looked the same. It was hard even to be sure what was permanent; here was a house under demolition; there another, to his eye scarcely different, being erected with much hammering and even more cursing.

At last he saw the name he had been seeking, painted on a wall-stone just above head height. Already he must be growing used to the City, for Old Tanpits Lane seemed quiet, though such a bustle in Delven would have been called a jamboree.

Garam's house—the name was painted on a board that hung from a projecting rail above the door—was on the left at the lowest point of the lane, which then turned sharply uphill again for no clear reason. Three steps led down into a long, low chamber, with the cool feel of stone all around. It was almost cave-like, and thereby homely. He had learned what inns were; they had figured in Holdren's tales, and they had spent the last three nights of the journey at inns. This seemed as clean and orderly as any of them.

A few men sat with mugs of drink at plain wooden tables. In an alcove four oldsters clustered silently over some kind of patterning game. A low hum of talk seemed to come from no one in particular.

At the back of the room the lamp-light was scattered and multiplied amid shelves of bottles and glasses; in front of them was a long enclosed table across the room; between the table and the shelves stood a girl. She was the only one to show any interest in him, so he approached her.

She was bare-headed, only a narrow band of cloth holding her hair back. Customs were different; he had learned that by now, but he was slower in learning not to be embarrassed. With luck the light would not be bright enough to show up the warmth in his cheeks.

She smiled. Her lips were very red and her teeth very white. Her blue eyes and black hair were strange to Rodal, whose folk were mostly sandy-haired or fox-red like himself, but it did not take him long to see she was handsome.

"Good day," she said. Her voice seemed pleasant, not so curt and hasty as most of the folk he'd spoken to in the streets.

"Greetings," he returned. "I seek Garam."

"I'm sorry, my father's out just now. He spends more time at the brewery than behind the bar, these days. Can I help you?" She did speak quickly, as everyone seemed to; but she was clear. Oft-times the snatches he'd overheard seemed no more than gabble.

He hesitated only briefly before deciding that, if Garam was to be trusted, then so was his daughter. "I was told to come to this house—that one like me, a newcomer to the City, would find lodging here at a fair price."

"And so you would," she said with an answering smile, "But I'm afeared all our rooms are taken for the next few days."

He said nothing, but his face must have given him away. She laughed merrily. "It's not the end of the world, friend; ours isn't quite the only decent house, though you'll surely find none better... Listen, at the top of the stepway there's an inn called The Fighting Cocks. They're sure to have a room free. It willn't be so clean as here, but it's safe, and it should be cheap. If they try and ask more than three bronze a night, you just mention my name. Annyt, that's me; Garam's Annyt's how they'll know me."

"My name is Rodal," he replied. It seemed to be expected. Then he was silent, and there was doubt in his mind.

She gave him a shrewd look. "Aren't you happy?"

She asked more than she knew, but he only said, "I was told to come here, and nowhere else."

"And right advice it was. If we can't commodate you oursel's, we'll see you right somewhere else. Do I look less than honest? Have I any reason to advise you ill? Listen, Rodal of..."

"Of Delven."

"—Rodal of Delven, you don't look soft to me." She looked down at his arms with a frankness that took Rodal quite aback. "I'm sure a lumpy mattress willn't kill you. You'll have a room for next to nothin'—and don't pay in advance; as soon as we've one free here it's yours. And come down here for your meals. No one who values his stomach would eat at the Cocks. If you were to go up there now and sort out your bed, I could have a fine supper waitin' for you when you get back. Now how does that sound?"

"That sounds... fine," he replied, forced into trust by her open manner. " And I thank you for your kind concern."

"Think nothing of it," she said gaily. "That's how we keep our customers."

Rodal had scant difficulty finding the 'Fighting Cocks', or in securing a place to sleep, though it was far removed from his idea of comfort; one low bed of a dozen in a long chamber at the top of the house, reached by a twisting, treacherous stair. There were no walls, only the under-slopes of the roof, beams and laths and slates open to inspection. It did not feel solidly enclosed, but the chamber was uncomfortably hot. He tried to open the movable part of the glass window set in the end wall, and when it would not move assumed there was some trick he did not know; he had never seen such a thing until a few days ago. However, the proprietor—a pot-bellied, lank-haired fellow—only laughed and assured him, "Bin stuck for years."

Rodal was glad to escape into the relative cool of the lane as twilight descended and lamps were kindled at street-corners. Garam's seemed doubly clean and cheerful now. Annyt's smile was waiting for him, and she had a foam-crowned mug on the bar-top before he reached it. "There. Did whoever it was also mention that, as well as bein' the most honest house in town, we also serve the best ale?"

"I think not."

"Then find out for yourself while I fetch your supper. There's steak pie and parsnips and pickled beets, if that's to your likin'."

The names were unfamiliar, but Rodal did not care. He eased himself up onto a tall stool at the bar. "I haven't had more than a bite since dawn. I swear I could eat raw fircones, if that's what you set before me."

"How d'you normally have 'em? Boiled?" she enquired with a wide-eyed innocence which he saw through even before she laughed. She turned with a swirl of her short, full skirt and disappeared through a doorway behind the bar.

Rodal tasted the ale, and a second draught followed swiftly. So there were good things in the City. This Annyt, too; outlandish in her ways, by Delven's standards, but surely there was no harm in that. You were never likely to forget she was a girl, yet you could talk as if she were not. In that she was like—*no*, he told himself firmly, *she's like herself, no one else*.

Then she came back and laid a plate before him. "That's a challenge to your appetite." The plate was deep, halfway to a bowl, and well-filled, with a great chunk of fresh bread, almost half a loaf, balanced on the rim.

"Sometimes I like a challenge." As she moved away to attend to another customer he made a forkful too large to be strictly polite and engulfed it. It was delicious. For a while he did not think of anything else.

Some time later he found Annyt regarding him with what seemed to be admiration as he mopped the plate with the last of the bread.

"Well," she said, "You can put it away, and no mistake."

"I've always had a fair appetite."

"I'd have guessed as much," she said, and again looked unashamedly down his arms. *Well, why not?* he thought. All women looked, besure; why should they have to pretend otherways?

"That was gradely," he said. He drained his mug. "This, too. This City has more to commend it than I was ever told."

He looked at her as he said it, then thought that could sound amiss; but she took his words at their face, merely smiled and said, "I hoped you might think so. Will you be here long?"

"Well, I... hope so. I can't say exactly." He explained briefly how he came to be in Carwerid, saying only the barest minimum about Jerya.

"Poor girl," said Annyt, "It must've been altogether bewilderin'; one day quiet and ordinary, the next dragged off to strange places with her hair all hacked off." She passed a hand through her own dark tresses as if reassuring herself they were still there, then picked up a cloth and began polishing glasses. "Was she very upset?"

"No, she conducted herself with great dignity."

"You mean she didn't dare show her true feelings."

Rodal dipped his head: she was more right than she knew, but all that had passed between Jerya and himself was secret and would always remain so. He wished Annyt would pursue any other subject, and wondered rather desperately how he might steer their talk away. But Annyt persisted. "I s'pose she had no chance to refuse?"

"Nor wish to, I'm sure," Rodal said, not quite concealing his affront.

"I'm sorry... I didn't mean... wouldn't it be a terrible thing, though, to steal someone's life like that if she didn't truly desire to serve? It'd make a mockery of the Dawnsong, and no one could want that."

"No, indeed not."

"Well," she went on brightly, as if sensing his wish to talk of something else, "I needn't hope nor fear it'll ever happen to me. We're hardly like to run short of Dawnsingers here, with hundreds o' them all singin' every mornin'." That was a thrilling prospect, though Rodal had the feeling he might manage to sleep through it on the morrow.

"But what of yourself?" she asked suddenly. "What do you do in Delven, when you're not escortin' Postulants of the Guild halfway across the Sung Lands?"

"It is very different there," he said. "Here... we came into the City with a man who spends all his days driving a cart. Others, it seems, do nothing but keep houses of hospitality, or brew ale. Others make shoes or sell fish—true, is it not? In Delven each man does many things. Perhaps if one is specially adept at... at making shoes, say, then another will relieve him from the hunt or the herding for a day in exchange for a pair. But a man must be ready and able to do everything."

"But what is 'everything' there?" she asked.

Before he could reply there were calls for more beer; she was busy filling glasses, loading trays, carrying them out to the drinkers. Rodal watched her with pleasure. In Delven... but you could not imagine a girl in Delven going about in a skirt that ended closer to her knees than her ankles, half-sleeves, throat bare, only a band on her hair.

She came back, deposited soiled glasses in a sink on a side wall, then picked up her cloth again. With no more than a lift of her black brows she indicated he should continue.

"I never had to list of my tasks before. I just... grew into them. As soon as I was old enough to leave my mother and go with the men I went out gathering forest fruits and mushrooms. Later I learned to tend the fields, and to help look after the sheep and goats, but there was not so much I could do as my father did not own a dog. I became fairly adept at fishing, and when I grew tall, I... I do not wish to boast, but I took well to the hunting."

"That's not all, is it?" she said when he paused. She sensed what he was about to say and took his mug to the cask to be refilled, talking on over her shoulder. "All you've said is to do with providin' food... but you don't seem like you've had to struggle every day just to keep your belly filled. You have time for other things."

"Indeed. Our land is not as rich as those round here, but it is enough for our numbers. The old ones say the winters are less fierce than they once were, and the summers not so hot; they say we have a soft life."

She laughed. "That's the sort of thing old folks always say. I 'xpect they're the same everywhere."

"And we'll be the same when we're old, no doubt." Thinking to shift the subject from himself, he asked, "Have you travelled much?"

"No," she said, "This is a bad business for holidays, and, asides, we are not rich. Oh, we make day-trips, of course; boat-rides on the river, and on the canal down to the sea."

He had seen boats, in the last few days; they had even crossed one wide slow river on a 'ferry', a broad, flat, creaking thing only slightly less alarming to ride than to think about. He wondered what a 'canal' was; there was so much to learn. But the sea... that, at least, he had heard of.

"I've never seen the sea," he said. "What's it like?"

"S'pose you think that's an easy question... Perhaps in one way it is. It's wet and it's big." She laughed. "Is that answer enough, Rodal of Delven? No? Then... It stretches to the horizon and all you can see is the edge of the world and on the clearest days the hills of Elannin. From the highest hills, North along the coast, they say you can see all the island and then limitless ocean beyond... From a distance, that's all the sea is—a hugeness. Grey when the sky's grey, blue and sparkling when the sun shines. But go down to the shore and it's like somethin' alive. People say it has moods, quiet, playful, angry... It's beyond me to describe it. You'll have to see it for yourself."

"I'd like that. Would you... mayhap you could show it to me?"

Then he was surprised at his own boldness, but Annyt only looked pleased. "I'd love to. The first free day I have... it needs a whole day, you see, and I don't get many. But I often have half a day, and there are other places we can go. We must go to the fayre before it moves on... that's why all our rooms are taken, in case you didn't know, while the bar's half-empty."

He had no idea what a 'fayre' was, but if Annyt, having lived in the City all her life, thought it was exciting, he was sure he would find it doubly so. Before, he had hoped that his stay in the City would be as brief as possible. Now, he was beginning to think again.

CHAPTER 9

JERYA

The dormitory was on an upper floor, a long room with white walls and dark beams. Jerya was grateful to find her allotted bed in one of the corners, where she might feel somewhat enclosed, but it was still very different from the cosy stone embrace of her own cave-cell. Curtains were drawn across the high windows, but they could not mask the fact that it was still half-light outside. Yet most of the girls were in bed and some seemed already to be asleep.

The ones who were still up seemed as shy with her as she was with them. Ten or eleven, they must be, twelve at most; still children to her eyes, but they were marked as Dawnsingers. The easy talk that had begun with Railu's warmth seemed far away now; but they were helpful enough, answering her few questions, showing her where the washroom was, and the privies—though there was brief confusion here, and much giggling, as they referred to them as the 'necessaries'.

By the time she had made use of 'necessary' and washroom, and changed into the nightgown she had found waiting on her allocated bed along with a clean white robe, all the others were settled, and the candles were out. It gave her no pause; the room was hardly dark, certainly not for one who had been happy navigating the low, twisting passages of Delven with no more illumination than well-spaced rushlights.

She settled into her bed, glad to find the mattress firm, unlike the over-soft one at Thrushgill, or the lumpy palliasses of the following nights. A last few whispers and hushed giggles gave way to a low murmurous background of breathing.

She missed her cosy cell deep in the earth; she missed the strand of hair which she had been wont to chew on. She even missed Rodal's broad back, which had given her a kind of shelter on that night in Thrushgill. There was nothing but a thin sheet and a coarse blanket; she threw her arm awkwardly over her eyes to shut out the light.

She did not think she would find sleep in a hurry, but almost the next thing she knew was the sound of a chime. She sat up to grey light, much like it had been when she went to bed; briefly it seemed as if mere moments had passed. But the room was full of girls yawning, stretching, knuckling sleep from their eyes, talking softly in voices still drowsy-vague. Soon they were beginning to dress. Jerya shrugged out of her nightgown, into her robe, stepped into her sandals. She had nothing else but the white cloak; the others seemed to be dressing warmly, so she pulled the cloak on as she joined the downstairs file.

The courts whispered everywhere with the sandalled feet of women and girls. Pale grey in the half-light, they were all moving the same way, towards the hilltop that rose behind the buildings.

The top of the hill had been levelled; a square space, as wide and smooth as the main courtyard, three sides lined with trees holding on to blackness. To the East it was open, and they arranged themselves in rows facing out over the great dark stillness of the land. The Eastern sky was milky over the mauve outline of mountains, tiny with distance but sharp and clear. Jerya's heart lifted at the sight. They were not the same mountains she knew from home, but they *were* mountains.

Nearest the East stood the Tutors; Jerya recognised Perriad's tall figure, her high-crowned head. Before even them was another rank, maybe a dozen. These, she supposed, were the Masters. Behind these ranks, the girls were ranged roughly by size or age, youngest to the fore. Jerya felt conspicuous among the little ones, but everyone seemed to be looking ahead, not at her.

Behind the distant mountains, the light swelled. Jerya could hardly breathe; it seemed as if the sun must be about to burst into view before it was summoned.

Then in front of her a low voice tiptoed into the first notes, and on that purple skyline a sliver of incandescence trembled into being. After the first stave other voices joined the lone alto. Around her the girlish trebles were fragile but clear. Jerya knew she should join in, but it was not so easy. She had heard the Song a hundred times and on every other day had felt as if she had absorbed it without hearing it. At Stainscomb she had been lost, doubting herself awake or alive, when the sun rose in silence; only later, walking the full length of the straggling village, had she understood that their Dawnsinger's house was simply too distant. The power of the Song evidently reached further than that of hearing. *How much further?* she'd wondered. Soon, perhaps this very day, she would begin to gain some answers; she could only hope that she was capable of understanding. Well, the old Dawnsinger must have thought so.

She knew the melody—knew it so well that she had sometimes caught herself humming it unthinkingly on her solitary wanderings, and had always been shocked, shamed, scolded herself. Now she could barely believe that it was not a dream, that she, Jerya, belonged among these white-robed, shining figures; that she could join in—that she *must*. She began quietly, almost under her breath, her voice lost in the swelling chorus. No one turned, no one looked askance; all was well. She threw back her shoulders, filled her lungs, and Sang.

The sun grew; it was becoming impossibly huge; it was about to encompass the whole sky. Then its narrowing underside appeared and Jerya realised that her eyes had been almost falling into it, into that light softened by haze just enough to be looked at, though already too bright to have real colour.

The sun sprang clear of the horizon; the Song fell to its end.

In the shocking hush which followed Jerya heard the sounds of the waking world: girls breathing all around her, the chatter of the trees in the light air, cocks crowing, the first stirrings of the City below, hidden by the edge of the songstead but sounding close. She heard dogs, geese, horses, cattle, quiet and almost conversational; there were human voices too: greetings, curt orders, laughter, sleepy grumblings. She could hear everything but the actual words.

When the girls around her began to file back down the hill, she followed them in a daze, barely knew how she found herself once more at table with the senior Novices. She wanted to talk of her feelings, the wonder of the Dawnsong and the new, growing, wonder of finding herself part of it, but they were full of their own talk: commonplace chatter, so far as she could follow it, as if they were untouched by the majesty they had just shared in creating.

She reflected that they had sung the Dawn every day for seven years and more; perhaps they had forgotten how the first time had felt, or perhaps they had been too young... was it possible that they had *never* felt quite as she did?

She was too *full* to make any effort to follow the talk. Last night's talk—perplexing, occasionally disturbing, frequently exhilarating—had been a gift, she thought; it would hardly be so easy, so much on her terms, again. But as she learned the ways of this place she would grow closer to her companions, better able to follow their talk. It had never been like that in Delven; she had felt herself, if anything, growing more and more distant from the chatter that went on around her. Detached... She recalled Railu's reference to a Principle of Detachment, and almost laughed.

Breakfast ended, and the others began to drift off to their lessons. Jerya realised she did not know what to do now. She had to see Perriad again, but she did not know when. She stifled a flicker of panic. There was no good in that. Anyway, the solution was simple. She could see Perriad still at the head table, so if she went now, straight to the Tutor's rooms, she must be there before her. If she had to wait, well, she had been given nothing else to do.

As it turned out, she had not been standing in the passage very long before Perriad appeared.

"You're early," the Tutor said with faint surprise. "I... ah, I think I see. Never mind, come in." She indicated a chair and seated herself behind the desk.

"I heard you Sing this morning," Perriad added. "You would seem to have good potential." Jerya did not know how anyone could have picked one voice out from the hundreds, but of course she still had no real idea what a Dawnsinger's arts might stretch to.

"Still, if we are to make use of you, you will require further instruction. And knowing the Song is not sufficient; you must, above all, know *when* to Sing. Aye, the essentials of a Singer's praxis; these above all must be mastered without delay, so that you are sufficiently prepared if... As for the rest, we shall see, but I have asked each of the Tutors to submit you to assessment. You'll go first to Tutor Yanil, for mathematics. She won't complain if you arrive early."

❋

Yanil was a short, wiry, nut-brown woman. Her face was deeply lined, but her eyes—behind glass lenses bound in metal—were still youthful, lively and, Jerya thought, kind. She quickly felt at ease with her, in a way she thought she never would with Perriad.

The room was small, though with a high ceiling, and one wall was all windows. The morning's light streamed over dark wooden desks and halfway up panelled walls that were mostly covered in paper charts. Their intricate designs conveyed nothing to Jerya's glance.

There were other girls in the room, five of them, bent silently over books and papers. Yanil ignored them, giving Jerya her undivided attention, seating her on a tall stool at her own high desk. "I hope you're beginning to settle in," she said. Others had said the same, but Yanil's concern seemed genuine. "Now, Jerya, what do you know of mathematics?"

"Nothing, I think." It was not a good answer, she thought, but it was an honest one, and that was the only kind she knew.

Yanil chuckled softly. "If that's true, you're quite the rarity... But perhaps you just don't know the name."

"I don't, besure."

"Don't worry, girl, it's not your fault. Mathematics, Jerya, is the most important subject you can study; and I don't say that just because it's *my* subject. Mathematics is at the root of everything. A Dawnsinger who knew no mathematics... but the very idea is preposterous.

"Now, let's see how much you know of this subject you've never heard of... How many fingers have you?"

"Ten," said Jerya, "If you count thumbs."

"Aye, my dear, I certainly count thumbs. And how many toes?"

"Ten again."

"Then, if all of us in this room are whole, how many fingers and toes all told?"

It took her but a moment. "One hundred and forty."

"Hm. Forget thumbs for a moment, and tell me how many fingers are in this room."

"Fifty-six."

"This is too easy for you, is it? Well, one more to be sure. If each Postulant has three robes to her name—"

"I have only two, Tutor Yanil." *And the other one, the one I travelled in, is hardly fit to be counted.*

"I said, 'if', Jerya. And by tonight you will, if you remind me before we part to see that it is attended to. If each Postulant has three, but I as a Tutor have seven, how many could we bring to this room between us?"

"Eighteen, Tutor Yanil."

Yanil looked disappointed. "Are you sure of that, Jerya?"

She was sure. The answer... the answer just *was*. She could not be wrong. Yanil must be testing her. "We have twenty-five all told, and seven are already here, because we are wearing them."

The Tutor laughed. Startled, the other girls looked up from their work; Yanil sent them back to it with a mock-scowl. "Perfectly true, Jerya. I was looking for the answer 'twenty-five', but of course you're right—depending, of course, on what one means by the word 'bring', but that's hardly a mathematical point, is it?"

"I do not know."

"Hmm... perhaps you don't. Well, let us move on." She shuffled papers on her desk, many of them covered with strange symbols and a scattering of words, until she unearthed a blank sheet. With a pencil mounted in a kind of metal bracket she drew an almost-perfect circle. To a casual glance, it would have been perfect indeed. At last, thought Jerya, she was seeing the real art of a Dawnsinger.

"Now, Jerya, without measuring it, how wide would you say that circle was?"

She considered it, and as she had been told not to measure she was careful not to look at anything else for comparison. "It's close to four inches; less rather than more."

"I won't quarrel with that, though we'll have to teach you centimetres sooner rather than later... Now, if you measured round the edge of that circle, how far do you think it would be?"

This was harder but, having been right with her first figure, she was quite confident. "It's close to a foot."

Yanil looked at her sharply. "Jerya, did you estimate that or calculate it?"

"I... I'm not quite certain."

"Really..." Yanil laid her hand down on the paper, covering all but a fragment of the line. "In that case... if you had a circle that was eight inches across, how far round would it be?"

"Just over two feet," she answered without hesitation.

"Are you sure?"

Last time she had been challenged thus, she had been right. "Aye, I'm sure. It's twice the measure for the small circle, anyway."

"Just so! And you say you know nothing! Ha! Well, let's go further... Consider the two circles, one four inches wide and one eight inches. Now, imagine if you can that those circles are the bases of two jugs, whose sides are ver—exactly upright. Both are, shall we say, ten inches deep? You have that picture?" Receiving Jerya's nod, she continued, "Then if you fill the small jug to the brim with water, and pour it into the larger, spilling none—it will fill it to halfway, will it not?"

Jerya held her breath. Yanil was wrong. It must be another test... still, it was hard to say, "No."

To her relief, Yanil smiled. "More, then, or less?"

"Oh, less."

"How much less? Put it this way; how many times would you have to fill and empty the small jug to fill the larger one, if not twice?"

She closed her eyes in order to 'see' the two jugs more clearly. "It seems to be about... four times?"

"Not 'about', Jerya—exactly. As you knew, didn't you? Never be shy to give me an answer—whatever answer comes to mind. Even when you are wrong it may tell me something about you, which is what's really important at this stage."

"Aye, Tutor Yanil. It did seem to be four, but I could not say why—I had not the words—so I was not certain."

"We'll give you the words soon enough, it seems to me. And we shall have to introduce you to the metric system in short order, too." Yanil pondered a moment, one brown finger pressing her underlip. "Are you sure you've been taught none of this?"

"Not that I remember."

"Read it in a book?"

"No, and of that I am sure. Delven had few books; I read them all many times, and there was nothing like this in any of them... but guessing at the lengths and the weights of things is an art all women need—at the loom, in the kitchen, everywhere."

"True, no doubt... Did you never observe that you were better at such 'guessing' than those around you?"

"I can't say... a little quicker, perhaps."

"And a deal more accurate, I should say, unless Delven is infested with idiot-savants."

Seeing Jerya's face darken, Yanil held up a calming hand. "Take no offence, girl. I call no one idiot. 'Tis an unfortunate expression, no doubt, but 'idiot-savant' merely means one who knows without being taught. That's you, to be sure... Did Sharess know?"

"I can't say, Tutor Yanil. It did seem as if she knew everything about me. Almost more than I knew myself. But we only talked the once, and not for long."

"Poor Sharess." Jerya suspected she had not been meant to hear, but she could not help it. "Let's try something more ambitious, then. A little elementary algebra, perhaps."

Later, a distant bell intruded on Jerya's thoughts. She glanced up. To her surprise, the other girls had left, clearing their desks, and the sun had moved round to leave their end of the room in shadow.

"Which bell was that, please, Tutor Yanil?"

Yanil glanced at her wrist. "Bless me! Twelve already... already! It should seem like an age. You've done half of first-year mathematics in three hours... You must be hungry after all that."

"I am, but should I not go first to Tutor Skarat? I was meant to go to her at the eleventh bell."

Yanil laughed. "Skarat won't delay going for her lunch on your account! Don't fret, I'll speak to her. It's my fault, really. I was enjoying myself too much. Hardly had so much fun since Sharess and I were Novices tog—"

She stopped short and stared keenly at Jerya. Her lips moved, but this time even Jerya's ears could catch no sound. Then Yanil gave herself a little shake, like a dog coming in from the rain.

"No," she said, still softly. "Coincidence... and I haven't seen Sharess for a quarter of a century anyway. Now—" She sat up straight and made herself brisk. "Does that timepiece of yours not work? Let me see..."

Obediently Jerya unslung the chain from around her neck and handed it across. Yanil turned the medallion around in her hands, eyes and fingers inspecting both its faces and around its edge.

"Do you know what this is, Jerya?" she asked. Her fingers played with the small button set in one edge of the medallion.

"Only that you just called it a 'timepiece'."

"As good a name as any. I can't see anything wrong with this, except that it hasn't been wound. Sharess didn't tell you its use?"

"No, Tutor Yanil."

"Well, then, I think I shall say no more about it until tomorrow. We'll see how much you can work out by then... I suggest you look at it from time to time—" She smiled again. "—Especially when you hear a bell. There. It should work now."

She returned the *timepiece* and Jerya slung it around her neck again. She did not know what Yanil had done, but the needles on its face were in new positions, and as she lowered it over her head she felt a faint vibration. Holding it to her ear she heard a regular, insect-like, ticking.

Yanil smiled at her wondering look. "There, Jerya; I expect you to tell me tomorrow just what it's for. Without picking anyone else's brains, I may add. I'm intrigued to know just how much you can deduce for yourself... Come now. I have a timepiece in my belly and it's time to go to Refec."

CHAPTER 10

JERYA

There was more than one North; this was hard to grasp. Magnetic North and True North; these were hard enough, but she thought she was getting the way of it. But there was something else called Cartographers' North, and she did not understand why the map-makers could not simply align their maps to True or Magnetic. *Not yet, but I will.*

And which of these had they meant in Delven when they spoke of North? That was hard to say; harder still, because in Delven 'North' was a men's word. That was to say, she had never heard any woman use it, had learned it herself in her usual way, by listening; listening, often, to things she was probably not meant to hear. North was in a couple of the books, too... Between these, she had put together her own notion of what North was. No one in Delven used a compass, as far as she knew; that had been a word only found in books. Her mind's eye had formed no clear image of a compass, let alone how to use it; but she had a good sense of North. You could overhear a good deal in nineteen years, if you listened, and watched, and learned.

By night—if the sky was clear—the North Star was a perfect guide, though often hard to see if you were in the forest. She had learned that by listening, but had discovered for herself that the two end-stars of the Skillet made a pointer if you needed help to find the North Star; the Pole Star, as Tutor Jossena and the astronomy books called it. "Though North Star's a perfectly apposite name, too," Jossena had said.

That was all fine by night, but what if you wanted to find North by day—as the men of Delven mostly did—and you had no compass, as they didn't? There were other indications; which side of a tree or one of the rock-towers grew most lichen, for example, though that was a rough guide at best. And she knew now that when the sun stood at its highest, that was South, and therefore North—*True* North—was the opposite direction. This was not something she could have spelled out before, but it did not come as a surprise; it felt like something she had *almost* known for a long time.

Now, in the College, she never passed a sundial—of which there were at least half a dozen scattered around, some mounted on walls, some on their own pedestals—without at least a glance. A sundial was a kind of timepiece, a simple and beautiful one; that she grasped as soon as Jossena showed her the basics. It was also, therefore, a link between Astronomy on the one hand—which she would happily have studied in almost every available hour if it was permitted—and Horology and Calendrics on the other.

The sun at its zenith showed you where South was, but the Sun was hard to look at—and dangerous—and knowing when it was at its highest was also hard; you could never be truly sure until it had passed the zenith. A sundial saved you the pain of looking directly at the Sun, and seeing when the shadow was shortest was easier too. And that shadow pointed North.

You did not even need a specially-made sundial. Anything that cast a clear shadow could be used. The rock-tower they called The Finger, the last one she had passed on her way out of Delven; there was clear ground to the North of it. She had seen its shadow often enough. It would be in clear view from the Dawnsinger's tor, too. But any rock, any tree; even your own shadow, if you could stand still for long enough: any of these would work, on a clear day.

She wondered if the men of Delven knew all this, or if their idea of North was as imprecise as lichen on trees, as her own had once been. Precision had been missing from her life and now she sought it greedily.

North was even stranger, or richer, than that. There were places on the Earth where, at certain times, a sundial would cast no shadow at all. By the logic of her earlier understanding, that would seem to suggest that South was directly overhead, and North was directly beneath one's feet, but this was not how it worked. It was often like that; one lesson would seem to undo half of what she had learned in the previous one, undo it and remake it in a new, deeper, picture. More difficult, more perplexing, but also richer.

The strangeness—the wondrous strangeness—went on. Having gone so far that the sun stood directly overhead at midday... if you then continued South, the sun would begin to stand to the North of you, and the sundial's shadow—*all* shadows—at noon would point to the South. (And in those places you would not be able to see the North Star at all).

Stranger still: suppose you went North instead of South, walked North. It had to be True North, taking direction from the sundial, or from the North Star, not from the compass. The further North you went, the further Magnetic North would deviate from True North. Walk North and keep on walking—if there were dry land all the way, and not too much snow and ice, and a good many other ifs; but this was all about the thought, like some of her question-tests, which she now knew to call *experiments*; this was an experiment of the mind, a question-test of the imagination.

Keep on walking North, and eventually you would come to the Pole. Many things were strange here; day and night each lasted six months (*a poor place to be a Dawnsinger!* she thought). Strangest of all, if you kept on walking in a straight line, all at once you were heading South. North became South in a single stride. In fact, if you started at the Pole, whichever way you faced was South.

It made her head spin, sometimes, but she kept on wanting more.

❋

She might have felt she could study Astronomy all day—or all night!—but there were so many other things that also called to her. First, of course,

Mathematics. Her first lesson, her favourite Tutor, and the subject where every lesson seemed to be revealing things which in some sense she had already known.

There was so much else, too. The making of the sand-glasses; she could have watched that for many hours too. (Aye, *hours*. How had she ever ordered her days without knowing about hours and minutes, without bells telling off the hours, without a timepiece to keep track of the minutes too?)

Tutor Mazibel had not explained the manufacturing process, but she had explained what the sand-glasses—clepsammia—were for: like watches and clocks, like sundials, they were another form of timepiece and, if properly made, a surprisingly precise one. Jerya had grasped almost at once how they worked; well, it was clear enough to see. And therefore it was also not hard to understand that by making the glass larger or smaller, you could control the time-interval it measured. Now she was learning that there were other variables too; the grade of sand used, the diameter of the aperture between the chambers.

And the reason the Guild devoted so much time and effort to manufacturing these things was simple, too, in its way. The effort was obvious: she saw three or four Tutors about the manufactory. She did not know all their names, but she knew they were Tutors because their robes were trimmed with silver thread, as Masters' were with gold. There were dozens of grey-clad artisans at work too.

The reason: people outwith the Guild—both women and men—also had need to measure time. How long to boil an egg; that was the first example Mazibel cited. Jerya had quickly learned to enjoy hens' eggs since arriving at the College—the occasional duck-egg, too, for a treat—so she appreciated that. There were many other examples from the culinary realm. Baking was another example Jerya could relate to; she had seen too many under-baked and over-baked loaves in her life in Delven. But she had been scarcely better than anyone else at judging the time exactly. How easy it would be with a sand-glass, or a combination of two or three—because you could measure any number of minutes with a few glasses. A sand-glass or

two would be a good thing to take with her on her return to Delven, she
thought.

※

Every Tutor's first session with her had begun not with telling but with
asking. Her first Astronomy session had been no exception. Jossena didn't
have Yanil's warmth, but Jerya soon sensed a kind enough heart behind the
gruff manner. "Yanil said, 'the girl will say she knows nothing of astronomy,
but ask what she knows of the moons and the stars'. Hmph. Well, let's see,
shall we? Let's start with the moons and how they move..."

"The Three move together," said Jerya. "You can watch as long as you like
and you won't see them move, but go back the next night and they will be
in a different place. The One, though... if you sit—or sometimes I lie on the
ground and look up—if you watch long enough you can see that it moves."

"Moves relative to what?"

"Relative?"

"Against what do you see it move?"

"Against the trees or the crags when it is low, or against..." She hesitated,
but Tutor Jossena smiled encouragingly. "It seems to me that it moves
against the stars. And it can catch and pass the Three."

Jossena just nodded. "Anything else you have observed about the One?"

She thought. "It... turns on itself as it goes. Like a tumbling stone, but
many times slower."

The Tutor hmphed again. "'Like a tumbling stone'. Well, well...go on."

"And sometimes it seems brighter and sometimes not so bright."

"And anything else concerning the Three?"

She frowned in concentration. "Sometimes you can see them, faintly, in
the daytime. They seem brightest... sometimes you see them in the East
when the sun is falling in the West. And sometimes in the West when the
sun is rising—and at those times it looks very much as if it is the sun that
lights them. But I don't think it can be..."

"Why not, girl?"

"Because they shine brighter still at night, when the sun is gone by altogether."

"Hmph... we'll come back to that. Let's talk about the stars."

"The stars mostly move all together; they make the same patterns every night. Only the North Star seems fixed; the others all move."

"You said 'mostly'. So not all the stars are fixed?"

"No, sometimes you will see one fall. And there are... there are just a few that move, but do not fall."

"How many of these do you know?"

"Five, I think," she said.

"Really?" Tutor Jossena sounded surprised, but then said in an encouraging way, "Go on, girl."

"There is the morning star, and the evening star. The red one. And two more. One of them is—apart from the Three and the One, it is the brightest thing in the deep night."

"Hmph, well, I did wonder if you'd seen Mercura. You'd have to be lucky with your timing, as well as sharp-eyed, but it's possible. However, 'morning star' and 'evening star' explains the five. Well, my girl, you've seen a good deal. Still, we can show you a great deal more... But is there yet more that you have observed all by yourself in your wild mountains?"

Jerya blinked slightly. She had never really thought of the lands around Delven as 'wild'. Perhaps she was simply ignorant, did not really know what 'wild' meant. The more she learned, the more she grasped how much more there was *to be learned*. She had made a flippant comment once, to Rodal, about wanting to know everything. Even then she had sensed that it could hardly be possible; now she knew it. But still she wanted to try. You could never get there, but the journey...

She recalled that Jossena had asked a question.

"Something I have observed, aye," she said. "I have seen the Three and the One from here in the evenings, and occasionally in the mornings also. I have seen stars, though with other lights always around..."

"Aye, my dear, that is a problem. But we do our best to shield our observing-stations from all extraneous light. Though it's not possible to do that to perfection without also blocking some of the field, obscuring anything that lies close to the horizon... That's why we have a separate Observatory, well away from the city. But there's plenty you can see from here; you'll see for yourself soon enough. If we ever get a clear night again... But you said that there is something else you have observed...?"

"Aye, Tutor Jossena. In the winter, mostly, and even then rarely. On clear nights when the Three are not showing, there is... It is hard to describe, but there are bands—veils—of light. Of different colours, too. And they seem to move, almost to dance..."

"Well, that sounds very much like the Aurora to me. Do you have any notion what it might be?"

"I wondered once if it could be some eldritch radiance from the Blistered Lands, but I soon saw this could not be true."

"Why not?"

"Because all tales tell that the Blistered Lands lie to the East, over the mountains. While the lights in the sky could be seen in almost any direction, including sometimes directly overhead, but most often to the North."

"Hmph. I cannot fault your reasoning. You're quite right; they do not emanate from the Blistered Lands. But then the Blistered Lands are... well, that's another story. The question for now is, can I explain to you, based on what you've learned so far, what the Aurora is?"

Chapter 11

Rodal

The sea was everything Annyt had said, and more.

Even getting there had been a source of wonder. The 'canal' she had mentioned so casually was like a river of still water, no wider than some of the roads he had travelled, but so long that it took half the morning to traverse it. They had travelled scarcely faster than walking-pace, he thought, but they had travelled in a boat.

A boat... well, he was learning that boats came in many shapes and sizes. But this one had been... he had stepped from solid paving onto something that dipped a little under his weight—a very little, but enough to notice—and then down and along into a construction like a long wooden hut. There were wooden benches along the two long walls, beneath lines of glass windows. There were people already seated, and more waiting to enter behind them. Annyt preceded him inside, and they sat down together.

When all the benches were full, he heard voices from outside, via the open door; a tone of command, an acknowledgement. Then there was a faint jerk. He looked about, through the windows, and saw that the stone edging of the canal was sliding past. It seemed quite natural to put an arm around Annyt, protecting her and reassuring himself.

Later, they had been able to step out through another door at the other end of the room they'd been sitting in, emerging at the front of the boat, to see the whole world moving past them. It was only the same as riding in a cart, he told himself, and after five days of that he had become quite accustomed to it. But it was not the same. This was a cross between a house, and a cart, and... he lost the thought as he saw something else. The whole thing was being pulled along by a long black rope, and its farther end was attached to a great grey horse that plodded along a path at the side of the canal, seemingly quite as accustomed to it all as the cart-horses.

Out there in the open it was easier to speak to Annyt without thinking that others would overhear, perhaps laugh at his ignorance. She knew and understood that many things in this city were new to him. He learned another welter of new words, like *towpath* and *foredeck* and *cabin*. He wondered if there were any end to the words, if any man could learn in one life all the words that there were for all the things in the world. But he also thought that perhaps there were words that he knew—words *and* things—that other men did not. That was consoling.

And now, after they had *disembarked*—now *that* was a word worth learning—and walked down a steep cobbled lane, and come out to the edge of the ocean; now there were dozens, maybe hundreds, of new words to learn, new things to absorb.

Annyt had asked if he wanted to take luncheon first, but he had taken one look at the crowd heading down the street where she pointed, and turned towards the ocean. Food could wait.

There were rocks between them and the water here, a low sprawl of them, grey and green with white veins. They looked glossy and slick even where dry, and the lower parts were covered in masses of green and brown vegetation, trailing limply towards the water. They moved on a little, until they found themselves overlooking a crescent of pale pebbles, with steps leading down to it.

It was a little tricky walking on the rounded, shifting, stones, and they held on to each other for balance as they progressed slowly to the water's edge, or as close as they dared. For the 'water's edge' was also a shifting thing. Rodal knew the tiny waves that sometimes ruffled the surface of the forest tarns, the greater ripples that swimmers made; he knew the turbulence of Delven's mountain streams. But this was quite beyond anything he had seen. Beyond a few dozen yards out, the whole ocean seemed to be pulsing up and down, rhythmically but not mechanically; but, closer in, the motion changed, and there were waves rolling towards them, growing, swelling smoothly and then suddenly fraying, their crests falling into white streamers even as the water lifted behind full of green light.

Again and again and again. Each one the same, and yet different. He felt as if he could watch all day, as if he would never be able to tear himself away. But there was Annyt's hand, still on his arm, and eventually he dragged his gaze away and looked at her, hair pushed back by the breeze, smiling. He felt exhilarated—and also a little embarrassed. Lost for words, he shook his head.

"Let me show you something else," she said. "I think the tide's right."

"Tide?" he queried, finding his voice at least for the one word. She nodded to their right and they started to walk, parallel to the water. There was easier footing lower down, where the pebbles were finer and more solidly packed, but sometimes the remnants of the broken waves ran up the beach to threaten their shoes.

She was frowning. "Now how do I explain tides? Well, the level of the ocean changes."

"I can see that."

"Aye, but it changes in a different way. Greater, but slower. The whole ocean is higher or lower. Sometimes the waves break farther out, sometimes they break right up against the sea-wall. I think it depends on the moons; it's highest when they're together, or something."

He only half made sense of this, but now they had come to the end of the *beach* (another new word), where rocks shouldered through the pebbles, and here they found several little pools, the biggest three or four yards across. Green fronds in the water; were they the same as the ones that draggled limply on exposed rocks close by? And among the fronds all kinds of life. There were little fish flickering about, different from the minnows he knew from home, but not so strange. But there were stranger things, things Annyt had to name for him. *Crabs*, with disproportionately huge claws and a bizarre sideways scuttle. *Starfish*, which looked like neither fish nor stars. *Anemones*, like fleshy flowers. And apparently the things which looked like nothing more than a kind of crust on the rocks were also alive; he added *limpet* and *barnacle* to his ever-growing list of new words.

It was all becoming almost too much for him, and he realised he was growing hungry too. Perhaps it was time for a break. They walked back over the crunching pebbles, climbed the steps, along the road to the village. He thought about new words. Would he even remember them all? *Shore. Beach. Ship* (a boat had brought them here, but the ones that sailed the sea were ships, Annyt said). *Wave, spray, foam. Island* (there were several of them out there, shadowy outlines only half-solid in the capering light). *Tide. Driftwood, flotsam, jetsam. Harbour, quay, wharf, jetty.*

And then there were *mussels* (which of course he heard first as 'muscles'), *cockles, whelks, shrimp*. All edible, apparently, and indeed people appeared to be doing so with relish. But Annyt saw his hesitation and laughed, not unkindly, and said, "Fish and chips is what you need."

A little shop, its wooden doors folded right back on this warm day, where activity centred on great seething cauldrons of oil. A fillet of fish, dipped in some pale liquor or sauce, slid into one of these. A short span later it was hooked out again, but now its coating was puffed up and golden brown. A ladleful of *chips*—slivers of potato cooked in a second cauldron—joined the fish on a square of stiff brown paper; its edges were gathered into a rough kind of pouch and it was handed to him.

They walked back part of the way towards their beach before perching on the sea wall to eat. Even after that interval, the chips were still almost too hot to handle, let alone to eat, so he picked at the fish first, the flesh flaky and white inside the crunchy *batter*. Then he copied Annyt, picking out one chip and waving it in the air to cool a little before biting into it. Crisp on the outside, fluffy on the inside.

Eventually he stopped eating long enough to smile at Annyt. "It's delicious." He thought about it, and about a few other things, and it seemed entirely right to add, "I do believe I never ate anything finer."

❋

They stood on the foredeck of the boat. Rodal was reluctant to go into the cabin while they could still see the ocean. The sun was close to the horizon now, throwing a long trail of light over the ocean toward them. Earlier, it had been the colour of butter, but now it was closer to the honey that the women of Delven harvested.

Finally a bend in the canal and a rise of the ground on that side robbed them of the ocean view. He knew it would soon grow cool under the clear sky, but before they went in he turned to face Annyt.

"Thank you," he said.

"What for?" she smiled. "For having a good time?"

"Aye, if you like. Ah... just... it's been a wonderful day, is all I can say. Only thing..."

"Mm?"

"I don't feel right happy about you paying for all of it."

"It doesn't matter."

"It does to me... But you know how I'm fixed. The money I have isn't my own. It's just to keep me till I know how J—how our Postulant's fixed, how long before she'll be going back to Delven. Then I'll be able to decide if I return home myself, come back when I'm needed, or whether I try to find work here, in the city."

"Which would you rather?" she asked quietly.

"I'd rather stay," he answered firmly. "But I could only do that if I was working, earning."

"Well, they often need men at the brewery. Shifting casks, making deliveries. It's hard work, I'm sure, but you're strong. I'll put in a word with my Pa, if you'd like."

"That sounds like it would do very well, and thank you. But I need an answer first; they surely won't take me on if I might be called away in a few weeks. Need to know."

CHAPTER 12

JERYA

"Well, look at this. Jerya's still got her satchel." This came even as she was squeezing into a place at the long bench, between two Novices; she didn't see who said it. But it was Freilyn who continued, "Do you take it everywhere? Do you sleep with it?"

They all laughed: Railu, Veradel, all the others she could see.

She gazed back at Freilyn, trying to remain calm. "What would you have me do? I have nowhere to leave it."

"*Nowhere to leave it,*" another voice repeated, mimicking her accent too. "*Besure.*"

Suddenly she couldn't stand it; having just struggled into a seat, now she had to clamber out again, her mind churning. Once free, she leaned back into the gap, hands on the edge of the table, looking around at the faces opposite and either side.

"I didn't know what to expect when I came here, among Dawnsingers. I imagined many things. But I never imagined Dawnsingers would be *cruel.*"

The words fell into a pool of silence; they were all gazing at her. But at the other tables, further down this one, the general hubbub went on. Somewhere not too far away she heard a laugh. Surely it wasn't a reaction to her words, yet it echoed in her ears as she turned away, walked down the gangway between the long tables, dodged past a couple of startled servitors in the passageway, and out into the day.

She didn't know where she was going, but her feet took her to the terrace below the songstead. There was a pool here, with trees behind and beyond both ends, but its fourth side was open, giving a view over the city, the ridge dipping and curving as it rose again to the Western hill, rooftops cloaking its sides like the scales on a fish.

Towers poked up above the other rooftops, and she almost smiled as she recalled the day of her arrival, when she'd thought those towers impossibly high, when the truth was none were much more than a hundred feet—call it thirty metres, in the measures the Dawnsingers preferred, that did not yet come automatically to her. It was just that they sprouted from the higher ground, the natural hills that had long been hidden beneath the accretion of stone and brick, timber and tile.

But then she looked again at the pool in front of her; there were tiles here, too, lining its edges, marking out a precise rectangle. It was more like her place in the forest than anywhere else in the precincts, but it was nothing like it.

She sank onto a stone bench. She could still see the tops of the highest towers, but the water reflected only sky.

The she just sat and cried.

She had no sense of how much time had passed, hadn't looked at her timepiece since the morning, and had no intuition in her head. It might have been ten minutes; it might have been an hour. Then she heard foot-steps. At the edge of her vision she saw white clothing, a bald head. Even now there was a piece of her that said *Dawnsinger*, that felt she should hide her face or run away.

She didn't move, and already a voice was asking, "Do you mind if I sit?"

Jerya shrugged. Railu settled beside her, perhaps a foot away. "I'm sorry," she said. When Jerya didn't respond, she went on, "I don't think anyone intended to be cruel. It just... things sometimes go a bit too far."

Still Jerya had nothing to say. She looked at the water, watching for fish.

"I don't think anyone meant to be cruel," said Railu again, "But perhaps some people did want to *shake* you a bit."

"Shake me? Why?"

"Because they're envious."

She stared at Railu. "Why would anyone be envious of *me*?"

Railu gave what Jerya could only describe as a half-laugh. "You really can't see, Jerya? All that special attention you get from the Tutors. Even Perriad herself. All those individual sessions. Blood-moons, Jerya, I've been here seven years, more, and I haven't had that much attention from Perriad in all that time. Well, maybe I have, but it's been the kind of attention no one wants."

"Aye," said Jerya, finding a glimmer of understanding. "But... you *have* been here seven years and more."

Railu just blinked at her, her eyebrows dark quizzical arcs. Jerya continued, "You talk about envy. Can't you imagine...? I haven't even been here three weeks yet." Her laugh was curt, mirthless. "A couple of weeks ago I barely knew the word 'week'. And I may only be here a few weeks more. A few months if I'm lucky."

She drew breath, looked at the water. A spreading ripple told her she'd just missed seeing one of the fish break the surface. She thought about the word she'd just uttered: 'lucky'. "All that time... Do you know how many books there are in Delven, Railu? Could you take a guess?" The response was a helpless shrug. "Twenty-three. Ha, it's a prime number. Something else I didn't know until a few days ago.

"Twenty-three books, Railu. Believe me, I know their number; I've read them all enough times. *That* was my education: twenty-three books. And then I came here and I found the Library and there are more books... it feels like more than I could ever count, let alone read. I feel paralysed sometimes, not knowing which to pick out next. And you... you all take it for granted. People treat books like they don't matter. Turn the pages with fingers sticky from eating syrup-cake. Lay them upside-down to keep their page...

"And it's not just books. It's all of it. All the things you already know and I'm desperately trying to catch up with. I'd never even seen a telescope before I came here. I just lay on my back on the cold earth and gazed at the stars with my bare eyes. And in a few weeks or a few months I'll go back to Delven and I'll probably never see a telescope again, let alone look through one." Railu's gaze was fixed on her, and she saw tears in those eyes; but she could not stop now. "And I thought, just for a little while, like the first night I was here... I thought I'd have people to talk to. Talk about books, about the stars, about numbers, about... well, everything. And what happens? People make fun of the way I talk and the things I don't know."

Railu was honestly weeping now. They both were. But Jerya hadn't finished. "And I'm still sleeping in a dormitory with the youngest girls, because no one's offered to share a study-chamber. When I want to read, or work on whatever task Yanil or Jossena or one of the others has given me, what am I supposed to do? I try and find a corner in the Library, but it means always having to carry everything I might need with me—and then people laugh at me for carrying my satchel around! Well, I ask you, what else am I supposed to do?"

"Jerya, I... I'm so sorry. I never thought..."

"No, it doesn't seem like anyone did." She wasn't quite ready to accept an apology, however heartfelt. "I swear... I was often alone, back in Delven, but I could always have stayed with the other women. It was my choice to be solitary, to wander. Alone is not the same as lonely, you know. I swear I've been more lonely at times here than ever I was before."

"I'm so sorry," said Railu again. "I really am. I try not to be cruel, but I have been heedless, and maybe that's almost as bad." She moved her hand on the stone between them, creeping it closer. "Is it too late? Can we be friends?"

Jerya looked at the hand a moment, then laid her own across it. "If you really mean it... then I'd like that. I'd like it very much."

For a little time they sat there side-by-side, hands clasped. Jerya gazed at the water again, and this time was rewarded as one of the black-and-gold fish shot up from the depths, snatching a fly from the surface.

"I can't offer to share with you," Railu said then. "I'm already sharing with Freilyn, you see. Since fifth year. But I can talk to the others..."

"I don't even need to sleep in the same chamber. It's just to have somewhere to work."

"It'd be better if you did, though. Keep everything in one place. I'll see what they think, anyway. I can't promise more than that."

"No, I understand. Thank you." They looked at each other and smiled.

"Don't you need to get to a class now?" Jerya asked.

"I'm supposed to be down at the Lower Infirmary. What about you?"

"Private study. I suppose I'm studying the fish at the moment."

Railu smiled again. "So you don't have to be anywhere right now?"

"No, not really."

"Then would you like to come with me? I want to show you something."

Railu's mention of a 'Lower Infirmary' had sparked Jerya's curiosity, even with everything else that was going through her head. Thus far she had been aware of only one Infirmary, on an upper floor at the rear of the main College range, where ailing Singers, Novices, and Postulants were cared for. But Railu led her in the opposite direction, down a flight of steps beyond the pool, then along a descending leftward path.

The path ran between high walls, then ended at a tall doorway. Beyond an anteroom and a short corridor, they turned into a larger chamber, with beds ranked along both side-walls. It had some of the same atmosphere as her one brief glimpse of the other Infirmary, but the beds were closer together, and there was more bustle, more noise.

And the women in the beds were not Dawnsingers. Some wore caps, of various colours, but many were bare-headed, with hair bound back or in a few instances hanging loose. There were grey-clad servitors moving around as well as two—no, three—Dawnsingers, one of whom was now talking to Railu. Railu beckoned Jerya to come closer.

"...hasn't been here very long," she was saying to the Singer.

"So I've heard," said the Singer, a shortish woman, dark, somewhat stout. She wore a white apron over her regular Singer's garb. "Who hasn't? Well,

Jerya, have you come to lend a hand? As you can probably see, we're permanently overstretched here."

Jerya didn't know what to say. Fortunately Railu saw her problem, and came to her aid. "Jerya has a heavy workload already, trying to learn everything in no time. I just brought here her to see. She ought to know everything that goes on, I thought."

The Singer nodded. "I wouldn't dispute that, as I'm sure you surmised. Well, Jerya... oh, I don't believe Railu introduced us. I'm Sister Berrivan."

Jerya bowed her head politely.

"As you can see, what we do here is treat women from outwith the Precincts. Family of our serving-people, mostly. Women who have little or no access to any other kind of care... as you may know, male physicians are often disdainful of what they refer to as 'women's complaints', and many women are understandably reluctant to submit to any examination by males outwith their immediate family."

Jerya nodded. She hadn't understood all of this, but a glance from Railu seemed to say, '*We can talk about it later.*'

"And then, of course," Berrivan went on, "Women—and indeed men—from poorer homes are often unable to pay a physician anyway. Whatever my opinions on the competence of male physicians..." She sniffed. "They are still, probably, better in most cases than the alternatives open to such unfortunates. Quack-practitioners with no training whatsoever. Nostrums peddled by unscrupulous—" She broke off as a passing servitor addressed a few words to her. "—Of course, I'll be right there. Well, Jerya, Railu can tell you the rest. It's been my pleasure to meet you and if you ever do have time we'd love to see you again."

"Thank you, Sister," Jerya said, but Berrivan was already turning away. After a couple of strides, she stopped, glancing back. "I'll need you in ten minutes if you're going to assist with the surgery, Railu."

"Of course, Sister." Railu faced Jerya again. "Sorry, but you see how it is. And for every woman in one of those beds there are hundreds more in the City who need help just as much."

"And beyond the City," Jerya observed.

"Aye, of course, but that's why—" She stopped herself. "No, I mustn't start now. Ask me tonight at dinner."

***

"Well, you saw a little of how it was. There are forty-two beds in total in the Lower Infirmary."

Around them, Jerya saw darting glances, rolling eyes. She thought she understood; the others had all heard this before, and more than once. But she had not, and she was happy to listen to Railu.

"Berrivan and the other Sisters down there are forever trying to get the Guild to expand the Infirmary. But if it was ten times the size, *and* if there were enough Sisters to staff it, it still wouldn't meet the need."

"And that's just in the City," she said, reprising her own earlier observation.

"Aye, of course. There are outposts, but smaller, in a couple of the larger towns. Still... you can surely see what a need there is, just to take care of women and girls. And Berrivan and the others talk about recruiting more Sisters to train as physicians."

"Like you?" 'Physician' was not a term Jerya had heard spoken, growing up in Delven, but she thought she understood, at least roughly, what it meant.

"Aye, like me."

"That's something you can be proud of, besure."

"I am. But of course, if you draw more Sisters to the Healing Arts, you have fewer for everything else. And however highly I value being a physician, I wouldn't argue that everything else the Guild does isn't also important."

"So what else would you do?"

"Well, maybe we could recruit more girls to the Guild generally, and then there'd be more scope to train physicians. That's part of it, maybe. But how many more would we need to really make a difference? Forty-two beds; would forty-two hundred be enough? How many Singers would we need?

Where does it end? Half the female population as Dawnsingers? Can you envision that?"

"I don't know. I'm too ignorant of too many things." She thought about it all the same. "But in a place like Delven... I can't see it. The Dawnsinger's only the Dawnsinger because she stands apart."

"Jerya's right," said Veradel, giving her a tentative smile. Jerya smiled back; she was in a forgiving mood, now. Veradel was small and slight for a senior, green-eyed, her pale skin liberally freckled. "Surely we—Dawnsingers—we have to be... have to *appear* special? Maybe we are—I do believe the Peripatetics seek out the brightest and best—but that's not all of it, is it?" She gave Jerya another smile, but this one seemed to ask a question.

"Brightest and best? Are you asking if *I*...? How can I tell? I could read; I don't know that anyone knew more about me than that. Most girls in Delven can't, or only with difficulty. But as much as anything I think the reason I was chosen was simply because I wasn't spoken for."

"I suspect you're too modest," said Veradel, smiling again.

Jerya shrugged. "That's kind... but as I say, how can I tell?" She noticed that Railu was looking impatient. "I think Railu has another idea..."

Veradel smiled. "Oh, she does. I wonder what you'll think of it."

Jerya looked at Railu again. "It seems obvious to me," Railu said. "I can believe we can't create that many more Dawnsingers... but there are other women working in the Infirmary already. Making beds, cleaning, feeding the patients. Doing all the menial tasks. Why not train some of them as physicians too?"

Jerya pondered. At least, she thought, she now had a clearer idea what Railu's 'awkward questions' might be, even if she had little sense of what the answers could be. "This is truly a moment where I feel like an ignorant Backland girl. I know nothing of the City beyond these walls, except the little I saw on my way here, for... no more than an hour, I think. But I do know Delven, and I suppose there must be many places which are more or less like Delven... And I'm thinking now... if it's my destiny to return to Delven as its Dawnsinger, why should I not use my time to care for the health of the women and girls? And why should I not teach them, so that they might care for themselves and each other?

"Well, I have one answer; I have had no training in the Healing Arts, and as far as I know I am not scheduled to receive any in my time here, so I will return to Delven knowing no more of this subject than any of the other women there.

"But then again, the present Dawnsinger; she, I am certain, was here for the full term, for eight years. And all of you receive at least a grounding in the Healing Arts—I have that right, don't I?" Railu and Veradel both nodded. "Then the obvious question must be, why does the present Dawnsinger not do this?"

She looked at the two of them; and she saw that others were beginning to listen now. "Without asking her, I can only guess. But I can say that there is almost no contact between the Singer and the people. In all my life, the first time I spoke to the Singer, or heard her speaking voice, or stood close to her, was the day I was Chosen. And it was much the same, so far as I can tell, in the other villages I passed through on the first days of my journey."

"Surely that's taking the Principle of Detachment to an extreme," said Veradel.

"I don't know enough about the Principle of Detachment," said Jerya carefully. "There are so many things I still need to learn." *And, unless I am very 'lucky', too little time.* "But I am not sure if this... separation... was of the Singer's choosing anyway. I do know that I was taught, from an early age, to stay away from the Dawnsinger. To move quickly around the base of the tor, to avoid the paths she used... so I think that, whatever the Singer herself may have wished, separateness was also very much enforced by the people themselves."

"Including the women?" asked Veradel, sounding as if she asked merely for confirmation.

"Certainly. It was the women who taught me. So I think that if I—as Dawnsinger there—ever tried to teach the women anything, be it the Healing Arts or anything else, I would find it hard even to gain their attention. And..." She paused a moment; she felt a little as if she were being disloyal to the women who had raised her. But the truth was the truth. "And how could I teach them anyway? When most can barely read, or know any but the simplest arithmetic? Where would I start?"

"How is it you can read, if none of the others can?" That was Freilyn.

"Well, perhaps I should not say they can't. Only that I have never seen them do so. And that girls in Delven are not *taught* to read. Nor all the men, either."

"Then how did you learn?"

"I learned by standing at the headman's feet as he read to us from one story-book or another. Watching his finger following the words." She smiled. "I learned to read upside-down, as it would seem to you. And for a few years, when I purloined one of the books to read it to myself, I continued to hold it upside-down. Until one day, watching him read, I thought how he must be seeing it all the other way, and that must be the proper way. But it was hard, at first, to read the other way. It felt like learning all over again. And I thought, sometimes, that it made no real difference, so why bother? I hardly know why I persevered, but I suppose it is a good thing, now, that I did."

"Can you still read upside down?" asked Veradel.

Jerya shrugged. "I haven't tried in a while, but I should think so."

"I should like to see that."

CHAPTER 13

JERYA

"I've received reports from all the Tutors who've assessed you, Jerya," said Perriad. "And very interesting reading they make."

Jerya stood mute. She had no idea whether 'very interesting' implied good news or bad.

"I might even say 'startling'," Perriad continued, only prolonging her suspense. "In some cases, at least, the word is entirely apt. Quite remarkable considering your background, or should I say, lack of it? Yanil in particular is delighted. She says you're as natural a mathematician as any she's seen in sixteen years as a Tutor... says it's a crime you weren't Chosen at ten years old. Tutor Jossena, too, would dearly love to welcome you into her Astronomy classes on a regular basis. I'm sure you'd like that, wouldn't you?"

"Indeed I would." Jerya's response was instant. *To know all the secrets of moons and stars and sun...*

Perriad tugged thoughtfully at an earlobe. "It's all very pleasing in its way, and you have every right to feel proud, but it does complicate the question of what we are to do with you."

As her first reflex response faded, Jerya felt a pang of guilt. Sometimes now, whole days could pass with barely a thought of Delven, or the old Singer, or anything else outside the walls. The Precincts were a world every bit as complete and self-contained as her old one had been. She could barely believe herself to be the same person for whom Delven's horizons had been the limits of experience. Sometimes she almost forgot she had not been here for years, like those she was, finally, beginning to think of as her friends.

But...

"There's what you want, girl, and there's what's right, and they bain't always the same thing." One of her Aunts, in Delven... but which one?

Doesn't matter, she told herself. True was true, no matter who said it. She squared her shoulders, looked straight at the Senior Tutor. "But the D—Singer Sharess intended me for Delven."

"Hm, so she did, mayhap. But village Singers do not have the authority to dictate these matters. And one may wonder whether Sharess's thinking was at its clearest—" Seeing Jerya's face, she stopped; then, in a tone clearly intended to be kind, she went on, "Well, she sent you to us. I'll not pretend it didn't strike me as strange, at first. Now, however, it seems she may have been wiser than I thought. Though the question does arise, why not send you before?"

She didn't wait for an answer. "Still, one must wonder how much she could have foreseen... You must have had little direct contact with her, prior to your Choosing?"

"In truth, none."

"Aye, and that is well and good. It surprises me not at all that Sharess honours the Principle of Detachment. And therefore she would have known little of you. I suppose she would have asked the headman, or his—hm, what word do your people use, the folk of Delven?"

"I am sorry, Senior Tutor." She felt colour rise in her cheeks, felt ignorant and out of place as she had on her first few days. "But I don't understand... the word for what?"

"For a married woman."

Jerya frowned. "We just say 'married woman', I think. Married or wedded."

"Really? No special word? Won't a man say, 'my wife', or something?"

"Well, he might say, 'She's my Own'."

"Own..." Perriad repeated with a note of satisfaction. "Does that not imply that the men feel that the women belong to them?"

This didn't sound right. Perhaps some men might feel that way; she could not know. But women spoke of their Own, too. Unbidden words flickered through her mind: what might have been: Rodal's Own, Jerya's Own.

And in that moment, Perriad pressed on, and Jerya lost the chance to clarify the point. "Often, I believe, it is the headman's spouse—his Own—who keeps the Dawnsinger apprised of the doings of the women—and the girls, of course."

"I see... but Holdren—Delven's headman—he had no Own."

"Is that so? That's most unusual, I should think...?"

"I suppose so." She shrugged. *I hardly know what's usual; I only know Delven.*

"Mayhap it's immaterial. The point is... Sharess could hardly have foreseen how you were going to blossom here." Perriad laughed softly. "Blessings, girl, I'm sure you yourself had no idea."

"No, Senior Tutor... if truth be told, I had very little idea what to expect here, in any regard."

"I dare say you did not." Perriad gave another low chuckle. "You have surprised us all, including yourself. And, that being the case, it seems to me—and to the other Tutors to whom I've spoken concerning you—that it would be a grievous waste to send you back to a place like that. You can be far more valuable to us than just one more Singer on a backland songstead."

Jerya realised she was shaking her head. She stopped herself at once, but Perriad had noticed. "What is it, Postulant?"

"I swore a Vow. To serve the Guild and its Knowledge, but also to serve *my community of Delven*."

"The Guild serves the entirety of the Sung Lands, Jerya, and therefore every Singer serves every community." Perhaps that was true, though it did not seem quite good enough. She thought that Analind might call it *sophistry*.

Perriad allowed her no time to form an objection. "There are things you should know, Jerya. I do not mean that you are at fault for not knowing, only that you need to be enlightened now. I mentioned the Principle of Detachment earlier.... There are excellent reasons why we take girls at ten or eleven for Guild training. Leave it any later and most will be forming other attachments, other loyalties. I suspect that in a place as small as Delven it was little short of a miracle to find someone like you."

Jerya stood outwardly meek and silent, but in her mind she protested, *Perhaps I did have other loyalties; you never asked. No one did.* Not even the old Singer, though she had seemed, somehow, to know well enough.

"There are excellent reasons why a Dawnsinger must hold herself apart, aloof, from the community she serves. Perhaps this is especially so in smaller, more isolated places." She glanced at the clock. "I have not time to go into this in depth. We must find time for you to attend Tutor Milag for some grounding in the Principles..." She sighed. "Ah, but any coherent plan requires that your future is resolved.

"For now, Jerya, take heed of this. In accordance with the Principle of Detachment, it is highly unusual for a Singer to be placed in the same village from which she was Chosen as a girl. From a purely practical standpoint, too, it is rare that a Singer's Ordination will coincide with a vacancy arising in her place of origin. But, even if it did, we would not routinely send that Singer to fill that vacancy. It is not easy—I do understand—for a Singer to maintain Detachment in any placement, still less in smaller or more isolated communities. It could only be harder, probably *much* harder, if she were required to live in proximity with those who were her mother, her sisters, her childhood friends."

I never knew my mother and I never had a sister. The thought flickered through Jerya's mind. But the image that lingered was the image of Marit, at Thrushgill. It had not seemed as if she wore Detachment lightly.

"That being so, Jerya, understand that it would be most irregular—even if we were to place you in a village, which I think now we should by no means take for granted—for you to be sent back to Delven."

"But..."

"But what?"

"But Delven must have a Dawnsinger."

"Of course it must," said Perriad briskly. "And so it shall. Have no fear on that account. Due arrangements will be made, as and when they become necessary. Though we hope and trust that it shall be many years before the necessity arises in fact." Her smile was doubtless intended to reassure.

The Senior Tutor leaned back in her chair, forming her long hands into an inverted V. "It seems to me, Jerya, that the first issue we must address is your anomalous status, bearing the title of Postulant but attending many of the classes of the older girls—and of course, quite naturally, your free time is mostly spent with those nearest your own age. I believe you are now sharing a room with another Senior?"

"I am, Senior Tutor."

"Aye, good. So I think we should advance you to the standing of Novice without waiting for a year to pass. Rules can be waived when circumstances require it. You will take your Novitial Vows with the other current Postulants at the Equinox. Among other things, that will bind you deeper to the Guild—and will allow you to be initiated into some of the mysteries that are closed to Postulants." Perriad smiled. "That will answer some of the questions I suspect you are already formulating. You'd like that, wouldn't you, Jerya? You like answers, I think."

CHAPTER 14

RODAL

R odal, perched on the tall bar-stool he'd begun to call his own, began to read the letter a second time. All was well, Holdren wrote. The crops grew apace, and just yesterdayday Kelbrick had hooked the largest salmon any of them had ever seen, as thick as his thigh and almost as long as his entire leg. "*We're smoking much of it, we'll save some to celebrate your return*," he continued. "*I hope, however, you are not in too great a hurry, that life in the City is not too disagreeable, for there are signs your return need not be so soon. Our Dawnsinger is stronger, and the weather is better. If she weakens again, and winter draws nigh, perhaps then will be the time.*"

"'Not too disagreeable'," Rodal repeated to himself with a soft chuckle. Life in the City was just fine, and seemed all the better now Holdren had eased his one nagging worry. He might be here all through summer, and harvest-moons, and leaf-fall. Time enough for many things.

Time enough for wooing...

He would, of course, be obliged to return to Delven to fulfil his duties as Escort. It would he good, by that time, to be sure, perhaps to bring Annyt with him rather than sending for her later. But—and this was a new thought—then, perhaps, he and Annyt would return to the City.

He knew, with barely a moment's consideration, that Annyt would never take to life in Delven. Having to sit all day in the stonecourt and bind her lovely curls in a rag... he did not want to see her like that, face prisoned in dull cloth, body shrouded. It was wrong to stifle such loveliness; it was not wrong, whatever they might say in Delven, it was ten times right for her to dress as she had today, loose yellow trousers gathered at her ankles, red blouse and gold-embroidered gilet.

And when they stood on the rocks in the breeze off the sea, the wind that raced the waves, the world salt-keen and full of life, and she had pulled off her hair-band and let the curls blow free, he had known it was not wrong, was a hundred times right, to pull her close into a kiss.

She had just gone upstairs to change. He had scarcely wanted her to change those clothes in which she was so bright, so beautiful... yet he was eager to see what new delight she would find in her wardrobe.

He swigged from his mug. That was another City pleasure he would miss, back in Delven...

He swung round in his seat to look down the bar. He wanted to share something of his pleasure; but though he was on nodding terms with several regulars here in the bar, and his workmates at the brewery were friendly enough, there was no one in whom he could confide.

Then a figure darkened the doorway against the evening light. (There was just a spell, late each afternoon, when the sun found its way into the narrow cleft.) It was a slight shock, but oddly pleasing—in the light of his recent thoughts, very odd—to see one dressed in the manner of the women of Delven, even to the precise way the headcloth was wound. Only the colour was different, a dull brownish-grey.

He smiled. It might be amusing, for a while, to see Annyt so dressed, when they visited Delven. Already the word 'visit' had established itself; he no longer thought 'returned home'. Aye, for a short time it might be amusing. Through sudden stranger's eyes, this woman's clothes now looked staid and dowdy. To think he had once been shocked to see Jerya without her headcloth...

Jerya.

She stopped at his side. Her hands gripped the edge of the bar-top, knuckles whitening. He concentrated on her hands, did not look at her face.

"I hoped I'd find you here," she said.

Rodal was no longer the ignorant Backlander who thought it impossible to speak to a Postulant... She herself had started to teach him. Still, it was hard to find his voice. "What brings you here?" he managed, then winced. His words sounded harsh, unwelcoming.

She hesitated. Her hand moved towards the letter, lying beside his glass. "News from home?"

"Read it if you like," he said, trying to sound kinder.

She read quickly and silently, like a man—some men, at any rate. Many Delven-women could not read at all; the few who did formed the words one by one, sounding them aloud or mouthing them silently. "That's good," she said, handing back the paper. "That Sharess is better... and Kita's baby. It was so terrible when she lost her first. She was so young... she still is. Younger than I..."

For a moment she fell silent, lost in thought. Rodal had his mouth open to speak when she resumed abruptly, "I need to talk to you. It's about this, in a way. And important... Is there anywhere private?"

Before he could reply—though in truth he didn't know what to say—Annyt came though the curtain behind the bar, bright in blue. Her smile faded when she saw his face. "Is something the matter?" Bangles clashed and glinted on her wrists as she laid her hands on the counter.

"I don't know," he replied. He glanced at Jerya, who had turned to Annyt with a startled expression. "We need somewhere to talk in private, if that's possible."

Whatever Annyt thought to this, she concealed it well. "Come into the parlour," she said, lifting the flap at one end of the bar. "It's free; Father and Mother went out as soon as we returned." She led them through, bade them sit, asked, "Can I get you anything?"

"I would like a mug of ale," said Jerya. Then her face fell, "Ah... I'm afraid I've no coin."

"Let me," said Rodal quickly, hoping his surprise did not show. Annyt drank beer, of course; most women did, in the City. But women in Delven never touched liquor of any kind, and he had never considered that Dawnsingers might do so.

Her request only served to fuel the vague but ugly suspicions stirring in his mind. What if Jerya were in trouble of some kind? If she had somehow failed, been found unsatisfactory... it was suddenly all too easy to imagine that she had been too independent, too flighty, to settle to her new role... He could cheerfully contemplate leaving Delven to settle here, but that did not mean he no longer cared about it.

He meant to demand her news, bad or good, but she spoke first. "Isn't it strange? I've worn these things most of my life, yet now I can't bear it... Do you mind if I take it off?"

He shook his head; he would welcome it. The headcloth did not please him; at best it was a disguise, at worst it might be a mark of disgrace.

She unwound the cloth quickly, just as Annyt came bustling in with her drink. She stopped short at the sight of Jerya's bare scalp. Her mouth formed an 'O', but no sound emerged. Another time, Rodal would have laughed, but now he wondered anxiously what was going through her mind.

"Please, don't worry," said Jerya, regaining her self-possession. "The only person who might get into trouble is me, and even that's not likely."

Annyt relaxed, at least enough to move again. Jerya accepted her mug with a smile, tasted the ale at once. "Thanks. That's good."

"Thank you, Dawnsinger." Annyt glanced at Rodal. "Call if you need me."

As she left, Jerya returned her gaze to Rodal. Then, bewilderingly, she laughed. "Rodal, you're a picture! Don't look so worried."

"I *am* worried. What am I to think, seeing you here?"

"Didn't you hear me say it's all right? I... I'm here because I may have a hard choice ahead of me. Since it concerns you—concerns everyone in Delven—and you're the only one here who can speak for them... I had to talk to you."

He heard this with no joy. How could he speak for Delven, when he himself was thinking of forsaking it?

"It comes to this," she went on. "When the time comes, it's possible that you may not have to escort me back to Delven after all." She held up a hand before he could protest. "No, don't worry. Another Dawnsinger will be sent."

"But when... surely you were made Postulant because no other Dawnsinger could be spared?"

"That's not quite true. In every community, from time to time, girls are Chosen to be trained as Dawnsingers, but..." She paused. "But I have learned that it is not the custom to send them to serve the same community as Singer when they are Ordained."

"But we all thought..."

"Aye, just as I did. It is what Sh—what Delven's Singer led me, us, to expect, is it not? But in truth that is not how it usually works, for at least two reasons. One, if a girl is Chosen at ten and Ordained at eighteen, it's not very likely that the place she came from will be in urgent need of a new Dawnsinger just at that time. Whereas other places may be. And second..."

"Second... it's felt that a community may find it harder to give their Singer the full measure of respect if they remember her as an ordinary girl, a mewling babe... And—not in my case, but for most—it would be a little strange, probably more than a little, to be sent back to live alongside her own mother, father, perhaps sisters or brothers, and yet always to be apart... you know how it is."

She glanced up, and just for a moment their eyes met, and he had the strongest feeling that he knew what she was leaving unsaid; that it would also be more than a little strange for the two of them, Rodal and Jerya, to live so close and yet to be always apart. Of course, that would not apply if he made the City his permanent home, but she could not know that his thoughts had taken such a turn.

He understood her line of thinking. Understood it perfectly, in fact; on their journey it had seemed fairset to drive him mad at times, the impossibility of reconciling the two Jeryas: the Jerya he had always known, had played with when they were small enough for girls and boys to play together, the Jerya for whom new feelings had flickered into life at the worst possible moment... and the Jerya who walked or rode alongside him, the Postulant of the Guild of Dawnsingers. To have that contradiction before him every day of his life; no, he thought, if Jerya *did* go back to Delven to serve as Dawnsinger... that would be another reason, and a compelling one, for him to choose life in the City.

But what she was telling him was that she might *not* be going back, and this part he did not yet understand. "But why? Why can't you return? Have you...?"

"Oh no," she replied, understanding what he hesitated to say.. "On the contrary, if anything I've done too well." When he said nothing, she added, "Aren't you going to congratulate me?"

"I am but a humble man. Is it for me to congratulate you?"

She sighed. "So we cannot be friends as once we were. Yet you haven't forgotten so quickly, have you? I thought you'd be at least a little pleased."

"But I am, naturally."

"Aye, it shines out of you like the sun!" she snapped sourly. A brief chill silence was broken by a gust of merriment from the barroom.

Jerya shook her head. Lamplight slithered across her scalp. "I'm sorry, Rodal. Everything's different, isn't it? You can't guess how different... Everything's changed so much for me. I came running to you thinking you'd be just the same. It was wrong to expect that of you. Wrong to expect you just to have been sitting in your lodgings waiting for me."

"It's all right," he said. He wasn't sure that it was, but he had to say it. "You've had much on your mind, I can see."

"No reason to think I could share it with you... There are things I'm forbidden to tell you in any case. Though I don't know what I might have let out if... Never mind. At least, if I don't return with you to Delven, you can set folks' minds at rest."

"I'll do that, of course. And I do... I can see why you might wish to talk to me. I want to tell you something, too, though I doubt you have need to know it... It may be that my own return to Delven will be but brief."

She had begun to rise; now she dropped back into the chair, mouth hanging open. *Not exactly all the dignity of a Dawnsinger*, Rodal thought with fleeting amusement. She did not speak, but her face asked the question. "I find I like it here," he said. "There's nothing to keep me in Delven anyway, hasn't been since the day you were Chosen. And now I may have another reason to remain."

"She looks handsome," she said. *She's sharp*, he thought. *Always was*. "I can't say more, not on a moment's meeting. But you're no fool, Rodal... And it's no business of mine in any case."

She sat up straight. For a moment she looked directly at him. "Rodal, I will come again before you... before the summons comes from home. When I know who'll be sent if I remain here, I will bring her. And I will make you be friendly to her."

She laughed. "I intended her to have a friend in Delven. At least she will have a friend for the journey... I think I should go now."

As she reached for the latch, he stopped her. "Aren't you going to put your headcloth back on?"

She burst out laughing. "Choss, I'd forgotten!" Then she looked straight at him, and he knew she was remembering another time. Then, too, she had forgotten her headcloth. "You see, I've not changed so much."

I'm not so sure about that, he thought, fetching the cloth for her from the arm of the chair. He watched as she wrapped it around her head. She looked much like the old Jerya—much like, but not exactly.

They went back into the cheerful racket of the bar, halted at the flap. Annyt glanced over as she hauled on the beer-engine. "I'm rushed off my feet! Could you help me when you're finished, Rodal?"

"We're finished now," he said. He held out his hand to Jerya and she clasped it firmly. Only afterwards did it strike him as strange; handshakes were for men. Yet it had seemed quite natural.

She looked at Annyt for a moment. If she said anything, it escaped his ears, but Annyt's face got a startled look. Jerya was already turning away, slipping through the crowd and out into the street without a backward glance.

CHAPTER 15

JERYA

Jerya traced the secret way back into the College, changed her clothes in the bushes, then hurried to the chamber Railu shared with Freilyn. To her relief it was Railu's voice calling "Enter!"; to her added relief her friend was alone. She had never truly warmed to the pale girl, who still seemed to hold herself aloof in a way none of the other Novices did, as if practising the Principle of Detachment she kept hearing about.

More importantly, she needed to talk freely. "You aren't too busy, are you?" she asked, seeing Railu was at her desk.

"Not I," Railu answered. "You know me. Model student... well, there's still some hope I'll do so well in Final Catechisms, they'll find it hard not to keep me here."

There was no bitterness in her tone. This had puzzled Jerya before. There could be no doubt Railu yearned to remain, and one who excelled in the Catechisms might indeed be retained in the College. But for all her evident yearning, she seemed strangely tranquil about the very real prospect of a different fate.

"And if I can clinch first in Physician's Catechism... Which isn't beyond the bounds of possibility, by the way... If I do that, Berrivan and the other Sisters'll fight to keep me here. I mean, I'd like to think they'd fight for me anyway, but if I'm first, it makes their case stronger."

"That would be wonderful..." She hesitated. It wasn't easy to say it. "It seems as if I may be here longer than I'd expected also."

Railu's eyebrows rose, but she said only, "Glass of wine?"

"I've already had some ale."

"You've been Out." It was hardly a question.

"Just got back."

"If you've been Out, you definitely need wine. Sit here with me..." She pointed to the bed, which was certainly more enticing than the alternative, the upright chairs which sat at the desks. Jerya subsided gratefully. Railu fetched a flask from behind the window-curtains where it was keeping cool, filled a glass and topped up her own.

They clinked their glasses together; one more thing she'd learned. Railu looked at her expectantly.

"I went to see... Rodal. My escort... my friend from Delven."

"And...? Your Dawnsinger's recovered?"

"Aye, at least somewhat, but that's not it... I went to give him some news, rather than receive it." She sipped at the wine. It was sweet, almost syrupy, not greatly to her taste; thus far, among the many new flavours she had encountered, she preferred both ale and cider to wine, and if wine was the only offering, she would rather have dry than sweet. Still, it was cool, and it gave her a moment to order her thoughts.

"I didn't tell you before," she said, "But Perriad called me in yesterday. She seems to want me to stay on here..."

Railu's eyes widened, and a grin took charge of her face. She shifted in her seat as if resisting some urge to move. "That's wonderful! At the very least we'll both be here until Ordination."

"I suppose so, but... it feels somehow strange. That they do want me... I ought to be full of pride, and I can't find it yet... But haven't you thought what it means? Our Dawnsinger is stronger. It probably means there'll be no summons from Delven until after your Ordination, but that means..."

"I'm the most likely person to be sent? Don't be afraid to say it, it's true."

"How can you sound so calm about it? I keep thinking about you imprisoned in that little tor-chamber."

"It's not really a prison, is it? I can get up and take a walk any time I want."

Jerya winced. Saying 'can' rather than 'could' made it sound as if Railu felt her future already sealed. *But just a moment ago she was talking about Berrivan and the other Physicians fighting to keep her...*

"No, listen. You could go for a walk, aye. But everyone would bow their heads and stare at the ground as you passed. No one would ever speak to you—except the headman, when he needed to know about the weather, about harvests and suchlike; maybe the Elderwife, once in a while. That's all the converse you'd ever have with another human being. No one ever passes through Delven. It's at the edge of the world."

"Don't you know the world is round? It has no edges."

Her gentle mockery was too much. "I don't care what the Tutors say," sobbed Jerya. "The world does have an edge. The skyline of the mountains. What do the maps call it? The Sundering Wall. If you go beyond, you come to the Blistered Lands, and you die."

Railu moved across to the bed; dimly she felt an arm slide behind her shoulders, draw her close. "*I don't care what the Tutors say:* you're beginning to sound like me... But if you don't want me to go beyond the edge, I won't."

"Delven would be like death to you anyway. I hardly know how *I* could face going back—even though it's my country and I've always loved it... and I've always been content with solitude. But you... you've been surrounded by people, all the years you've been here. A strange country, strange people, people who won't speak to you, won't even smile at you... How can I consign you to that? You mean too much to me."

Railu said nothing. Instead she turned Jerya's shoulders until they were facing each other. Then she slid her hands to Jerya's head and pulled her forward until their lips met.

At first Jerya did not know what to do, even what to think. But *Railu* knew, and Jerya let herself be led, imitating, linking her hands behind Railu's neck and giving herself into the kiss. She knew nothing about ways of kissing; yet what was it but one more new thing to learn? When Railu tugged at her earlobes with a force that should have been painful but was instead thrilling, Jerya eagerly responded in like manner. When Railu's hands strayed once more across her scalp, Jerya sent her own roaming over smooth stretched skin.

When Railu released her, Jerya's sense of loss was acute; but then Railu said, "Take off your robe." All at once Jerya felt as if she were breathing the winter air of the mountains, chill and rarefied. In a stillness like the heart of the forest she heard her own heart pounding. She knew what was developing, though she had no vocabulary, no experience, only a nameless, instinctive, vision of enwrapped bodies.

That men and women did such things, she knew. That it was scandalous if they were unwed, she also knew. She had never heard of such things between women. Of course women hugged, held each other; sisters, especially, might share a bed. But she had gleaned no inkling that such intimacies could shade over into something... but she lacked the word. And the thought slipped from her mind, as she was seized by impulses deeper than words.

In a moment they were both naked. Jerya felt sudden doubt; her body had always served her well enough, but its lithe slenderness was not what men desired. What *women* might desire, she had never really considered. She almost laughed. *Why do you ask so many questions, Jerya?* Aye, she had asked many questions, but there were far more she'd never even dreamed of.

But Railu was kissing her again, and her hands were roaming over her body, and then there were no more questions.

They were together and Railu's weight was over her and seemingly all around her; she no longer knew where one body ended, where the other began. Something—fingers?—was creating miracles of sensation, each stroke sending waves of chill and tingling down her spine, like the first shock of diving into her forest tarn repeated again and again and again and again. The rhythm was everywhere; in Railu's hands, in the slow shifting of Railu's weight above her.

The rhythm was everywhere, filling her. It swelled, accelerated, became almost insupportable... then suddenly it crashed all at once into stillness; a moment of unbreathing, a moment of soaring, a moment which held a thousand unnameable feelings. In the middle of it she heard a cry; to her ears it sounded anguished, but it had left her throat as joy.

They lay side by side on the bed. Jerya saw their two bodies agleam with sweat. In the lamplight they were near enough the same colour, and their shapes seemed in some way simplified, not so different at all. The valley where their flanks touched was just another shadow; she could easily imagine that their bodies had merged. They were breathing together; they had been one; they were still not yet two halves again.

"*Stars above*... I never knew there was anything like that... Is that what men and women do, also?"

Railu chuckled. "How would I know?"

Jerya pondered. Perhaps men and women might twine themselves together in the same way, animals and angels all at once... but no one had ever spoken of such things to her. And men were made differently; stronger, harder. Without setting out to eavesdrop, she had heard occasional snatches of their talk. They spoke of 'doing' things to women, 'having', 'taking'. Somehow she had known that what they said was not the truth, was barely even a part of the truth; she had heard only the loudest, most boastful, snatches of their talk. Still it did not seem it could be the same. Between Railu and herself there had been no 'taking', only a great giving.

"I don't know either," she said then. "But it surely can't be the same." She half-sat and twisted over to kiss Railu and sent a lazy hand trailing over one round breast. She wished she could be more like Railu. There had been moments when she had almost felt she knew what it was to be Railu, felt her angles rounded, felt herself broad and strong in a comfortable coppery skin.

"I couldn't lie like this with a man," Jerya said. " I'm sure I couldn't do this..." With a delicate finger she traced the crease under one breast.

"I'd be a funny-shaped man if you could!"

"I didn't mean that... I mean just to touch you in that way. Like playing. I don't think a woman can play with a man so easily. I don't think with a man I could so easily have... Choss, I don't even know what to call it!"

Railu laughed again. "I'm supposed to be the innocent one. Over seven years I've been here and you've been Outwith. How is it that I have to teach you these things? You're supposed to have all the experience of the world."

"Of the world?" Jerya repeated. "Why does everyone think I know so much of the world? I know Delven, that's all. The rest... I just got a few glimpses on my journey."

"Well, what about Delven? Did you never... were there no men there?"

"Well, of course, but mostly our lives were quite separate. They went out into the land, herding and hunting and so on; women stayed in the village, carding and spinning and weaving, cleaning and cooking and a dozen other things. Mostly never venturing further than the hives or the berry-thickets. Not very interesting things... at least, not very interesting to me. I always felt... how can I say it? That what I was doing was... not enough. Do you know what I mean? Not enough... I would hurry my work and steal into the chamber where the books were, or go wandering, alone. I don't believe any of the other women ever... they never seemed to want any of that. Their lives seemed to content them, but not me... right or wrong, I felt there must be something else. Now I know I was right."

"You haven't answered my question. I still want to know about men."

"What do I know of men...? I could tell you a little about one man, that's all. One man is not *men*. Would you ask me to tell you about women?"

"No, but then I know something of women. Tell me about this one man, then."

"He was the only one I ever touched..."

The sweat was drying on her body now. She felt a sudden coolness. She must have shivered slightly, for Railu languidly pulled a blanket over the two of them. Jerya, grateful, turned on her side and snuggled closer, feeling her breasts against Railu's side. She felt ready to tell Railu anything, everything, whatever she wished to know.

It had begun that day in the forest. How distant it seemed now; distant in both time and space. That day she had sensed the possibility that her innermost thoughts might not always need to be hers alone. But that idea had barely formed in her mind before it was closed off again.

"I only kissed him once," she said. "And not like kissing you just now. I held his hand on those first days, when we were walking alone. And one night when I was... frightened... I lay down near him—but there were still blankets between us.

"That's all I know of men; next to nothing. I have only a guess at what happens between men and women in their private chambers. But what I guessed or imagined was not so very different from what we have just done—only I could never imagine anything so... so glorious."

"So we still don't know the answer. We can only guess what it might be that they do. But we do know what we have."

"Even if I still don't know what to call it."

"There are many names. I like best to call it 'making love'."

"Making love... that's nice." Jerya slid her arm around Railu's waist. "Only love was there already, wasn't it? We didn't make it, only released it."

Railu chuckled softly. "You're too clever by half... No wonder they want you to stay."

Jerya frowned, not welcoming this reminder of the cold and complex reality outside the newly discovered reality of love. She was about to say something when the door banged open.

Freilyn came in carelessly, as if expecting the room to be empty, humming a tune. As she saw them together in the bed, she stopped in the middle of a phrase. Jerya felt strangely tantalised, missing the rest of the melody.

"Oh, I'm sorry!" cried Freilyn, but her tone was at odds with her words. Whatever she was truly feeling, it wasn't contrition.

Railu sat up slowly, pulling the blanket with her, keeping herself covered. Jerya remembered how proudly naked she had been. She did not seem so proud now. "You said you wouldn't be back till eleven."

"And what time do you think it is now?"

"It isn't! Is it?"

"Almost twenty past." There was a strange note in Freilyn's voice, almost as if enjoying Railu's discomfiture. "Calls herself a Dawnsinger but can't keep track of time." She laughed unpleasantly. "I hope you had at least finished your business."

"Business! Don't say that!"

"Why not? A pretty piece of business for you, wasn't it?"

"What do you mean, business?" demanded Jerya.

"Business: an arrangement or transaction intended to bring mutual benef—"

"—I know what the word means, but why do you use it here?"

"Because that's what it was. A simple transaction; even a simple Backlander can understand. If she could ensure your wish to stay here... Her black marks would be discounted. So she'd be able to stay on, too."

"Who was this? Whose promise?"

"She promised nothing," said Railu.

"She implied it clearly enough," countered Freilyn.

"But it was all hints and suggestions."

Jerya had her doubts about the value of a hint from Perriad—'she' had to be Perriad—but another question came to the fore. "If you can stay and I can stay, what happens about Delven?"

Freilyn shook her head. "You still don't see, do you? Delven's of no consequence."

Delven's of no consequence. The words were meant to wound, and they did.

"They'll send whoever's most dispensable," added Freilyn, and that was hard to hear also. The idea that anyone, least of all a Dawnsinger, could be dispensable; she rebelled against the cruelty. The hardest thing was, she was ready to believe the cruelty wasn't only in Freilyn's mind.

Jerya slipped from the bed, taking care not to disturb the blanket that shielded Railu. She kept her back to both of them as best she could as she retrieved her skirt and smock, wriggled hastily into them. Undergarments were of less import; she bundled them in one hand.

Only when she was covered again did she turn and face them. Railu's look was pleading, almost abject; and, despite the gloating tone she'd adopted, Freilyn looked no happier. She was, if anything, even paler than normal.

"Jerya..." said Railu. "Please believe me—"

"I hardly know what to believe any more."

"*Please*... You don't think this last hour was just business, do you? You can't suppose I was merely pretending, play-acting."

"I don't know about play-acting. We never went in for that in Delven. You can call me a simple Backlander. Why not? It's what I am. I know I'm ignorant of many things. I still can't read a clock-face at a glance like you all can, and I certainly can't spell half the words I hear every day.

"But I'd rather be simple than deceitful. Aye, we may be simple folk in Delven, but we value honesty above almost anything else. I was warned it was different in the city, but I never thought I would meet deception in these precincts."

"I haven't deceived you!"

"Haven't you? You certainly didn't tell me all the truth."

"I know. I'm sorry... but when could I have told you..? Everything happened so easily—so *naturally*. Perhaps if we'd had more time..."

"Oh, forgive me," Freilyn said acidly. "It's all my fault, I see."

Suddenly Jerya wanted only to escape. Freilyn's bitter ire was unpleasant, but Railu's forlorn pleading—Railu who had so recently seemed to intermingle mind and body with herself—that was beyond endurance.

She smoothed her skirt, resettled her smock, reasserting her own dignity as best she could. "I'm going now."

Railu stared at her as if fearing the worst. Jerya, or part of her, wanted to bestow a comforting smile, but her face felt paralysed. She could think of nothing more to say. She slid past Freilyn, who made no move to make her passage easier. Remembering how the door had banged when Freilyn burst in, she was careful to open and close it quietly. Then she was alone in the corridor, in the midnight stillness of the College.

As she made her way to the room she now shared with Analind, she found herself thinking of the forest where she had always been able to take her problems and rediscover the company of herself. Suddenly she longed for the forest. Briefly, she wondered how long it might take to walk back to Delven; a week? Ten days? Without coin, she would have to get water from becks, exist on fruit; well, it wasn't a bad time of year for that. Where to sleep might be more of a problem... But it was a foolish notion.

Wasn't it?

She eased the door open silently; the interior was dark. After a moment she heard Analind's quiet breathing. Closing the door left the interior close to pitch-black, but Jerya had not lost her Delven-bred ability to move surely in darkness. She found her own bed, shed her garments, slipped under the covers, all without waking her roommate. Analind was a kindly person; no one else had offered to share with her, and she thought it must have been no small sacrifice to give up the luxury of single occupancy. For that very reason, she had tried to impose herself as little as possible. They had shared few confidences, spoke mostly of straightforward practical matters.

In many ways, Analind seemed an ideal person with whom to share the space; but just now, Jerya could have done with someone who would not mind being woken; someone whose shoulder would not mind receiving her tears. Well, she reminded herself, she'd bedded alone for many years, dealt with her troubles and sorrows by herself. Why should she expect things to be any different now?

And if she could not go to the forest... well, there were other ways to lose herself. Books, for one.

CHAPTER 16

JERYA

Jerya went along the passage to the great tiled stove that filled the angle at its corner. There were always enamel jugs of water sitting in its niches, too hot to grasp without wrapping a cloth round the handle. She carried one back to the room, emptied half its contents into the basin, then bent, scooping water over her head, gasping at the heat. She took up the bar of soap, massaged it in her hands, lathered her scalp thoroughly.

Shaving yourself was not easy. Analind had never seemed to mind doing it for her, but Jerya was not entirely comfortable accepting a favour she could not reciprocate. It had puzzled her at first, why her hair—and that of the younger Postulants—grew back, stubble greying the scalp within two or three days, yet the Novices' did not. When she'd fumbled out a question, Analind had looked blank for a moment, then smiled. "Postulants shave," she'd said. "But when you become a Novice, they give you a pot of cream. You rub it into your scalp every day and after a month or two your hair never grows back at all." Thanking her, Jerya wondered if she would truly be counted as a Novice after the Rite of Elevation, now only weeks away, when Postulants who had measured up were accepted as Novices. Perriad had suggested it a while back, but nothing more had been said.

Was it even possible, she wondered, if it was decided that she was to return to Delven after all; was it possible she would vault straight from Postulant to Ordained Dawnsinger? She did not feel ready for that, not at all—but perhaps she knew most of what she needed to know as the village's

Singer. After all, she knew the land and the people better by far than Railu or anyone else; that might count for something.

One thing she had learned very quickly was that shaving yourself was easier if you *didn't* use the mirror—especially for the back of the head, which you could only see with two mirrors, which made everything completely back-to-front. She could impress her friends by reading upside-down—and mirrorwise too, they had found—but she could not control the blade when using two mirrors. The mirrors had their place, for checking you hadn't missed anywhere, but for the actual act of shaving it was better to work entirely by feel. Ten fingers were often smarter than two eyes.

And not to hurry; that was the other key. A nick on the scalp was not only painful, it left an embarrassing mark, out there where everyone could see it. It took a lot of concentration; you could not really think of anything else. Yet sometimes it seemed as if her mind carried on anyway, thinking thoughts she didn't even know about until afterward.

Thinking herself finished, she towelled her head, then ran hands carefully over her scalp. The sensation, that had been so strange at first, was almost familiar now. Aye; she had done a thorough job. The mirrors confirmed it. She wiped off the blade, folded it back into its own handle. She would need to sharpen it before next use, but that could wait. The trick had worked again, her thoughts coming clear while her attention was elsewhere.

It was time to find Railu.

She carried the basin out to the sluice, emptied it, swilled it clean with the rest of the water from the jug, returned the basin to the room, filled the jug with fresh water, toted it back to the stove to warm up for whoever needed it next.

She did not, of course, know where Railu was at this moment, but she knew where to start looking. As she headed toward the Infirmary, she smiled vaguely at everyone she passed; scurrying servitors, chattering Postulants, a couple of younger Novices so deep in talk they seemed not to notice her at all. That reminded her of her first moments in the College. She smiled more broadly, was still smiling when she entered the Infirmary.

"Come to help?" Sister Berrivan was ever hopeful.

"I need to see Railu," she said. "To talk to her."

"And if there was some task the two of you could do while you talked...?"

She raised her hands in acquiescence. "Why not?"

She did not know, of course, whether Railu wanted to talk to her. Over the past few days, Railu's looks, whenever their paths crossed, had gone from imploring to despairing to—finally—resigned. And when she, following Berrivan's directions, found Railu in a supply-room, her friend's expression registered only mild surprise and then tentative expectancy.

"Sister Berrivan said I could help you," she began.

"You finally found time to help out down here? I thought Perriad had you studying every minute of the day."

"Perriad can't watch me every minute. And I didn't come down here to help out. I came down here to find you. But if I can be of use as well..."

"Aye, well, there's nothing much to do for a few minutes, till that's finished." She indicated a large vessel from which a thin dribble of steam was leaking, a clepsammia on a shelf nearby. "So..."

"Railu..." And then she simply did not know what to say next. "Choss! Twenty minutes ago it seemed clear as anything."

"I suppose you want me to go first."

"I came to you... but if there's anything you want to say...?"

"Oh, Jerya, there's a ton of things I want to say. But I suppose I'm like you, I don't know where to start."

They looked at each other. The steam-vessel filled the silence with its sibilant seething. Then Jerya stepped forward, and Railu moved to meet her.

"Well," she said, slightly breathlessly, after some moments. "I'm glad that's all cleared up, then."

Railu smiled. "Stars above, I can't tell you how much I... look, Jerya, you have to believe me... aye, Perriad said—hinted—I mean, it was the broadest possible hint, you'd have to be stupid to miss it... but it was a complication more than anything else, because she wasn't talking—hinting—about anything I hadn't wanted to do anyway. I've been thinking about it ever since... I suppose since that day, by the pool, the first time I ever touched you. Or you touched me."

Jerya hadn't really thought about it, but, aye, that had been the first touch, her hand on Railu's, honey over copper over grey stone. Had there been a promise there? She'd been thinking only of friendship, herself, in that moment.

And maybe friendship was what truly mattered.

"I wish you'd told me," she said.

"I understand, but how was I to say it? 'Perriad wants me to seduce you, but don't worry about that because I want to do it anyway.' How would that have sounded?"

"Ah, well." Words were slippery, sometimes. She ran a hand over Railu's head in lieu of words. Always smooth, no need to shave, never the drag of stubble. Aye, it would be fine to be a Novice. And not just for that. "If Perriad wants to seduce me, she can do it with books and telescopes and incunabula. She doesn't need to drag you into it."

Railu kissed her again, then looked aside. "Time's up. Better get on."

"Tell me what to do."

"First wash your hands. Over there."

"I washed when I came in."

"Not to Berrivan's standards, I'll be bound. Then take a cloth from that chest. I'll drain the steamer." Before they began drying the instruments from the opened vessel, Railu also made her put on a cloth mask, covering nose and mouth. Jerya, always keen to learn, asked several questions about the whole procedure.

Then, as they settled to a routine, she said, "Have you spoken to Perriad since?"

"No, but I've felt her watching me—at Dawnsong, in Refec."

"Me too. Listen, Railu, tell her whatever you think best. If it might mean we can both stay..."

"Aye, but..." Railu turned away, transferring a handful of scalpels to a drawer. "It feels like lying to her."

"Telling her you seduced me? Pardon me if I've misunderstood. I am still an ignorant Backlander, after all. Maybe I need to look it up in a dictionary. But isn't that exactly what you did?"

"It didn't feel like it. It felt like it just happened. After that first kiss, nothing was... you know, planned, premeditated. Didn't it feel that way to you?"

"I reckon it did, but how would I know, really? I'd never even been kissed before, not like that."

"Then how had—no, don't answer that!" Railu giggled softly, briefly. Then she was serious again. "There's another thing. If they don't send you, and they don't send me... then someone else has to be sent."

"Aye, but maybe not immediately. Sharess is much recovered. There's no hurry. And besides... seems to me, some of the girls..." *Girls!* she thought. *These are* Dawnsingers. *Not so long ago you'd have fallen flat on your face or run headlong rather than look one in the eye. Now you casually call them 'girls'.* "Some of them may not mind it so much. Some people suit a quiet, contemplative, life. Sharess seemed content. I could have been, too, I think."

"But you've been seduced by incunabula?" They laughed, behind their masks, and went on with their task.

The seventh bell sounded as they made their way, arm-in-arm, up steps and pathways towards dinner. A soft drizzle was stippling the paving-stones, coolly tickling Jerya's fresh-shaven scalp. Railu was speculating whether Freilyn would agree to move in with Analind: "It's not comfortable for her either now, still rooming with me. I'm sure it'd be better all round." *Except possibly for Analind*, Jerya thought. Perhaps that was uncharitable towards Freilyn; but she knew she, herself, had done her very best to impose on Analind's goodwill as little as possible. She could not guarantee that a disgruntled Freilyn would be equally unobtrusive. She thought this, and of course she thought it would be a fine thing to share a room and a bed with Railu. But above all, she was just glad they were friends again.

And there was something else, an undertow tugging at the current of her thoughts. She couldn't yet put her finger on it. *Perhaps I should go and shave my head again. Then it might come clear.*

That was silly, of course; and now the lesser bell was sounding for dinner, and she was suddenly all too aware that she had entirely forgotten about lunch. She leaned closer to Railu as they turned into Refectory Court together.

"I know you're all panting with eagerness to begin your calculations and then prepare your fair-copy maps," said Skarat. "But you'll have to tolerate my detaining you here by this... roaring fire."

Jerya smiled at Veradel beside her, sharing appreciation of Skarat's sly humour, but appreciating the warmth even more. It was ironic that the first true outdoor lesson of her time in the College should coincide with a decidedly unseasonable day, a sharp North wind making it the coldest since she had arrived in the city, more like late autumn than high summer.

She was chilled, but elated. In her mind, thoughts of angles, of sight-lines and alidades, jostled with images of the class moving through the orchard, low sunlight filtering through the golden leaves and flickering on white robes and bald heads. Then—and now, huddling with the others—she thought she had never felt more entirely, more comfortably, a part of it all.

"And while I detain you," Skarat continued, "I may as well say something about the applications of what you've learned today, and what you'll learn in the coming weeks. Ere now, only a few Singers have made much practical use of the surveying and cartography they've learned. It has been the domain of the specialist. But for some time I have had the vision that a combination of village Singers and Peripatetics would enable us to map the entire land both more accurately and more precisely than hitherto. Dawnsingers' tors and towers are ideal bases for trigonometric stations. They're typically the highest point in a given town or village; and, particularly in more populated regions, often intervisible."

She broke off momentarily as a couple of servitors entered with trays; coffee, and jai. In that moment, Jerya thought of the implications. Singers whose towers were—in that fine word—*intervisible* could communicate by heliograph. Might that have alleviated Marit's palpable sense of isolation? Would it be beneficial for Sharess too—or her successor? Probably not, because she very much doubted Delven's tor and Thrushgill's cottage were intervisible; but she could not be certain.

As steaming mugs were handed round, Skarat resumed. "Some of you will be taking up posts as village Singers next year, while others will be embarking on a year or two as a Peripatetic-in-training. More than a third of you will therefore be—potentially—in a position to forward this scheme. Exactly how many will in fact be able to do so will depend on progress in the production of new, lightweight, surveying equipment."

Jerya still had only a rudimentary idea of the role of a Peripatetic. She had heard the word many times now, but there had always been some other question demanding to be asked first.

Still she had gathered something, by inference, from those passing mentions. Peripatetics travelled the Sung Lands, normally in threes (a 'troika'). At each village, they would bring companionship to the resident Singer (something that Marit, for one, had seemed to sorely miss); they would also assess those girls who were around the right age, possibly Choose one, or very rarely two. She had also heard some reference to assessment of tithes, but this she hadn't fully understood.

I need to know more, she thought suddenly. To travel the land... If her one journey had taught her anything, it was that what she had seen was the merest fraction of what there was to see. The map of the Sung Lands that adorned the Library wall was close on two metres long; she'd traced her own journey in a few hand-spans.

And perhaps, as a Peripatetic, she might be able to visit Delven. To see Sharess again, even if only for a few hours... *Well, that would be something. It really would.* The intensity of the feeling took her quite by surprise; but was it the chance to see Delven again that really thrilled her, or the wider prospect of travel?

CHAPTER 17

JERYA

J erya settled herself in a window-recess in the deepest reaches of the Library, back against an oak panel, and began to read. The leading between the panes cast intersecting shadows across the page, and imperfections in the glass itself made their own watery imprint, but before she had read half-way down the first page all these distractions were forgotten.

Chapter One

Historical Sources

Like any other subject, history can be framed around two simple questions: 'what do we know?' and 'how do we know it?' First- and second-year studies were directed almost entirely at the first of these, presenting an outline of our knowledge both of the Present Age of the world (Posthistory) and of the Age Before (Forehistory). It will, of course, be understood that this is just the beginning, and there is a great deal more to learn.

However, at the beginning of the third year, it is now time also to begin to consider the second of the two great questions.

In history, as in most other subjects, the foundations of our knowledge rest to a large extent on writings and other material which have been preserved from the Age Before. Other subjects, however, offer us the chance to test and verify at least some of what these writings tell us, through experiment and observation. History is different, because we can never directly observe the past, and we most certainly cannot perform experiments upon it.

But history does *test stories about the past. History looks carefully at how the ancient knowledge we study and cherish was preserved for us in the first place. It examines what we, historians, call the source material.*

Every subject has its own source material, not just history. In fact, the source material of history tells us a great deal about where the source material of other subjects comes from and how it was preserved. Also, we can consider all surviving material from the Age Before, whatever its ostensible subject, as source material for historical studies.

It should already be clear that, the further we look back, the less source material we have to work with, and—often—the harder it is to understand. There is a particularly sharp divide between the end of the Age Before and the beginning of the Present Age. In fact, from a historian's perspective, it can be argued that there is no better way of defining when the Present Age began than by the richness of source material. This in itself is a question of great interest and complexity, and one which continues to exercise the finest historical minds of the Guild.

With rare exceptions, historians all accept that defining the Division of the Ages in this way can only ever give us an approximate date. First-year Calendrics as well as first-year History will have made it familiar that our numbering of years—the Guild Reckoning—dates from the Foundation of the Guild; we often write or speak of dates such as 320GR (the year in which this text is being written). It should also be fully understood that—with even fewer exceptions—historians agree that the Division of the Ages should be identified as falling before the Foundation, though there are at least three main schools of thought about the interval, ranging from a single genera- tion (perhaps thirty years) to somewhere between three and four centuries. Detailed consideration of these arguments, and their implications, will be encountered in fourth-year studies.

This agreement (that there was an interval) initially strikes many Novices as odd, because there is no question that our supply of source material becomes very much richer from around Year 1 GR. With the birth of the Guild, proper records were created and systematically conserved in a way that had not happened before. It should therefore, be understandable that a small (but passionate!) group of historians argue that the Division of the Ages should be dated at Year 1 GR; not only do we have much more, and clearer, source material from then on, we also have an exact date to work from in a way we do not before.

Even so, the majority of historians both now and in earlier centuries of the Guild's existence believe that the Division of the Ages should be identified as occurring at least a century prior to Foundation. Perhaps most tellingly, none of the first generations of historians to work within the Guild, such as Master Iroline, identified the Division at Year 1 GR.

Another consideration is as follows. Having already observed that the quantity of source material from the centuries before the Foundation, i.e. Year 1 GR, is significantly less than that created thereafter, we should not overlook the fact that it is also qualitatively very different.

It must be understood that the use of the word 'qualitatively' is not a judgement on the quality (in the usual sense) of the source material from different periods. The quality of source material is in itself an important element of historical study, and for those who choose to specialise it will form a significant part of fifth-year studies. For now, let it just be said that 'quality' may refer to any and every aspect, from the physical state of preservation of the material (is it fully legible? Is it so fragile as to require special handling? and so on) to its comprehensibility and the density of information embodied therein.

From this perspective, it would be easy—but facile—to say that the material from Year 1 onwards is of better quality than that from earlier times. One is tempted to say, 'well, of course it is'. From the Foundation onwards, our records and writings have been collected and conserved by our Librarians and Archivists. Naturally the material is both abundant and well-preserved.

It should also be no surprise that, from Year 1 onwards, comprehensibility is hardly ever a major problem. We are now dealing with material created and compiled by Dawnsingers. Though the early years were emphatically not without challenge, historians, record-keepers, and the rest of the Guild's

*investigators and researchers were operating in an intellectual environment
which, though different from the present in many ways, would not be wholly
unfamiliar to Novices or Singers of today.*

*As soon as one steps back, so to speak, across the threshold of Year 1, the
source material is not only much less plentiful, and much more variable in its
state of preservation; it is also much more variable in its comprehensibility.
Quite simply, the further we go back, the harder it is to understand, or at
least to be reasonably confident that we understand correctly. Reading this
earlier material is more challenging in all sorts of ways. There is more scope
for divergent interpretations. The second term of Year 3 will bring Novices
into direct contact with selected examples of this material, and invite them to
form their own conclusions about its meaning.*

*For any true historian, of course, the fact that this material presents harder
challenges than that from the years after 1 GR is not a reason to shy away
from it; it is just the opposite. The greater the challenge, the greater the reward;
and, the stranger the material, the further it takes us from our own familiar
world, the more we have to learn. This is what we mean when we say that it
is qualitatively different.*

*Perhaps nothing illustrates this better than the documents known as the
Four Fragments. These are permanently displayed in the Library and should
be attentively and reverently viewed by all Novices.*

❈

Jerya had been in that room scarcely half an hour ago. She had felt duly
awed, the obvious significance of those survivals from the Division of
the Ages being underlined by the reverential way they were displayed; in
glass-topped cabinets, the curtains drawn back only while they were being
inspected, and only far enough to admit the bare minimum of light. The
windows faced North and the Singer-Librarian had told her that no direct
sunlight was ever allowed to fall on any of the relics, and that only senior

Singers engaged in approved research or conservation work were ever permitted to open the cases, let alone touch their contents.

She looked down at her hand, resting at the edge of the page, poised to turn it, not to waste a second's reading. She felt the smooth fine paper under her fingertips. It seemed to have no texture at all, unlike the coarse soft pages of the books in Delven, their corners frayed and rounded by long handling. Under the book was the soft white worsted of her skirt, tinted faintly green by the light through the glass. Again she thought of the goat's wool of her old garments.

She read on, dutifully continuing to the Introduction, restraining her impulse to skip ahead to the transcript of the Fragment itself.

Chapter 2

Introduction to The First Fragment

One of the tragedies about the First Fragment is that we know next to nothing about its author, not even a name. Nor do we know much more about her main collaborators in the great work; throughout the surviving text they are referred to only by their initials, M, R, and C. Beyond the fact that all three are female, there is very little that we can say with confidence about any of them. As for the author herself, not even an initial is ever given. She is normally referred to as the Journal-Keeper, though some particularly fastidious historians prefer to call her the Author of the First Fragment. Collectively, the four are usually called the Forerunners.

These gaps in our knowledge are almost certainly a result of the greater tragedy; the reason why the First Fragment is a fragment, not a complete journal. Like most ancient documents, the pages of the First Fragment appear almost charred at the edges. This is almost certainly not the result of exposure to fire, but simply a consequence of great age. (Incidentally, this is often adduced as supporting evidence for a longer Division interval, but we should not forget that over three hundred years have now elapsed since the Foundation.)

Others of the Four Fragments appear to have suffered rough handling at some time (opinions vary, even among the most expert, as to whether this occurred close to the time of their creation, or at a later date); pages are torn, and in some cases missing entirely. There are some torn pages in the First Fragment, too, but the greater tragedy is the fact, obvious even at first glance, that the cover and a number of the early pages are stuck together by a congealed mass of some unknown substance.

No one can say with certainty what this congelation consists of. Attempts have been made to analyse a few flakes which have become detached, but without success. It is fairly clear that it was originally a liquid, which would appear to have been spilled or otherwise deposited over the journal when it was closed, and to have soaked through a number of pages[1]. Whatever happened, it was left long enough to dry completely and become something like the congelation we now see, though the passage of centuries has no doubt rendered it even more impenetrable.

There are two main theories about the origin of the congelation. The first is that it was nothing more than a heavily-sweetened drink, such as a cup of sugary jai. This would suggest that the defacement of this precious relic is due to nothing more than carelessness. To us, now, it seems unthinkable to expose a document of such value to the risk of this kind of damage; still less can we imagine not taking immediate action to clear up the spillage and minimise the harm. This does make us think, however, about the frame of mind of people at the time (which historians should, surely, do as a matter of course).

---

1. It is not even possible to say how many pages have been affected. At first glance, the congelation appears to amount to almost a third of the thickness of the whole, which would suggest that it encompasses as many as forty pages, but many have suggested that the apparent thickness is greatly exaggerated by the congelation itself; experiments on a similar (but modern) screedbook suggest that even a heavy spillage would not completely penetrate more than six or eight pages, though this is very dependent on what exactly the original liquid was.

The second main theory is that the substance which caused the congelation is blood. It is certainly true that spilled blood, if left, can dry to a similar dark and crusty appearance, although experiments again suggest it would not soak through many pages. If it is blood, it is not possible to be sure whether it is of human or animal origin, but most writers who propound this theory incline to the view that it is human[2]. This does of course encourage speculation about the circumstances in which a significant quantity of human blood could be spilled on the Journal—and not only spilled, but left to congeal. However, speculation may be tempting, but without at least some evidence it has little place in serious historical study.

Whatever the spillage consisted of, it appears to have had more effect on the lower edge of the pages than the upper. The edges of several pages are distinct at the top, but still bound into the mass at the bottom, and staining affects a number of pages beyond that; even though these pages are separable, some of the text at the bottom of the page cannot be deciphered.

Some have suggested that it might be possible, where some pages begin to be separable at their upper margins, to detach these portions, and that doing so might reveal text that we have not seen before. This of course would inevitably inflict further damage on our most precious relic. The counter-argument is that we have any number of copies of the text which has already been extracted, and as such there is nothing further to be learned from the Fragment in its present state. Even the slender possibility of extracting some further knowledge from the Fragment should therefore outweigh the preservation of the physical object itself.

---

2. In truth, there is little, if any, real evidence either way. And one may well ask, does it really matter? The answer, in this writer's opinion, is that it is immaterial to our understanding of the text itself. It might tell us something about the circumstances at the time of its composition, but we currently have no way of knowing whether the spillage occurred moments, or weeks, or years, after the author made her last entry.

The opposing view—and the one which has so far prevailed—is that the Fragment has value beyond the information it contains. It is one of very few tangible links to our past and to the Forerunners themselves.

Reading the First Fragment

The text which has been extracted from the First Fragment is barely 12,000 words long. For comparison, first-year essays are normally no more than 1000 words, but final-year Novices are routinely required to compose essays of 6000 to 8000 words. It may well be asked how much there is to be said about it, but at the last count (327 GR), more than 40 books in the Library catalogue are devoted to it.

Jerya smiled, though she could almost have wept. More than forty books on this one subject! In her whole life, until a couple of months ago, she had seen only twenty-three. Well, there was one phrase to hold on to: *making up for lost time.*

She read on.

While the field is extensive, Sister Cressyl's Concordance to the First Fragment *is generally regarded as the standard work. From fourth year onward it is one of the essential texts, especially for those who choose to specialise in Forehistory. It is not necessary to read it at an earlier stage, and some Tutors strongly advise against it, arguing that it is as likely to add to confusion as to lessen it.*

On the other hand, as will soon become evident, attempting to read the First Fragment without some kind of exegesis is a thankless and potentially soul-destroying endeavour. The 40-plus books mentioned above are only one indicator of a vast enterprise. Since the discovery of the Fragment early in the history of the Guild (probably in GR56), Sisters almost beyond number have devoted large parts, sometimes the entirety, of their working lives to making sense of it. Any Novice rash enough to plunge into these deep and murky waters without a guide would surely feel as if she were drowning in incomprehensibilities.

To take just a few examples, all drawn from the first two pages of the Fragment:

what is a 'ghost-town'?;

what month or season is indicated by 'October'?;

what is a 'petrol station'?;

who or what are 'looters' and 'squatters'?;

and so on and so forth. In some cases we can make a persuasive inference from the immediate context: a 'bungalow' is surely a type of dwelling-house, for instance, and 'Scotch' some kind of drink, pretty definitely alcoholic. However, persuasive inference is not the same as certainty, and even these interpretations have, quite rightly, been chal—

Somewhere, perhaps in the next room, a bell chimed. Outside, she dimly heard the greater bells. She almost groaned aloud. She'd never liked wrenching her head out of a book, still less this one. But it would not do to be late.

Carefully she closed the volume, returned it to the shelf and then gathered up her things, reflecting as she did so. It was only right and proper that the College ran to time, that Dawnsingers—including Novices and Postulants—should be subject to it.

CHAPTER 18

JERYA

"I read the First Fragment," said Jerya, "And one thing puzzles me."

"Only *one* thing?" said Analind, sceptical.

"Well, no. Lots of things, of course."

Analind laughed. "If you hadn't been puzzled, never mind Yanil or Jossena or Galirran, I think all the history tutors would have been begging you to stay so you could explain it to them once and for all."

"I don't know," said Railu, "What would they have to write about then?"

Jerya joined in the laughter. It was muted, because it was late, because some Sisters might already be abed, but it was warm. For herself, with Sunday to come, and Dawnsong getting comfortably later as summer drifted towards autumn, she would be happy to talk for another hour or more. She sipped at her porter, smiling at the faces around her, wondering if she could express the pleasure—the *joy*—she felt in something as simple, and yet as rich, as talk.

Before she could frame the thought, Analind—unusually animated tonight, from some combination of beer and fellowship and ideas—spoke again. "So what is it, Jerya?"

"What's what?"

"What's puzzling you if it's not what's in the *Concordance*?"

"Oh, aye..." She sipped again, set down her glass, smoothed a hand over her scalp. Sometimes it seemed to help her organise the thoughts within. "Before I read the *Concordance*, and the Fragment itself, I read the first chapters of the Third-Year history textbook."

"Thelwig's?" said Arvelyn, sitting comfortably cross-legged on an oaken chest. Bronze-skinned and dark-eyed, she had a figure that Jerya's aunts would have approved. Some might even call her plump; but she could put either foot behind her neck with apparent ease.

"That's the one."

"I'd almost forgotten that. Never use one word if three will do."

"Show some respect, Sister," chided Analind, sternly; but then her dark face relaxed into a smile, and Jerya saw the sternness was feigned. It had taken her a little while to realise that Analind was not only the darkest person she had ever been close to, but also one of the most beautiful. She felt a surge of affection for her onetime roommate, the urge to reach out and give her a hug. Even leaving Railu out of the reckoning, she had never touched people as much, in all the life she could remember, as she had in this last six weeks.

But they were looking at her expectantly again. "There's a line early in the first chapter. Something about testing what we know, or think we know, from historical sources."

"Aye," said Veradel. "It says... I may not remember verbatim, but the idea is clear: we can't perform experiments on the past as a natural philosopher may do to test a hypothesis. But this does not mean that historical scholarship lacks rigour. We must always test what we know, or merely believe, against all available evidence. We must continually ask, can we be certain that this is how it was?"

"As Brinbeth says in class, beware the assumption, beware the lazy inference," said Analind.

Jerya nodded. "That's it. So... the question I've been wanting to ask is... how do we know that the author of the First Fragment is female?"

She was not surprised by the ensuing outcry. Not at all.

Hastily Analind hushed everyone. "Remember people may have retired." Then she focused on Jerya. "But you can't blame... Are you *serious*, Jerya?"

"Doesn't it seem like a pretty serious question?"

"It seems like a *ludicrous* question to me," said Veradel.

"And yet you just said—about one minute ago, I should think—we must continually ask, can we be certain that this is how it was? That's my question: how can we be *certain*?"

"That the Journal-Keeper was female? How can we doubt it?"

"Surely common sense—" began Veradel.

"Common sense?" repeated Jerya. "Aye, sure, my common sense, my intuition, whatever you want to call it, they tell me that the Journal-Keeper was female. When first I read the Fragment I never questioned it—"

"—Well, then—"

"—But the book says... if I understand what the book says, common sense isn't good enough. Common sense is not scholarship, is not evidence; it certainly isn't *proof*. Especially..." Her mouth was dry; she reached for her tankard again as she finished, "Especially when the Fragment tells of a time so distant, so different from our own. So *strange*."

She sipped once more. The glass was almost empty; Analind offered more. Jerya hesitated, then shrugged. *Why not?* "Just halfway, please... And then I asked myself a question, and I went back, and I read the Fragment again. And of course, the Journal-Keeper never says, 'I am a woman'."

"Why would she?"

"Well," Jerya said, "It is a fragment. We have neither the beginning nor the end. Perhaps at the beginning she would say more about herself."

"You're saying *she, herself*."

"Aye, well... I have to say something. And I do think it likely—I do *feel*—that the Journal-Keeper is female. But I can't say I *know*..."

"I get the feeling there's something else," said Railu.

"Aye. When I read it the third time, I looked very carefully at... of course, the Journal-Keeper only ever identifies the people around her by their initials; that's no clue."

"And the names from back then are strange," said Arvelyn. "So it'd be hard to know someone's gender by that."

"So, often, the only clues we have are pronouns—that's the word, isn't it? She or he, her or him."

"Aye. And there are whole books about the problems of historical names."

That sounded fascinating, but Jerya already had a long list of things that sounded fascinating, that she hungered to know more about. *Never enough time.* And she had still to finish what she had begun. "The Journal-Keeper's three main friends, collaborators: M, R and C. Unless there's some evidence that I don't know about—and which isn't mentioned in the *Concordance*—we don't know their full names, their ages, or very much at all about them." She gazed around, harvesting a couple of confirmatory nods. "And I found that R and C are referred to as *she* or *her*. I never found M referred to by pronoun at all."

"So now you're saying M is male too?" said Veradel.

"Don't do that. Don't tell me I'm claiming something we can't possibly know. All I'm saying is how can we be *sure* that either M, or the Journal-Keeper, are female?"

"But the two of them share a room, a bed. There's a line about M saying something 'to me, while we were still in bed'. Something like that. You're not really suggesting one of them's male, are you?"

"I'm not *suggesting* anything," Jerya protested again. "I'm only asking how we can be certain." She scanned the room again, faces intent or indignant in the lamplight. Perhaps it was the wine she had taken talking now, a little. "It *is* possible, you know, that a man and a woman could share a bed. It happens all the time, outwith these precincts." If she'd said it under different circumstances, they might have laughed; now no one did.

"But..." Veradel's face was screwed up in concentration. "If we follow your thought all the way... It's also possible that *both* of them are male. Does that happen, Outwith? A man sharing a bed with another man?"

"I never heard of it," she said. "I'm sorry, I don't know everything about life Outwith. I really only ever knew Delven. And even there there are things I didn't know." *Like who my mother was.* It didn't often come to mind, especially not now; the College, these friends in particular, felt like more of a family than she'd ever known before.

❋

"This is decidedly concerning," said Perriad.

"Are we not getting a little ahead of ourselves?" said Yanil mildly. "Putting the cart before the horse... isn't that the vernacular expression?" Perriad turned to her, brows raised. "Pronouncing a verdict before we've heard the evidence, if I may be so bold."

"Very well; the evidence. Brinbeth, if you please..."

Tutor Brinbeth was as tall as Perriad, a gaunt figure, her face habitually serious if not stern. Analind, who wasn't much given to joking herself, once described something as 'rarer than smiles from Brinbeth'.

Brinbeth leaned forward in her chair, fingers interlaced over her walking-cane. Jerya had observed her with something like admiration, stumping about the courts without the slightest concession to her handicap, without ever seeking or expecting special treatment. A new word she had acquired seemed to fit: intransigent.

But Brinbeth's intransigence carried over into her teaching. "On Maurday last, Postulant Jerya asked if she might sit in with my third-year class. I understand that, in her unique circumstances, she has licence to audit almost any class when not committed to a specific Tutor."

"That's quite correct," said Perriad. "Though perhaps we should review that policy." Yanil shot her a sharp look, and Jossena also frowned. "Well, all in good time. You allowed her to sit in, Tutor Brinbeth?"

"I did. And she listened attentively to my introduction, answered adequately when I directed a question at her. It was only when I invited the class to question me that I became concerned."

"For what reason?"

"She said that she had been studying both the *Introduction to The First Fragment* and the *Fragment* itself."

"Nothing wrong with that," said Yanil.

"No, of course not. But then she quoted what the *Introduction* says about the Journal-Keeper: *The author, too, is female.* And she asked me, 'Pardon me, Tutor Brinbeth, but how do we know that?'"

Perriad fixed Jerya with a hard gaze. "Do you deny this, Postulant?"

"No, Senior Tutor. That's what I said, but I—"

"Kindly confine yourself to answering the question put to you. Tutor Brinbeth, please continue."

"I observed signs of... consternation... among some of the other girls."

Jerya thought back to that day in Brinbeth's classroom, dust-motes dancing slowly in the afternoon light from the tall window. There had certainly been surprised looks on the faces of the younger girls, twisted in their seats to look at her; there had been a few suppressed giggles, murmurs. But *consternation* seemed an unfairly weighted word. She wondered fleetingly if she dare protest it, but Brinbeth was already continuing. "I suggested that she withdraw her impertinent question, but she only said that she had also been reading Thelwig's textbook. And she quoted the opening line of the first chapter: *Like any other subject, history can be framed around two simple questions: 'what do we know?' and 'how do we know it?'*"

"As a matter of interest..." said Yanil quietly. "Did she quote correctly?"

"Aye, but that's beside the point. She then went on to say, "At the very beginning, the book requires us to ask *how we know*. But in the very next chapter, it states that the Journal-Keeper is female without telling us how we know that.""

"At this point, I instructed her to remain after the class so that we could address the matter privately. But I then had great difficulty in calming the other girls down and returning their attention to more appropriate matters. As soon as I turned my back for a moment I heard someone whisper, *but how do we know?*"

"That was not you, was it, Jerya?" asked Yanil.

"No, Tutor Yanil, it was not." She had seen who it was, spotted a cheeky grin, a round amber face, quickly reverting to deadpan as Brinbeth swung around demanding to know who had spoken. But as she didn't know the girl's name, she felt doubly justified in saying nothing. At that point Brinbeth, lips white with suppressed fury, had ordered the entire class to remain, on detention, unless the culprit's name were immediately forth-coming. With the room still full, she had coldly dismissed Jerya when she presented herself to 'address the matter privately'. For herself, she had thought no more about it until summoned to this colloquy.

"So, Jerya, what have you to say for yourself?" said Perriad when Brinbeth had nothing more to add.

She hadn't had long to consider her approach. *Tell the truth and hope for the best.* It went against her Delvenborn instinct to do anything other than tell the truth anyway.

"I'd already raised the question with the Senior Novices," she said. "And none of them could give me an answer. So when I realised that the third-year class were considering the background to the First Fragment, I thought I would ask Tutor Brinbeth."

"But when she told you the question was impertinent, and asked you to withdraw, you persisted. Is that correct?"

"Aye, Senior Tutor, but—"

"Wilful disobedience on top of impertinence," said Brinbeth.

"May I clarify something?" asked Yanil. Perriad regarded her a moment, yielded with a tiny nod. "I'm not a historian, obviously, so this may seem naive to you, but I'd be grateful if you could explain *why* you deemed the question so impertinent?" She smiled at Brinbeth, but received a frosty glare in return.

"I should have thought it was obvious."

"Forgive me," said Yanil. "Clearly, I'm missing something. And it *is* a long time since I studied the Fragments..."

"Are you saying you actually entertain the notion—the *outrageous* no-tion—that the Journal-Keeper might *not* be female?"

"I wouldn't say that. No, I would find that extremely hard to swallow. But surely the Postulant here—" she gave Jerya the briefest glance— "Did not ask if the the Journal-Keeper was female or not. She only asked *how we know*. And I must admit, now the question is before us, I'm intrigued also."

Brinbeth glowered, and Perriad also looked severe, but just for a moment neither spoke. In the silence, Jerya took a chance. "Might I say something, Senior Tutor?"

Perriad sighed. "Very well, then..."

"It's only this... I never sought to suggest that the Journal-Keeper was not female. As Tutor Yanil just said, I'd find that very hard to swallow. As she also said, my question was purely and simply; how do we know? Or is it just an assumption?"

"Remind me, Yanil," said Perriad, tone gentler now. "The term you use in mathematics for fundamental propositions which you can't prove but form the basis for everything else."

"I think you're speaking of axioms. But really we need a philosopher here."

With a languid wave, Perriad dismissed the caveat. "Axioms, of course. And surely we can say it's axiomatic that the Journal-Keeper was female?"

Yanil nodded slowly. "That's for the historians to say, of course. But I will observe that in mathematics, in formal logic, we begin by stating our axioms. They should always be clearly identified as such."

"Just so. And you, Postulant? Would you accept that the gender of the Journal-Keeper is axiomatically female?"

"I cannot fairly say, Senior Tutor." Perriad frowned. Jerya hastened on. *Be humble*, she told herself. "These words, axiom, axiomatic, are new to me; I never heard them until this moment."

"Aye," said Yanil, "We haven't gone that far into the roots... Perhaps we should rectify this, if you would attend me at the earliest opportunity..." Her eyes fixed on Jerya's, who thought she took the message: *straight away, if you will.* She tried to convey her understanding, her willingness, without actually nodding.

"There is still the matter of the girl's wilful disobedience," said Brinbeth. Even Perriad looked faintly put out by this.

"We must allow the girls, especially the older ones, some capacity for independent thought," said Yanil.

"But this girl, though older, is still a Postulant."

"Quite true," said Perriad. "Her... anomalous... position does perhaps create the potential for such inappropriateness. This may require further consideration among ourselves." She turned her cool gaze to Jerya. "Behaviour which may, on occasion, be acceptable in a Senior Novice is not appropriate in a third-year class. Is that clearly understood, Postulant?"

Those girls have been here over two years, thought Jerya. *I've been here barely two months.* But she only bowed her head and said, "Aye, Senior Tutor."

Perhaps she missed something while her gaze was directed at the floor. There were faint sounds of movement, and then Perriad said. "I think also that you should offer your apologies to Tutor Brinbeth for disrupting her class."

For asking a question... But she knew better than to protest. "I apologise, Tutor Brinbeth. It will not happen again."

"I should think not." Brinbeth said no more, but her gaze, and her tone, both left Jerya in no doubt that the Tutor would prefer it if Jerya left her classes alone entirely. *Well*, she thought, *maybe I'd prefer that too.* The historical question was fascinating, but so were a thousand other things. *And little enough time for any of them.*

❊

"I imagine you could use a drink," said Yanil, brandishing a bottle. When Jerya hesitated, she smiled. "Half a glass? I could use one, and I don't like to drink alone."

Drink alone... Jerya thought of Marit. Not that she imagined there was any risk of Yanil ending up like the lonely Singer of Thrushgill, but she acquiesced. The wine curled into the glass, a nearby lamp tinting it golden as honey.

Yanil waved to her to one of two easy-chairs by the window-bay. Outside, the lights of New Court were beginning to outshine the afterglow. "Well, that was interesting," said the Tutor, hitching her skirts with one hand as she sat. She watched Jerya's face a moment. "Perhaps not the word you'd choose...?"

"I hardly know, Tutor Yanil."

"Less of the formality, please. We're just two Dawnsingers sharing a glass of wine." She raised the glass. "Very good health... Well, let me say, *I* found it interesting. You know, we Tutors have our badinage, on occasions, and some of us—mathematicians, natural philosophers—do like to chaff our colleagues in subjects like history over their notions of rigour, of proof. And yet, before today, I had never for a moment considered the question you raise."

"I never expected it to provoke such... fuss," said Jerya. She sniffed the wine, then sipped, suddenly glad she had accepted it.

"No..." Yanil gave her a long, thoughtful regard. "No, I don't suppose you did."

"It is still only a short time since I arrived from Delven. And in Delven, 'It's the way things are,' was often the only answer to my questions. Here, I would be laughed at if I could not do better than that. In the very first sentence of the history textbook we are told to ask, not only, *what do we know?* but also *how do we know it?* And it seemed to me that all I was doing was raising that second question."

"Indeed, Jerya. And I can hardly fault you for that. Perhaps your timing, your choice of audience, were a little rash—impolitic—but no more than that. However..." Yanil leaned forward, cradling the glass in both hands now, just below her face, as if to enjoy the aroma even while she spoke. "Perriad was... well, she is not a mathematician, so perhaps she uses the word 'axiom' more loosely than I would. And I don't think this is the time to go into it all in full..." She glanced at a wall-clock. "No, we shall both have to be making our way to Refec in twenty minutes. Let us defer a full consideration of axioms to another time. But, since the word came into play, I must give you some notion... Do you recall how Perriad described it?"

"Fundamental propositions which you can't prove but form the basis for everything else."

"Word-for-word. I'm impressed. Well, that won't do for a mathematical definition, but in common parlance it serves well enough. I think one might also say that... if a statement, a principle, is to be axiomatic, it must be generally accepted as true. Perhaps to be seen as self-evident."

"And... it is self-evident that the Journal-Keeper was female?"

"Well, I've always taken it to be so. And perhaps all that would be necessary would be for future editions of the text, the *Concordance*, other relevant works, to observe that there is no explicit evidence to that effect but that it is regarded as axiomatic. Would that satisfy you?"

"I... think so."

"You don't seem entirely sure."

"I'm still trying to understand. As I said to my friends, common sense, intuition, tells me that she was. But are they good enough? I am sure it's 'generally accepted as true'. But is it really 'self-evident'? Especially..."

"Go on."

"It's just that... I mean, it seems to me, if there's one thing that *is* self-evident about that time, that might be axiomatic—" She stumbled slightly over the unfamiliar word. "—It's that it was very different from our own time. 'The way things are' could be very different from 'the way things were'. And I've already learned that 'the way things are' in Delven is often not 'the way things are' here.

"So... what is self-evident in one place, among some people, may not be self-evident in another place, among different people, And we are looking back to a time more than four hundred years ago, when everything was in chaos after the Shattering. Some people think it's much more than four centuries... How are we to know what might be self-evident to... to someone writing a journal, back then?"

Yanil regarded her steadily for a moment. "You are a most interesting girl, Jerya. A most interesting young woman, I should say. I almost wonder... if you might not be inclined to transfer your efforts away from mathematics. You would bring a most interesting—most *stimulating*—perspective to the study of our history."

"Oh no, Tu—Yanil. I—nothing interests me more than mathematics. Save perhaps astronomy, and of course the more I learn of astronomy, the more mathematical it becomes."

Yanil smiled. "I'm very glad to hear you say so. So perhaps it is still only Jossena with whom I need to wrestle for your attention." She sipped briefly, a smile still teasing at her lips. "But I do see, or begin to see, why Perriad is also speaking of retaining you here... And that is something you wish for, too, is it not?"

"With all my heart," said Jerya at once, but then her conscience caught up. "But only... I cannot leave Delven unprovided-for, and I am still a little less than easy to think of... someone... being despatched there in my stead."

"Such consideration does you nothing but credit. Hmm, Jerya... It seems to me you have been used to following your own counsel, but if you would accept some counsel from me..."

"Of course, Tutor Yanil."

Yanil smiled. "Originality of mind, such as you have displayed today, is surely one of the things which have inclined Perriad to take a particular interest in you... but still I counsel caution. *Particularly* if you wish to remain. I can do my best for you, but it is Perriad who holds the final power to determine the fate of any student. Only the Masters, in Council, could overrule her.

"If today teaches you anything, let it be that there is a time and a place—and an audience—where it is possible to speak freely; and equally, there are occasions when it may be better to bite your tongue. Do you understand?"

"I do, but..."

"Heavens, girl!" Yanil laughed. "Must there always be a but?"

"I am sorry... it is only that if I wish to act as you advise, how am I to know which questions are impolitic to ask, and which are politic?"

"I can't give you a simple answer to that. Keep your eyes and ears open, and if in doubt, err on the side of caution."

Watch, listen, learn, she thought.

"Well," said Yanil. "We have a few minutes yet. Finish your wine and let us speak of easier matters. Has Jossena invited you on her trip to the Kendrigg Observatory?"

Chapter 19

Rodal

Rodal had never written a letter before in his life. He had never been away from home long enough to require it. Still, he had thought it would be easy until he had the pen and paper in his hands. Then he was not even sure who to write to. Holdren it was who had written to him, but it seemed more natural to write to his own parents. His father could read, and only his parents would be primarily interested in his own adventures. Although another moment's thought told him it was highly likely his letter would be read to the entire village in any case.

'Dear Father and Mother,' he wrote, deciding, *'Greetings from the tumultuous city of Carwerid.'* That word 'tumultuous' pleased him enormously. He could almost hear the little murmurs of half-ironic appreciation at taletell in the hearth-chamber. He had borrowed a dictionary from Annyt to check the spelling of that and a few other words. *'We arrived here saefly and days sooner than expected, having ridden, in a seeries of carts, all the way from Stainscomb. A good thing too, as the crossing of the Scorched Plains was a terrible day. I conducted the Postulant to the presincts of her Guild and then found my way to these logings, as Holdren advised, though I had to sleep under another roof for the first four nights as all rooms here were ocupied. Now I have a very comfortable room, larger than my chamber at home and with a window, if you know what that is, so I can look out into the street. At night I draw a certain across to keep it comfortably dark. I eat very well here and each day seems to bring something new I have not heard of before.*

'I could not begin to describe all the wonders there are to be seen here, even if I had seen them all! It will be better to make a great telling of it at the feast when I return. I hope of course that our Dawnsingers health will last long years yet, but I also wold wish to see you again before I am much older.

'Which brings me to my heavyest news. I have had the best possible guide in my explorations of this city. Her name is Annyt and she is the daughter of Garam who keeps this house. Garam says Holdren will remember her before she was born. Those were his words. He wishes to be remembered to Holdren.

'I think of you reading this and you must have gessed by now that I have certain hopes of Annyt. Customs here are diffrent, and I cannot tell yet what they will come to. If my hopes are rewarded I intend to bring her to Delven with me.'

He chewed the end of his pen a moment; it was a metal writing-nib spliced into a carven stick, not a goose-quill. That last sentence was only half of the truth, and so felt disturbingly close to an untruth. But it was easy to let the words sit on the paper and pass on to another part of the message. It was not like facing his mother's gaze. It would, he thought, be easy to be a liar in writing.

He chewed his pen once more. It was one thing to slightly blur the truth about Jerya; not so simple either to hide or to reveal that he was thinking his return to Delven might be only a temporary one. Perhaps he could creep towards it.

'Annyt is a city girl, though in many ways you would hardly know it. I am not sure she wold he happy in the life of a woman in Delven. Think not hardly of her; it is a very diffrent life from the one she is acustomed to here. Women are surely more rooted to their homes than men...'

No woman of Delven would argue with that, he thought. Most scarcely went further than the gardens, the beehives, and the trodden paths in the fringes of the forest. Jerya had been different, but Jerya was no longer a woman of Delven, if she ever truly had been.

'I have enjoyed to travel, and life here in the city, though tumultuous and often bewildering, is exiting for me. I could easier plan to make a home here

than ask Annyt to spend the rest of her life in Delven. Surely when you meet
her you will aprove my choice and see the wisdom of this plan.'

He finished, read through the letter, then tailed it, *'Yours with all best*
hopes,' as Holdren had done. Only as he wrote his name did he become
aware of Annyt standing close by, arms folded, smiling as she watched him.

"Writing home," she said.

"Aye." He folded the letter.

"Have you been writing about me?"

"Perhaps I have."

She saw right through his 'perhaps'. "And what have you said about me?"

"I have not said too much." But perhaps, now, he thought, it was time to
speak out. "I said I hoped they would meet you soon."

"What? Are they coming here to visit?"

He smiled at that, at the thought of his mother undertaking such a
journey. "No... I hope you will come with me to Delven."

"Come with you..." Her face took on a rare, wholly serious look. At once
she seemed years older. "Why, I'd love to see your home—but how would
you expect me to get back? Or had you not thought of that?"

"I—" he began, and then felt something was missing, which he righted
by reaching across the stained and age-smoothed table for her hand. "My
thought is to bring you back here also. Delven will seem dull and cramped
to me now. I won't easily settle there again, besure. I *am* sure there is a life
for me here... and I hope, for *us*."

She dropped her gaze, fixed her eyes on the union of their hands. She
seemed to stare at it as if debating whether to pull her hand away. Her free
hand toyed edgily with the heavy embroidery on her bodice. "What are
you saying?" she asked in a voice suddenly dull. "Are you asking me to wed
you?"

"Just that."

"Is this how you do it in Delven? Just grab a girl's hand and say it?"

"It's not 'how I do it in Delven'," he said. "It's the first and only time I've
done it, anywhere." And, if the truth were told, he'd startled himself too.

"I should hope it is!" she sparked back. "But... Rodal, here it's considered strange for a man to offer troth to a girl until they've courted for a year."

"A year!" He was appalled; it hadn't been a quarter, yet; he and Jerya had arrived at the very start of summer, and summer it still was. "Do you think it's strange of me?"

"In truth, aye, I do. We don't... I hardly know you that well. I don't see how you can be so sure, so soon... What do you think you're asking? What does wedding mean in Delven? A few hundred of you in the place, how much choice can anyone have? But here... Rodal, think. I have no brothers, I will inherit this inn; my father's share in the brewhouse, too. That's the life that awaits me. Do you really want to spend the rest of your days here with me? After a couple of months here are you so sure you've seen all the other futures you might lay claim to?"

"Are you saying no to me?"

"Well, I'm not saying aye, not now. How can I? But Rodal... if my father consents, I'll travel to Delven with you. If you promise you're returning here as soon as you reasonably can... returning here, at least to bring me back, no matter what answer I may be going to give you thereafter."

Rodal looked down at the letter folded under his fists He could not send it now, he knew. No one in Delven would understand how he stood now in relation to Annyt. He was not sure he understood himself. The sophistication he had imagined himself to be acquiring seemed nothing but fancy.

Slowly, methodically, he began to tear the letter into smaller and smaller squares.

"What are you doing?"

"Feeling like a fool," he replied, concentrating his gaze and striving to concentrate his mind on the regular dismemberment of the paper.

"A fool? Why?"

"Because in Delven things are done one way, and here they are done always quite otherways. And when it really mattered I did not take account of that. I thought as if the differences would simply smooth themselves for my convenience.

"Think of this, Annyt. You say you wish to come to Delven. I can understand your wish, now I have travelled. In a few weeks, I have seen more of the shapes life can take than any man could in a lifetime in Delven. Just by living in this city, you have seen much, too. Yet you have never travelled far, never seen any place like my home."

"I want to travel for its own sake, of course. But I want to see Delven because it is the place that made *you*. Perhaps that will help me understand you better."

"But no one there will understand *that*. Come to Delven with me, and it will mean we are betrothed; what other reason could there be for a woman to travel? That's how they will think.

"I could not introduce you simply as... as my friend. They would not believe, or simply not comprehended. And they would make nothing of your wish to understand me better. They would not know what there is to understand."

"Rodal, you sound... You've never spoken of your home or your people before with anything but affection. Now you talk of wishing to stay here and suddenly... I can only say you sound bitter."

"Bitter?" He was startled, first by her, then at himself. "I am disappointed... I don't mean to be bitter, you have given me no cause to be."

He stopped. He had no idea what else he wanted to say. Annyt watched him closely. He felt her concern. She *did* care for him, he had no doubt of that, but had he mistaken the nature of that care?

"I'm sorry," he said at last. "You must think me a fool, not to consider that a man and a woman can be plain friends here..."

"I don't say that's all we are. Don't misunderstand me, Rodal; I'm very fond of you. More than I've ever been before... And maybe something more. *Maybe*. But you must see we need to wait some time before we can be certain."

"Certain!" He threw back the word. "In this city is anything ever certain?"

CHAPTER 20

JERYA

It felt a little odd to line up with the younger ones, hardly any of them even as high as her shoulder. But that was how it was. *The way things are*, she thought, smiling within. You could worry about feeling conspicuous, you could succumb to embarrassment—or you could stand proud and tall; and if you saw anyone smiling, smile back, take it for goodwill and not mockery.

She looked across to where the Senior Novices stood; looked for Railu and found her, her gaze drawn like a compass needle to Magnetic North. No doubting the genuineness of that smile. Railu had shaved her, with even more than usual care, barely an hour ago, before rubbing oil into her scalp until it shone. Jerya had dressed in a new lambswool robe, as soft as it was pristine. "You're beautiful," Railu said, and for once Jerya made no protest.

Now they ranged themselves before the high ones of the Guild. Twenty-six girls of eleven and twelve, and Jerya. Twenty-seven might be an auspicious number, if you thought of numbers that way; it was certainly a tidy one. Three ranks of nine, of three-times-three; Jerya at the centre of the rearmost line, looking over the gleaming heads in front. No doubt every one had been shaved as meticulously as she had; everyone wished to look her best for the Rite. She smiled, recalling how she once had supposed Dawnsingers to be without vanity.

The Hall of Ceremonies fell quiet as the Master Prime rose to her feet. Jerya had seen her many times, of course, at dinner and at Dawnsong, but never so close; she had never had such an opportunity to *observe*. The

Prime—she saw almost with shock—was not as tall as herself, even perhaps a little below average height. A nondescript woman, you might almost think, middling in colour, middling in build. If anything was notable it was the apparent absence of eyebrows, but she saw now that it was only that they were the same hue as her skin.

There was nothing nondescript about her voice, however. Surprisingly deep and resonant, it filled the Hall without apparent effort. "This is the eighth occasion on which I have presided over the solemnisation of Novitial Vows, and each year I take fresh delight in it. I truly believe there is no more uplifting occasion in the entire Calendar." Her eyes ranged over the girls as she spoke. "The Rite of Elevation is joyful occasion, certainly, but also a solemn one. By taking these vows you truly commit yourself to a lifetime's service. Service, of course, not merely to the Guild but to the entirety of the Sung Lands and all their people."

She smiled momentarily. "Of course such service is—or at least should be—not merely a duty but, for most of the time, a joy. It is not always easy—I do not suppose any life is always easy—but it should not be a burden.

"I know each and every one of you has had conversation with the Mistress of Postulants or with a chosen mentor; some may have spoken with several Tutors. And you have had three days clear of lessons, clear of all duties save for the Dawnsong, in which to contemplate your future and to discuss with friends.

"Still, I say it again; if you do not feel that the life of a Dawnsinger is right for you, and that you are right for this life, it is better by far to renounce it now. There is no disgrace in doing so. I would even say that it may take more courage, greater resolution, than to continue on the expected path.

"If any of you has doubts, speak now. There are several options open to you. You may defer your Novitial Vows for a further year. I can tell you that there have been Sisters who have done just this, who then went on to take their vows after the second year, and who subsequently rose to become Tutors and even, in at least one case in my personal experience, a Master.

"You may also decide, without disgrace, to decline the Sisterhood entirely. Far better to do so than to continue as a Sister against your inner inclination. If you make this choice, you may remain in service to the Guild as a Lay Sister, an extern, either here or in one of the Adjunct Houses in another town. You might find a place in some other outpost, such as the Kendrigg Observatory. There are many possibilities, and any girl who wishes to explore these will receive ample counselling and guidance in making her choice.

"Therefore I invite you, one final time, to examine the innermost recesses of your hearts, your consciences, to ask yourself; is this truly my calling? And I remind you again; there is no disgrace, there is only honour, in making the right decision."

There was a dense silence. A few soft sounds—the shifting of someone's feet, a hastily-suppressed cough—only accentuated it, as a stray sunbeam heightens the dark of the forest. The Prime's gaze passed along the three ranks, pausing on each girl in turn. Jerya felt that those eyes lingered longer on her than on the others, but she told herself that everyone probably felt that way.

No one moved; no one spoke. None of the girls stepped forward.

"Very well," said the Prime at last. "We shall now proceed to the Vow itself."

As they had rehearsed, each girl in turn stated her name before the cohort recited the Vows together. "I, Helfreda, born of Snelling"; "I, Lerys, born of Harroton"; "I, Evrith, born of Brinsey"; and so forth. Some spoke out firm and clear, some voices wobbled, some were barely audible even from a mere couple of paces behind. When it came to, "I, Jerya, born of Delven," she was relieved to get the words out with no more than a slight tremble on the name of her old home.

The rest they recited in chorus.

"In full understanding and after solemn consideration,

"By my own free choice and absolutely without duress,

"Do irrevocably bind myself and undertake to serve,

"The most perfect and immaculate Guild of Dawnsingers,

"And the land and community we are consecrated to serve.

"To this end I pledge as follows:

"I shall conduct myself at all times in accordance with the rules and practices of the Guild;

"I shall defer at all times to duly instituted authority;

"I shall cherish, preserve and seek to extend the wisdom and knowledge of which the Guild is guardian;

"I shall reveal none of this knowledge to persons outwith the Guild, save as sanctioned by authority;

"I shall serve in whatever capacity is required of me.

"All this I pledge, accepting no other loyalty to the end of my days."

Finally, each girl in turn advanced, knelt before the Prime, who laid a hand upon her head a moment and spoke a few soft words. Jerya's turn came at last, and she felt the hand settle upon her scalp, dry and cool. "Welcome, Jerya," murmured the Master. "I suspect you should have been one of us years ago, but that's put right now."

Having received the blessing, they removed themselves to one side. When the last few girls had joined them, the Master Prime declared the ceremony complete. Flute and viol struck up in a corner, and Novices, Tutors, and Masters began to move about the room, seeking friends, mentors, mentees. The buzz of talk threatened to drown the music.

A beaming Railu found her before she had moved more than a few steps. "Here you are then, Novice Jerya."

"Thank you, Novice Railu." They grinned at each other, both well aware that their newly equal standing would last little more than a month, when Railu and the others would be presented for Ordination.

"Here," said Railu. "I brought you a present. Now you need never shave again." She pressed a small pot into Jerya's hands.

CHAPTER 21

JERYA

"It is not yet dark enough for serious observing," said Jossena, "Though Venera is well displayed in the West, and would well repay a look through the fifteen-centimetre refractor, if you have the opportunity on another evening. And the last of the high cloud appears to be clearing to the East, so I have hopes of some fine seeing in an hour or two. But for now... I have a little demonstration planned for you, for which the courtyard will be quite dark enough. After that we shall take refreshment, collect our warm clothing, and attend to the telescopes."

She soon had some of the girls scurrying about, extinguishing lamps or drawing down blinds in those rooms which looked into the central courtyard of Observatory House. Others stood by, ready to douse the lamps in the court itself, while Jerya helped her carry a large ball from a store-room. It was very light, must be hollow, but large enough to be awkward for one to carry. Jossena unhooked one of the lanterns from a wall-bracket in one corner, and they suspended the ball from it, its top about head-height.

"Now, everyone—except those who are prepared to douse the lamps—gather so you have a good view of the globe. And you, Jerya, just remain there. Hold the globe just as it is, so it does not spin. " She moved away to the opposite corner. "Lights out, girls, please."

For a moment the yard seemed utterly dark, a blackness Jerya had barely known since leaving Delven. But there was still a deep violet glow in the sky overhead, and as her eyes adapted she could quite easily make out the white robes of the waiting girls, the heads of those with lighter skin.

Then Jossena unshuttered another lamp, and Jerya threw up an arm against its dazzle.

"I beg your pardon, Jerya." Jossena made some adjustment, narrowing the beam, so that it no longer fell on Jerya's face. With a few more adjustments, she contrived it so the beam illuminated the sphere, but little else.

"So... here we have the Earth—in the custody of Jerya—and the Sun, in my hands. A model, of course, and a very rough one. Just how rough, we shall discover in the coming weeks. For now, let us just say that my Sun is very much too small, and very much too close to the Earth, for this model to even begin to approximate the correct scale.

"Still, we persevere, and it will give us the beginnings... So, Jerya, how tall are you?"

"I do not know exactly, Tutor Jossena."

"Hm. Well, you must be above one-seventy, and the globe is half a metre in diameter, or a little more. Let us say, for ease of calculation, it is one third of your height. That being so, if the model were truly to scale, Jerya would be..." She paused a moment, for effect. "Jerya would be around thirty-six thousand kilometres in height." There were some gasps, some half-stifled giggles. "You are the tallest in the room, Jerya, but not by quite that much." The class dissolved in mirth. Jerya smiled, though she was sure no one could see her in the darkness beyond the beam of the lamp.

"I hope you will all now remember that the diameter of the Earth is close to twelve thousand kilometres. And therefore its circumference is..."

Multiply by pi. Jerya would have raised her hand, but she was holding the globe as directed. It took a moment before other hands appeared in the gloom. "Aye, Cressiel?

"Forty thousand, Tutor Jossena. Approximately."

"Aye, indeed. In fact the true figure, by our best estimates, is a little more, but we don't need to be pernickety about it just now. Forty thousand is a nice round number. And, if you think about it, it's also a very large number. Which is why, in everyday life, we do not perceive the world as a sphere...

"Now Jerya, if you would be so kind as to turn the globe... there. Now, can everyone see that?"

Most of the surface was grey, but one small portion, more than halfway up the upper curve of the globe, was painted green. Jerya could have covered it with her thumb.

"That, girls, represents the Sung Lands. All that we know, all that we have explored, all that is displayed on Tutor Skarat's maps, is contained within that small compass. Now, Jerya, will you please be so good as to rotate the globe to return the green patch into the shadow... just so. Now, girls, please observe closely... no, wait one moment. I want all of you to be able to see the terminator... does anyone know what I mean by "the terminator?"

Jerya saw a couple of hands raised, heard Jossena chuckle softly. "A small complication: I cannot identify whose hand is raised. Who are you, the one closer to me?"

"Kuallashe, Tutor Jossena."

"Ah, Kuallashe. And your answer?"

"The terminator is the line between light and shadow."

"Indeed, well done. Now, bearing in mind that this globe, however crudely, represents the Earth, what other words could we use in stead of 'light and shadow'? Is that you, Telleni?"

Telleni was almost as dark as Analind, but with a bouncing eagerness quite unlike the customary calm of Jerya's friend; two characteristics which made her readily identifiable even in the darkness. "Day and night."

"Just so, thank you, Telleni. Day and night... Now, if everyone can see the terminator on the right-hand side... Jerya, kindly rotate the globe to bring the green back into view—slower, please; as slow as you fairly can. Good. Now, girls, what are we observing here? What particular moment?"

With her hands otherways engaged, Jerya once again had to be content with knowing that she knew the answer—as, it seemed did most of the class.

"Sunrise," said Jossena. "But does the sun, in fact, rise?"

No, she thought, *if the lantern is meant to be the sun... it's not moving at all.* Jossena quickly coaxed the same observation from one of the younger girls. "We call it sunrise because that is how it appears to us, standing on the surface of the Earth. However, the appearance is deceiving; in point of fact, the Earth revolves around the Sun, and not as our perception might suggest. And the Earth also rotates—spin it faster, if you would, Jerya—and it is that rotation which gives us the cycle of day and night.

"Now, there are many things which follow from these basic facts... and they *are* facts. I must ask you to take my word for them for now, but will acquaint you with proofs in the next few weeks. Indeed, much of your study this coming year will be concerned with these matters, with proofs, and with details. But for now what I will say is... you may wish to think about what this may mean to us—and by 'us' I mean, specifically, the Guild of Dawnsingers. In particular, please keep this demonstration in mind when we Sing tomorrow morning.

"Now, I think we can have the lamps lit once more. We'll gather again in the dining room."

❋

The songstead that served the Observatory complex did not occupy the highest point; that was reserved for the telescopes themselves, in their twin domed buildings. But there was a great sense of elevation nonetheless. The hill on which the College stood was no more than seventy metres above the river and the lower parts of the City; its immediate overlook encompassed the College's own orchards and vineyards and kitchen-gardens, which spread out across the gradual declivity. The Observatory, on the other hand, stood close to three hundred metres above the rolling lowlands beyond, and it seemed as if most of that thousand-foot fall was a single precipice.

Even from the Easternmost edge of the terrace, there was nothing to be seen below unless you leaned beyond the parapet, and then there was a dark tumbling chaos of crag and scree. Even for Jerya, who had grown up among rocks, and scrambled the crags, the drop was impressive. Many of the other girls shrank from it, and despite Jossena's urging, stood back a pace or two as they readied themselves to Sing.

The sky was pale now over the distant hills, its pre-dawn lavender transmuted to a kind of silvery yellow, faintly echoed in the mists that pooled in the valleys far below. Jerya had first seen those hills the day before, sitting on the box beside Jossena as the carriages reached the ridge-crest after an hour of gradual switchback ascent. They had been insubstantial then, a weak sage hue in the afternoon haze. She had wondered if they were linked to the mountains behind Delven, but a preoccupied Jossena had met her question only by referring her to the Observatory's Library. This turned out to be little more than an alcove off the dining-room, but along with its dozen shelves—still far more books than Jerya had seen in her first nineteen years—it had a map-cabinet. Most of its wide, shallow drawers were filled with star-charts, but there were terrestrial maps too. And these showed that the hills she saw were connected with 'her' mountains, but only as a minor offshoot. The main ridge continued, further to the East, and it looked as if its peaks rose higher even than the ones above Delven.

Those peaks were lost to distance—not to visibility, she thought, for the air could hardly have been clearer. It must be the curvature of the Earth itself that hid them from view. Jossena had been prevailed upon, at dinner, to say a little more about the matters her demonstration had introduced, including the size and shape of the earth, and how these might be proved and mensurated.

I would like to see those mountains one day, she thought, considering again the appeal of spending a year or two—if not longer—as a Peripatetic. But her thoughts were interrupted by the first notes of the Dawnsong. After the soloist's first line, she joined in, watching for the first spark to tremble into being over the suddenly-dark outline of the hills. Today's sunrise was aligned to a narrow gap in the hills, and she realised that might mean that not all of them, ranged as they were along fifteen or twenty metres of the terrace, would see it at precisely the same instant.

The new day speared through that gap in the hills, throwing a distinct beam across the land, setting the river-mists aglow and making the autumnal woods appear almost to burst into flame. If a village lay in the path of that beam, she realised, its Dawnsinger would be Singing well before those in other villages to either side. She knew there were a number of settlements; she had seen lights here and there in the night, and there were one or two threads rising in the still air that could only be smoke. Those villages were East of them, but the sun would reach them later.

Looking out across the land, she saw that everywhere it was the higher places that caught the light first. The sun had reached their hilltop, lighting the faces that flanked her, shining off the copper-clad observing-domes, but below, in the long shadows of that line of hills, each village would have its own Dawnsinger, and she would still be waiting. *But the Sun has risen for us...* And its rise was occasioned by the rotation of the Earth, by motion of the entire globe.

She had another unsettling thought. Even though she could not look at it directly, she had seen well enough that the sun had come up behind the far-off hills. And surely that meant that the other sides of those hills must have been sunlit long before any light reached the part of the world where she, Jerya, watched. Over there, in the unconsidered country beyond the hills, the sun must have risen long before she and the other Dawnsingers around her had even drawn breath to start their Song.

Well, of course, she thought. She knew there were other villages out there, and other villages meant other Dawnsingers. But she had not properly seen before, had not considered, that the sun did not rise at the same time everywhere: that Dawnsingers across the the Sung Lands must not all sing at the same time.

But then...

She turned away and followed the other girls to breakfast in the breeze and brightness of the day; but all morning her mind kept returning to the puzzle. It seemed to do so whether she wished it or not, as a tongue keeps returning of itself to the gap left by the fall of a baby-tooth. Jossena had said, *'you may wish to think about what this may mean to us—specifically, the Guild of Dawnsingers.'*

Jerya felt, not that she wished to think about it, but that she could not stop herself.

✻

She did not doubt she was right. She *knew* it. Everything Jossena had said the night before, and everything she had observed before and during Dawnsong, pointed the same way. But she did not speak out. She remembered what Yanil had said, and her own question: *how am I to know which questions are impolitic to ask, and which are politic?*

She liked Jossena, but she wished Yanil were here. Five minutes', ten minutes', converse with Yanil would surely set her mind at rest. But she would not see Yanil for another five days, and there was no one else in whom she could confide. The younger Novices were... too young, and she did not know the four Sisters who were the permanent Observers, though two of them seemed little older than herself.

It was Jossena, or an agonising five days' wait.

✻

"The Earth turns, and the Sun rises... or we see it as rising." Jossena merely nodded. After searching for nearly half an hour, Jerya had found her taking the air in a small orchard a short way down the Western slope. "And you showed us—I held the globe in my hands, *I* turned it—the terminator, the line of day and night, spanned the whole globe. Half in day, half in night."

"And thus you conclude...?"

"I conclude... no, I don't, I only *ask*: why do we Sing? The Sun rises here, it rises behind the mountains, it rises everywhere in its own time and according to its own rules, or—I suppose I should say—according to the rules of the Universe. So what purpose does the Dawnsong serve?"

Jossena regarded her gravely a moment, then turned, with a small gesture of invitation, and began walking, along the line of trees, gently curving to follow the contour. "Let me turn your question back on itself. What do you suppose would happen if we did not Sing?"

"The Sun would still rise." There it was, in five simple words.

"Aye, it would. Not a second later, not a second earlier... But is that to say that there would be no consequences?"

Jerya had no answer. She had thought she had learned so much, yet now she seemed to know nothing at all.

"I know this is hard, Jerya. Perhaps it is harder for you, having lived so much longer with another account of it all."

"The way things are." She said it almost to herself, but Jossena's ears were sharp enough.

"The way things are. Is that what they say in Delven?"

"It is, Tutor Jossena." And she had come close to hating it... but now she was not so sure.

"Hmmm... imagine for a moment that you are still in Delven. You were never Chosen, nor was any other girl in the village. But one morning there is no Dawnsong...

"There is silence. And yet—as you now know must happen—the sun still rises. It's a fine day, neither too hot nor too cold. There is no Song to waken the people, yet the light rouses them."

Ah, now there you're wrong, she thought. *In the deep caves, where Delven sleeps, it's always dark.* She knew, though, that this had no real bearing on Jossena's argument.

"So... the people stir. Seeing it is a fine day, they go about their daily tasks. Nothing else is different... And so it continues. Silent dawn follows silent dawn. There are hot days, cool days, wet days and dry. Just as before. Apparently the absence of the Dawnsong changes nothing.

"And yet... Imagine yourself in this situation, Jerya, with your questing intelligence. You begin to wonder... what it is that moves the sun, why the seasons change, what causes the moons to wax and wane. The old simple answer no longer holds... You cannot rest until you have another. Of course, you're thinking just that now, aren't you?"

Jerya nodded, realising that she had already accepted that the old answer was in error. She felt as sad as if someone dear had just died. As if *Sharess* had died, and that were the reason for the silence Jossena's words had conjured... it seemed almost the same thing. All her life, Sharess had *been* that answer, even if she had not known her name. It was distressing, but she had lived through enough to know that what she might *want* need not be what *was*.

And she wanted to hear Jossena's new answer. "We do not intend to permit any such situation to arise. In every city and town and village in the Sung Lands, each morning is hailed in Song. Many people—especially those in remoter places, those who have never travelled—believe explicitly that the sun would not rise if their Dawnsinger fell silent one morning. They would not dare to sleep anywhere out of earshot of the songstead. There have even been reported tales of folk being stranded by some kind of mishap too far from home and simply dying during the night, apparently from pure terror. Whether there is truth in any such tale, I do not know...

"A more sophisticated belief, common among those who travel, recognises that there is but one sun, that it is hardly to be held susceptible to local influences... yet I doubt you will find any who believe all would be well were *every* Dawnsinger to fall silent.

"We do not compel people to believe that we have power—individually or collectively—over the Sun. We do not preach or proclaim this; we simply allow them to believe it. What else should they believe? Why—as you asked—why else do we Sing? Patience, girl, I'm getting there.

"We allow the people to make a perfectly reasonable deduction from observed facts—from *the way things are*. We Sing every day, in every populated place, and every day the Sun rises. No one need ask themselves the questions which you would have asked, in that hypothetical Songless dawn.

In the unlikely event the question arises spontaneously, it will seem that the answers are already known, and are in the most trusted and reliable hands. Because we are separate, because we are aloof, because we are the Guild, ordinary folk feel it neither necessary not even possible to inquire into our mysteries.

"That, Jerya, is the reason why we sing the Dawn. If ever you thought that our learning, our lore and our mysteries, were simply placed at the service of the Dawnsong... now you know differently. The Dawnsong itself is simply part of the strategy by which we maintain our custodianship of the mysteries.

"You look... disappointed, Jerya. There's no need." She paused, and her gaze sought Jerya's. Her eyes were grey, faintly flecked with green, and nested in fine lines. "We don't summon the Sun, we don't command her. Well, is that so terrible? Consider: a Sun which is at the beck and call of a few women is not so great a thing. Isn't it a mean, a trivial, even a vulgar notion, to reduce the source of all life to the status of a trained dog? The truth is, of course, that the Sun is so distant and so mighty that no power we could even dream of could affect it in the slightest degree.

"However—and you must, if you think about it, find this truly inspiring—we can *understand* the Sun. How it burns; well, we have some ideas about that, but there is much more to be done. But as to how it moves—or, to be precise, how Sun and Earth move in relation to one another; we understand that pretty well. We do not demean the Sun to something we can order about; we *elevate ourselves* to understand it. Is there not altogether more dignity in this? When we Sing, it is no empty performance. It expresses the awe and the wonder and the beauty of it all. And we remind ourselves of the surpassing importance of our task, and of the most perilous and glorious knowledge we hold in trust."

"Why do you say 'perilous'?" asked Jerya.

"Because it is, my dear. In the wrong hands this knowledge could destroy the Earth. And once it almost did so. It rocked the Earth—and it shattered the Moon, for once there was only one."

CHAPTER 22

JERYA

"In your First Vow, you pledged to serve *the ancient and secret Knowledge of time and space.*" said Perriad. "And in your Novitial Vows, you affirmed *I shall reveal none of this Knowledge to persons outwith the Guild.*"

Save as sanctioned by authority; that was how it continued. Jerya said nothing; Perriad had barely paused.

"*Ancient...*" She shrugged, "That almost goes without saying. We are well into the fourth century of the Guild Reckoning, and the events of the First Fragment—of all the Fragments—lie no small number of years further back; perhaps more years than we even imagine. No, Jerya, the word I wish to focus on is 'secret'. Have you formed any opinion on why our Knowledge is so firmly kept secret—why we do not share it even with other women, let alone with men?"

"Because it is perilous." She remembered Jossena's exact words; she did not think she could ever forget them: *It rocked the Earth—and it shattered the Moon, for once there was only one.*

"True enough—but, you might well say, is not all knowledge perilous?" Perriad shrugged. "That seems inarguable, to me. Knowledge is a treasure, but also a burden. Above all it carries great responsibility.

"And yet the ancients seem to have lost sight of that truth. And we believe that this is because those who are closest to life were excluded from power. Centuries ago... well, today, there is no authority over all the Sung Lands but our Guild. Villages have their headmen and their elderwives,

towns have their councils, trades and crafts have what they, too, call guilds...
but each of these has authority only in its own area, its own business. Once
it was different. Women were kept apart, disunited, each in her man's house
with her children. Of course women were not always literally bound to
the house, but still they were confined, limited; they could not truly come
together. It seems women often accepted this. I suppose it's not entirely
unnatural for a woman to think above all of her own children, of a home
for them. And when a woman did not fall into line, devote herself to home
and family... well, as I said, men are stronger.

"And, if the human race is to continue, women must lie with men and
bear their children." A fleeting expression disturbed the grave set of her
features. She sipped at her cup, and when she looked up again her face
was once more calm, her voice dispassionate. "But I fear I tell you what
you already know. Perhaps—surely, indeed—you know more than I about
men. I am sure you will recognise what I am speaking of... in your village,
Delven, did not the men believe that they ran things? Oh, they would bow
to the Dawnsinger, of course, listen to her words on the weather and the
seasons—yet strut around, convinced that the real business of life is what
men get up to."

Jerya nodded. This she understood. Some men, definitely, were like that.
"As if hunting were more important than cultivation, or shearing the sheep
more important than spinning the wool..."

"Just so. And it's little different, here in the city. Men busy themselves
with building things up and knocking them down. Carpentering and
blacksmithing and leather-working... And in trade, too. It's men, nearly
always, who spend their time moving things from place to place so they can
double the price.

"Most of what they do, of course, is of value; I don't deny that. But they
imagine that this—and only this—is what is really important. It has been
observed that what do is called women's work; what men do is called simply
work... And yet, you know, they could cease most of their activity tomorrow

and life would go on. If women ceased to do what women do, in perhaps eighty years there would be no one left alive.

"Yet someone must stand aside from that. Some of us must accept the wider responsibility.

"In those ancient days... in those days, the Knowledge which is now in the trust of the Guild, and—I must tell you—much more that we have lost, was in the hands of men. It seems absurd now, but they seem to have believed that women were temperamentally ill-suited, if not completely incapable, for scientific work. They may have believed it quite sincerely, but what's certain is that it was also *convenient*." She saw Jerya's face, and smiled. "Aye, absurd is the word, isn't it? In this Age science, learning, is our domain; in the Age Before, it was precisely the other way about. And if you have looked at the First Fragment, you will have the beginnings of an understanding of how that change was made.

"But let us be fair; those ancient men also made many things which worked for good ends: contrivances, and potions, which could cure diseases we can do nothing about today. Their ingenuity could strike off in any direction. They could cross in minutes distances that would take us days; your entire journey from Delven might last an hour or two rather than a week. It is said that they even walked on the Moon—as you know, in those days, there was but a single Moon."

She paused again, took another sip of her jai. "At least, that is how most scholars interpret the surviving records. You should ask Tutor Jossena about this if it interests you, but I think she would say there is little doubt about the single Moon; there are so many references scattered across the ancient texts, even a few images. As to *walking* on the Moon, that is more controversial, as you may imagine, but it keeps scholars occupied.

"Whatever the specifics of such matters, we can be sure that there were wonders we can scarcely now conceive. But many, perhaps most, of these wonders, seem to have arisen from a science that was devoted first and foremost to weaponry. And in the end, as far as we can understand, they built weapons that were like tiny suns..."

She uttered a brief, mirthless laugh. "Ironic, is it not? Men—in some places, at least—now believe that *we* control the sun; and we go to some lengths to ensure that all believe at least that we have a certain influence upon it. We know otherwise—and we know, too, that once they, *men*, could in some way mimic the sun.

"Even at its unimaginable distance from us, the sun's heat can burn your skin, can even kill you if you are incautious. You know this better than most, do you not? The sun had left its mark on you when first you came here, though we are nearer the Pole than the Equator. We can hardly conceive its true intensity; a heat far beyond any ordinary fire. Yet the ancients could harness, and unleash, some of that power. Their weapons, it seems clear, were like tiny suns, at least for an instant—a devastating instant. If one were detonated in the air above this city, it would leave... not even ruins. The very hill upon which this College stands would be vaporised, the solid rock at its roots would melt, the land for kilometres around would be wiped clean of all life.

"Not only did they make such weapons, Jerya; in the end they used them. I do not know how they could do so—how could any thinking being participate in the extinction of millions of other thinking beings?—but then I am not a man and cannot imagine how men think.

"Well, it happened. We live now in lands which were spared because in those days they were scarcely populated. Where their cities were—what do your Delven-folk call the lands beyond the mountains?"

"The Blistered Lands."

"As many do... and it's as good a name as any. However, the true Blistered Lands, it seems, were far South of here, as well as East. For all we know, the land directly East of your former home was always wilderness, and as such would probably have been spared. Some say the world is warmer now than it was then—whether because of the weapons they used, or for some other reason, is unclear, like so much else." She sighed. "But what does seem clear is that the regions where we live can support a greater population than they did before. In any case, the Earth recovers. It was all centuries ago; even millennia, by some readings. After the war, those lands were deadly to walk upon, but most scholars believe they would be safe to enter now."

Perriad's words lanced through her with an almost physical impact. She was sure she must have shown some reaction. But Perriad was sipping jai again and saw nothing.

Most scholars believe they would be safe to enter now. And that meant... *The mountains* aren't *the end of the world.*

They'd always been there, all her life. It wasn't very far from the village up onto the moor; through the upper forest, where the trees became smaller, sparser; past the last cluster of beehives nestled in a sunny spot where a band of rocks curled protectively over them. Up the rocks at the side; grey here, not rust-red and salmon-pink as they were lower down. An easy climb, almost like a natural staircase, though you had to be careful. Long skirts and sandals weren't ideal for climbing; she'd seen that long ago. Men's boots, men's clothing, must make it easier. But she could do it; and so you came out onto the open moor above. In her mind, always, the heather was glowing purple, as it did at the height of the summer. And there were the mountains, the nearest ridge clear and dark, but streaked with snow, some patches surviving even when the heat seemed to pulsate like the humming of the hives, on days when the bees themselves seemed sluggish. And another ridge beyond, appearing to the left where the first one fell away, always paler, not quite substantial.

And beyond that, there had always been nothing. Nothing but the Blistered Lands. Nothing but death.

"—Jerya! Are you listening to me, *Novice?*"

In a flurry she reassembled her scattered wits. "I beg your pardon, Senior Tutor," she said, dipping her head, trying to look submissive.

"Well," said Perriad tolerantly, "It's a great deal to take in, I'm sure." Jerya nodded. That she could agree to, with all her heart.

"Those lands may not be deadly to walk upon," Perriad said then, "But some of those places, especially in more Southerly latitudes, might be distinctly disturbing to visit. You would be walking upon the memory, if not upon the very ashes, of millions of people—not only the men who wrought such destruction, but millions of innocent children. And women; women whose only crime was to live too narrowly in their own lives... which is what we must not permit again."

Jerya nodded again, trying hard to keep her mind on Perriad's words. One lapse of attention might be condoned; a second would not be so easily forgiven. But at the back of her mind there hovered always the image of the mountains, and the way the sky looked bright above them.

"Now perhaps you can see why the Guild exists. Without science, humankind is in darkness; who would know when to plant crops, how to navigate on the seas, how to smelt metals? What sort of an exchange is it; the prospect of annihilation, or the brutish, miserable existence of our remotest ancestors?

"The world needs science, Jerya, but science is perilous. If you ever need a reminder of just how perilous it can be, the Three and the One are there for all to see almost every night. Beautiful, perhaps, but they bear witness to the shattering of the One Moon.

"Aye, science is truly perilous. We hold it in trust for all. The most perilous Knowledge is the most secret... Indeed, no one today knows how those dread weapons were made; our finest minds can barely guess at the principles. But men knew once, and what they discovered once they presumably can discover again, if allowed to roam freely in the province of science... So we have made that *our* province. Women, in whom reverence for life is the deepest of instincts, make the safest—the *only* safe custodians.

"The need to cherish knowledge, yet to contain it, is the fundamental guiding principle of all our doings. This is why we must hold aloof from those we serve... Knowing what we know, how can we be at ease with them? We have responsibilities they cannot even imagine. We hold their very lives in our hands, if you think about it—though not at all in the way that they devoutly imagine. And of course we cannot marry or bear children... We must hold ourselves apart, above all, from men.

"It is the deepest irony that we are custodians of life itself, yet we ourselves do not bear children. Yet we are still women, and we retain a woman's sensitivity to the rhythms of life. It is even said—on good authority, I believe—that before the Shattering, the orbital period of the singular Moon was the same as a woman's cycle. Imagine that, Postulant: to know that the phases of the Moon, the tides of the ocean, are echoed in the rhythms of your own body.

"They took that away from us. Perhaps it is an unsupported assumption that this was part of the *intention* of those who broke the Moon, but then again no one can say it wasn't. Who can say that men did not grow envious that women float in the deepest catamenial currents of the world, while they merely stand on the banks? Publicly we sing to the sun; in private, I believe, every Dawnsinger loves best the moons' light, the light of the Three and the One; broken though they are, somewhere deep inside we remember that once they waxed and waned in time with the rhythms of our own bodies... who could sanely deny that it's women who are made to be astronomers, who know the heavens not only with our eyes and our intellects, but with every fibre of ourselves?"

Perriad sighed, sipped at her drink. "And who else knows that every time we look upon the moons, we see a reminder of the ultimate atrocity that men once wrought? The Shattering of the Moon, Jerya. That is why we—why the Guild exists."

Jerya nodded. It was all she could do; she could find no words to express all that was flooding—cataracting—through her mind. In the caves of Delven at night there was only ever candlelight, rushlight, or blackness. Still, she had, from time to time, felt the impulse to walk out at night, even if she had never dared to go far, just to the edge of the moor where she had a wide view of the sky.

Certainly the night stirred and moved her, but she was not so sure she loved the moons. Only since arriving in the College, and learning to sleep in a room that was not fully dark, had she been so constantly aware of them. The Three were waning now, and each night was a little darker than the last. Still, with only a thin curtain to block out the moons-light, she found it an enemy of sleep, had taken to pulling a corner of the bedcover over her face.

She knew that it was not for the moons that she had wandered at night, but for the stars, and moonless nights were best for gazing at the stars. And now she had begun—barely begun—to discover how much more could be seen through a telescope...

Her thoughts had wandered, she realised, and Perriad was eyeing her expectantly; but she could not think of anything to say, unless it would sound hopelessly inane; 'that's very interesting...' Better to keep silent. She remembered a saying some of the women in Delven had used to chide their more gossipy neighbours: 'wise head keeps oft a still tongue'.

She smoothed her hands over her scalp; it was smooth, though she had not shaved since the Rite, but faintly sweaty. No inspiration there. She folded her hands once more in her lap.

Seeing her mute, Perriad shrugged. "It's too much to take in all at once, I'm sure. And so much that must be glossed over... Aye, it must be hard to digest. Perhaps you want to think about it before you question me... but if there's anything you'd like to ask now?"

"I don't think so... Though some of it is hard to believe. I don't doubt you," she added hastily, seeing Perriad's brows rise, "Hard to take in, I should have said; it's so strange. I can scarce believe the men I've known could do such things. They fight, aye, but they do not kill, save animals, for meat. And when they fight each other; even when it is a real quarrel, not a sporting match, it is usually harmless—a few bruises, no more. And, from what I've seen, they often seem better friends afterward."

Perriad's response, almost gleeful, surprised her. "Just so... It is not only for your intellectual potential that we wish you to remain here. You have lived Outwith, in the world, near twice as long as most of us, seen it through the eyes of an adult as well as those of a child. But let us not worry about that now. Don't burden yourself with too much new philosophy all at once. It's your own future which concerns us first. What you need to understand, before anything else, is the true nature of our Guild. We are trustees, I believe. The future of our people, their safety, their very existence, depends on us. We may allow people to nourish their superstitions concerning us, but at heart we are trustees of truth."

CHAPTER 23

JERYA

A s she pushed through the crowd in the taproom, Jerya was aware of Railu close as a shadow behind her, the hand tightly clutching her own. She knew that this close and rowdy concentration of men was fearful to her friend. But she was also looking out for Rodal and trying to catch the eye of Annyt behind the bar.

The girl's face gave a flicker of recognition, but nothing more, until she was free to come over to them. Then her eyes were very intent on Jerya, but otherwise she was careful to do nothing that might draw attention.

"If you're seekin' Rodal," she began, "I'm afeared you may have a long wait. I don't quite know when he'll be back." Her smile seemed strained.

"You don't know where?" asked Jerya gently.

"No, I'm sorry." Annyt shrugged.

Before she could speak again there was a burst of raucous laughter behind them. Jerya glanced back involuntarily, but the men were leaning in close around the table; there was no sign that they were interested in herself or Railu. She would have dismissed the moment completely, but for Railu's reaction. Under the brown, the blood had washed from her face. Jerya squeezed her hand but there was not much she could say.

The streets and the City were still strange to her, of course. She had expected that Railu, having known all about the secret way out of the precincts, would have more experience of the City. But it hardly looked like it; she had clung to Jerya's arm, only speaking to give directions, and then in a hasty whisper. In the face of fear greater than her own, Jerya found herself obliged to act as if she had no fear at all. She had allowed Railu to cling as she concentrated on finding her way.

In almost eight years, Railu had left the College only for trips to the Observatory, had never once spoken to a man. Men were, of course, rigidly excluded from the Precincts; all the staff were women, even for work normally considered male. She had watched the women who stoked the boilers, muscular, flushed and glossy with sweat, had failed at first to recognise them at the end of the day making their way out in skirts and blouses and demure caps, looking smaller somehow.

Annyt had not missed Railu's distress, though Jerya doubted if she understood its cause. "Why don't you come sit in the parlour a while? It's quiet. I'll send Rodal in if he appears, and..." She hesitated; Jerya encouraged her with a smile. "Well... I'll be free soon, when my parents have finished their supper, and I would... if you willn't mind, I'd like to talk to you myself."

"Of course." Jerya had no notion what Annyt wanted, but she felt herself warming to the girl, and she thought she would welcome the chance to talk to someone outside the Guild.

They went through into the cosy parlour, Railu still leaning a little. Annyt left them alone with welcome mugs of ale, but returned within a few minutes, closed the door and untied her pinafore. Underneath she wore a yellow blouse and full blue skirt—no, Jerya saw, it was another pair of what she now knew were called culottes; many of the serving-staff in the College wore them at times, even a few of the Singers (always white for these, of course).

Annyt's dark wild hair was pulled into bunches with blue ribbons. Jerya let her eyes dwell on the bright, free-swinging clothes, pale unblemished skin, unpainted but vivid lips, intense blue eyes. Suddenly she realised; she found Annyt very desirable. Almost angrily, she looked away, looked at Railu, saw her, too, regarding Annyt with admiration. Then she wanted to laugh; Railu was in no position to be jealous, then. It was strange, though, to find how she herself had changed. She seemed to be looking with eyes she had not possessed on her previous visit.

Oblivious to these attentions, Annyt drew up a chair, smoothing her skirt as she sat, back to the door, sipping at a small mug of ale. She did not look directly at them, except in quick shy glances. Jerya sensed that she was remembering that they were Dawnsingers.

"Don't be worried about talking to us. Forget we carry any other titles outside this chamber. I'm Jerya, this is Railu, you're Annyt." Annyt nodded, but said nothing; softly, Jerya prompted, "You said you wanted to talk,"

"Yes, thank you. I know it's impudent of me—I don't mean because you're... of the Guild, just because it's not what you came for... well, partly. Partly it *is* because you're of the Guild. But you said to forget, and I am trying." She laughed, a little nervously.

Jerya could not restrain her own answering smile. "Please, go on."

"Yes. It's about Rodal. I know you guessed when you came before... Jerya. That we've been very much together, almost since the first day he came. It's been a fine time, too. Everythin's new to him, and so for me it's almost like seein' things for the first time all over again.

"And he doesn't know how to behave—oh! That sounds worse than I meant... I mean, he doesn't know city etiquette, what we consider polite. He tends to just say what he thinks. I like that... Well, we've become friends, and maybe somethin' more. I say maybe—in me it was just startin'. Perhaps it meant more to him that I would hold his hand—and kiss him sometimes." She looked down, perhaps blushing lightly.

"In Delven you would not do that unless you were betrothed," said Jerya. *And little enough even then, not under the eyes of the whole village.*

"I was pretty sure it'd be that way. I thought Rodal understood that it's different here. Perhaps he did. Perhaps it was not in that way that I have misled him—if I have... Anyway, he asked me—asked! It didn't come out as a question. First I knew was when he told me he was writing in a letter home of hopes to bring me to Delven."

"Choss!" Jerya gasped. The old, familiar, oath eased the shock she felt. "He wants to wed you?"

Annyt nodded, the bunches of her hair bobbing. "At least, he did. But I told him... oh, it was sweet, in many ways, and part of me wanted to say 'yes' at once. But I don't have sole voice in this, and I know my father and my mother would tell me to think again. Not that they think anythin' but the best of Rodal; only that I am still but eighteen, and have known him only weeks. We do not decide such things in short time here; they would have made me wait until a year has passed... and I believe that is right.

"Still, I said I would travel to Delven, if he would promise to bring me home again, I am curious to travel, and curious to see his home—of course, it's your home, too, isn't it? To learn a little more about him, also. But he said it was not possible. I could not travel there with him were we not betrothed. Or perhaps I could travel there, if you were goin' too: what better chap'rone than a Dawninsger?—but how would we come back, just the two of us?"

"Tell me a thing," put in Jerya. "Did he speak of staying here in the City when—if—you were wed?"

"Oh, yes. Perhaps even if we were not. Assuredly if we were; he says I would never be happy with the life that would be mine in Delven."

"He has the right of it there, you may be sure."

"Oh, so I believe. And he was surely thinkin' of me, and then I felt more strongly that perhaps I could be his wife. But I also felt that if I han't seen his home as he's seen mine, we'd still be, in some wise, strangers. And since then we seem to have been more like strangers, not less so."

"How is that?"

"First we argued some more over this matter of goin' to Delven. I still don't understand it. Perhaps you can help me."

Jerya's hands toyed with the brown homespun skirt she wore in place of her now-accustomed white. Railu had known exactly how to lay her hands on their garments—their disguise—even if she had never previously acted on the knowledge and ventured out into the city.

Her hands had lost none of their old deftness in winding on the head-cloth, so long practised it needed no conscious thought. The old ways of her village were not yet lost to her. She could imagine herself back there, once again squatting with the women in the shade of the rock-courts. She could almost hear the chatter...

"Since I left Delven," she said, "I have learned things that you may have always known. Such as... that it may be possible for a man and a woman to be friends." She glanced at Railu. "Railu doubts me, I know, but... In another life, Rodal and I might have been such friends, but we did not understand that." *Perhaps we might have been more than friends, also*, she thought: but it was fruitless to dwell on what could never be. "When we were thrown together on our journey, we felt... ah, many things. Certainly a companionship I hadn't met before, might never have discovered had we remained in Delven. There, men and women lead such separate lives. Even those who are wed rarely pass their days together.

"And women do not travel. The men go sometimes to the nearer villages; sometimes one will take a wife in another village and settle there, just as there are a few men in Delven who were not born there. But not women. If you were betrothed to Rodal... even then, they might find it strange that you should travel—but strange in a... in a pleasing way. But if you were not, there would be more strangeness and no pleasure."

"But if we explained..."

"What is explanation? So many words. In Delven it is what you do, how you behave, that matters. *And* how you dress... I was born there. For nineteen years I knew only Delven ways... and still I found it hard, at times." *Perhaps that's what the Dawnsinger saw*, she thought suddenly.

"The only woman they have ever seen who does not dress that way is the Dawnsinger. And I'm not sure they scarcely even know she is a woman. I mean... what do I mean? It is hard, sometimes... I don't always have the words for what I feel." She laughed, but there was little mirth in it. "You see? Words are not enough, not always.

"Dress as you are now—dress any other way—and you will seem almost as strange as a Dawnsinger; but a Dawnsinger is permitted—expected—to be strange. But dress as they do, and how are they to know that you are different? You will be left with nothing but words, and words will not be enough. How can they understand—how can they understand your not being sure of Rodal? Anyone there who is not already betrothed would not hesitate to accept him."

"Would you?" The question had clearly slipped out; Annyt coloured instantly, cast her eyes down, muttered an apology

Jerya did not mind, however. *Well, perhaps a little.* But it was all becoming remote. A fire will always die, sooner or later, without fresh fuel. "Not now, of course; but then... not without hesitation, not without questioning. I could imagine things being different; I don't know why I had that power, but I did. But at the end of it all... I would not have been able to do better, not half as well, with anyone else. If I had remained in Delven, then my only choice, I think, would have been Rodal, or spend the whole of my life alone."

Annyt looked up again, her face still a little flushed. Again Jerya felt a tremor of desire, the impulse to stroke her glossy hair. It was hard to sit still and straight and keep her hands folded in her lap. *Railu, what have you made of me?*

"You understand me, don't you?" Annyt was saying. "So why cannot others in Delven?"

"I *think* I understand you, but how can I be sure? One touch of understanding between Rodal and myself, and it seemed like everything. We grew close while we journeyed; in particular, we shared a terrible day across the Scorched Plains. I had never known such companionship before... but I soon learned that it need not be unique." She glanced toward Railu, but without meeting her eyes. "I did not understand too well then. Perhaps I still don't. But I understand, at least, that there may be many kinds and degrees of friendship and affection and love. That you may seek something more, or different, in wedded life than is ever dreamed of in Delven... Aye,

I understand a little. I understand your wish to take time over your choice. I may even understand it better than Rodal does."

"I wonder if you could talk to him, then," Annyt said eagerly.

"It is one thing to talk... I don't know whether it will change anything. I say again: you cannot go to Delven with Rodal unless you are betrothed, or pretending to be. And such a pretence... Delven folk have a hatred of deception. I don't know if Rodal would be able or willing to take part in such a deception. I don't know if I would be able or willing to persuade him to do so."

"Ah, well," said Annyt with a sharp change of mood. "P'raps it no longer matters..."

"What do you mean?"

"We went this afternoon to the fayre, thinkin' to put aside disagreement and doubt, just to enjoy the day. And for a time we did... I've been to the fayre every year since I can remember, and it's all familiar now. I have my fav'rite games and rides and booths and sweetmeats, and I must visit them all, taste them all, each year. It's like steppin' back to childhood, I s'pose. But to Rodal, it was all so new; it made it like new for me, too."

Jerya had only the faintest notion of what she was talking about, but she could see how the recollection brightened Annyt's face. It made her very lovely, for a moment; but the seriousness took hold again, and it was like a cloud crossing the sun. "But we came to the wrestling booth. The challenge is to go three rounds with their champion, and if you last the time you win a bronze, and if you beat him you take five silver. Rodal just looked at me and said, 'That'll pay my board and lodgin' for a few months,' and started in to make his challenge. I grabbed his arm to stop him and said I'd rather pay his rent myself than see him hurt. I thought it would please him, but he looked at me, cold as a fish, said, 'I haven't been defeated for three years,' and stalked off inside.

"I could barely watch. I knew what would happen. I went to wait for him at the rear of the booth, where I could still see the ring but get away easy after. There was a delay while they 'sembled a crowd to cover the purse; after that it didn't take long.

"He wasn't badly hurt; he'd been so overmatched the champion didn't need to do any damage. A few bruises, pulled muscles, a sore head from bein' thrown. It wasn't his body that pained him: it was his pride. And—p'raps worse—that I'd *known* he would be defeated. But I've seen... last year when I went to the fayre I watched a challenger. It was no one I cared about, so I didn't mind so much... The champion's not so big, no bigger than Rodal—that's why so many think they can beat him—but he's so fast and cunnin'. Rodal said he cheated, but I didn't see him cheat. He didn't need to."

During this speech the door opened. Jerya looked up to see Rodal entering, but Annyt had been too caught up in her tale to be aware of his approach behind her. He swayed a little as he stopped behind Annyt's chair.

"In Delven we'd call him a cheat," he said suddenly, loud and close.

She jerked as if he had slapped her, gave a gasp that was almost a scream. But she recovered quickly, springing up and around to confront him. "Don't you dare do that to me!" she cried, brandishing an open hand as if she had barely stopped herself slapping his face.

"D'you command me?" he asked. His voice sounded strange, barely recognisable.

"I don't command," Annyt replied. She looked very calm now, rigid calm buttressed by anger. "But if you ever do that again..."

The threat was probably the more effective for being unvoiced. Rodal seemed to sag a little. "I'm sorry," he said at last.

Annyt said nothing, but took his hand and led him across the room to a settle against the far wall when they could sit together. He did not look at Jerya or Railu as he passed, and when he sat, he hung his head as if studying his own feet,

"Come," said Annyt, low and soothing. "Greet your guests."

He looked up sharply, and Jerya had the most disturbing sensation; he had looked straight at her when he entered, yet now he seemed to see her for the first time. "What are you doing here?"

She took a deep breath, trying to calm herself.

"I came to see you, of course," she said, striving to smile and sound unconcerned. "And to introduce Railu."

He rose with a show of dignity and bowed, marring the effect by almost toppling forward. "I am honoured," he said, then sat down again with a thump. Annyt caught his arm, looked close into his face. "Are you all right?"

"I'm perfectly well!"

"Rodal, are you sure? You said your head was ringin'..."

"I'm all right! Weren't you listening?"

She said nothing, but released him sharply and stalked back to her original chair. Rodal stared at her back; when she sat, facing him, apparently composed, he turned to Jerya.

"I'm sorry," he said, in another abrupt, unsettling, change of mood. "That's no proper welcome. Let's try again... I'm glad to see you. What may I do for you?"

Annyt gave us a perfectly proper welcome, she thought, but didn't risk saying it. "I wanted you to meet Railu. If I don't return to Delven, it's possible she will be sent in my stead. But I can't decide... and she needs to know—*we* need to see clearly what she'll think of Delven, and what Delven will think of her."

"And you're asking me?"

"I... I thought you might be able to help."

"I can't speak for Delven," he said. "And as for myself... well, it hardly concerns me, do it?"

All three women gazed at him. Railu's expression betokened distaste; Jerya and Annyt exchanged concerned glances. Both, in different ways, knew Rodal well; Annyt, clearly, found his present behaviour just as bafflingly out of character as Jerya did.

"No one's asking you to speak for Delven," said Jerya. "That's the head-man's job... I just don't want my guesses to be any more wild than they need be. I only know how the women think—and even that, maybe, not as well as I might. I'm not asking you to make our choices for us, only to venture how you think the men might take it if they found themselves with another Dawnsinger in my stead."

"They'll think precious little of it, if you must know," he flared with a sudden energy that looked like anger. "One way or t'other... S'long as the place has a Singer, I doubt they'll care what her name was afore. Gossan, Jerya, you don't think anyone was holding their breath for it to be you, do you? Could even be some wouldn't have been too happy if they'd known aforehand it was to be you. But no one—saving Holdren, I s'pose—no one guessed until you were presented to us. And then, well, a Singer's a Singer. Now, if they think twice about it at all... Oh, could be there'll be some talk of you turning your back on your home or some such nonsense... but some folks'll take anything amiss if there's half a chance. Maybe I don't have to tell you who I'm thinking of... But, draff, if you're called to higher things and they're too ignorant to appreciate it, hard luck on 'em. As long as Delven gets someone with a white robe and a bald head and a decent pair o' lungs—I doubt any of 'em'll think twice about it. Maybe not even once."

Jerya had begun to smile as he spoke of folk holding their breaths. By the end of his speech she felt like laughing. Then she caught sight of Railu's face.

She had been hoping—almost expecting—that Rodal would clear her lingering concern over the feelings of the villagers. That he had done, in a sense, but it gave her no joy now.

The prospect of remaining in the College, delving ever deeper into mathematics and astronomy and other mysteries, called her more strongly than ever. She had learned a few things, but knew she had barely even begun to grasp how much more there was to be learned. But, more than that, in the College she was *someone*: not just the remote figure she would be as

Delven's Dawnsinger. Rodal's words had underlined that. *I doubt they'll care what her name was afore.*

Oh, aye, Perriad had dangled a most tempting lure... and Jerya had allowed herself to be deflected from proper consideration of the wider implications. Once, only a week or two ago, returning to Delven had seemed beyond doubt, and as long as there was no doubt she had faced it with equanimity, though she had known since her very first evening in the College that she would sorely miss much about it.

As soon as doubt had been introduced, as soon as Perriad had dangled that lure, the ground had shifted. It was hard, now, to see how she could ever be reconciled to that lonely life. It seemed cruel, she thought, what the Guild asked of its Singers, especially in out-of-the-way places like Delven... Seemed? It *was* cruel. Perhaps it was necessary; perhaps there was no other way it could be managed. She wasn't sure, yet, how she felt about all that, about the justification Perriad had offered, for the Guild's strategy—and for the great deception at its heart.

There was all that to wrestle with. And there was Railu, also. She knew, now, that however hard banishment to Delven might be for her, it would be even worse for Railu. She could not ask her friend, her lover, to accept that.

Suddenly she was furious with herself. It made her feel almost physically sick. At once, she got to her feet. "We'd better be going. Best to be back before all settles down for the night." It was only the simple truth, yet the words had the sour taste of deceit. "And I'd say Rodal needs his bed also."

He frowned, but made no protest.

Annyt slipped quickly past them to open the door. Railu went ahead into the short dim passage. Jerya stopped in the doorway, facing Annyt. For a moment both were silent, then both spoke at once.

"Thank you for—" Annyt began, then broke off with a choked, embarrassed giggle as Jerya voiced the identical words.

Jerya was first to regain composure. "I must thank you. You've been most hospitable. Now you must worry no more about us. Think of him, instead."

Annyt waved a hand, almost as if dismissing Rodal. "He needs to sober up; that's what he needs. But I must say... thank you for talkin' to me—or listenin'."

She held out her hand and Jerya clasped it. The desire to do more than merely clasp hands was fierce, for a moment.

As she joined Railu, she glanced back, saw Annyt already moving back towards the parlour. Then the swing of the door blocked her from her sight.

CHAPTER 24

JERYA

"I think she's keeping us waiting deliberately," grumbled Railu, shifting her feet on the flags. "The longer I stand here the less sure I feel."

Jerya grabbed her hands. "Hold to what we decided last night. You know we were right."

Railu nodded slowly. "I know. But it's a lot easier when I'm holding you, in our bed... Jerya, this is *Perriad* we're going to challenge. I can't help but remember all the other times I've stood here in the last five years. It must be easier for you. You've never seen her angry."

"Maybe I soon will, eh?" Jerya laughed, but she knew it sounded forced. "Well, I've faced anger before. And if I speak for both of us... she may be slower to anger with me. I'll—"

The door opened. Perriad, smiling coolly, beckoned then to enter. Nothing was said until they were seated. The chairs, upright and uncushioned, had been placed well apart, and Jerya knew she could not very well begin the interview by shifting Perriad's furniture about. Perhaps she couldn't have held Railu's hand anyway, but it would have been nice to have been closer.

"This is somewhat unusual," the Tutor began, leaning back in her own upholstered arm-chair, making an 'A' of her hands in front of her face, long nails meeting in sharp ridges. "One might even say, irregular, but curiosity impelled me to grant your request. So... what can I do for you?"

Her glance dismissed Railu and settled on Jerya. She recognised the practised way in which Perriad had already put her at a disadvantage. It was not so easy to know how to counter it. *Tread slow*, she told herself. *Tread careful*. Like stalking a deer in the forest... She had done that, not to hunt, as men did; she had neither bow nor skill, and doubted also whether she would find it possible to loose a killing shot. She had followed the animal merely to observe.

"You asked me to consider remaining here in the College," she began. Perriad showed no hint of reaction. "I had to give it a deal of thought. When I was inducted by Singer Sharess I swore service not only to the Guild, and to the Knowledge, but also to the community of Delven."

"You mentioned that before," said Perriad. "And I am sure you recall my answer: anything which serves the Guild serves the community of Delven. In any case, your Novitial Vow supersedes your Postulant's Vow. But there should be no necessity for any such argument. You *will* serve the community of Delven—because you will serve the entirety of the Sung Lands."

"A Vow is a Vow for life," Jerya responded. "So I have always been taught." It was true that in Delven it was invariably said with reference to the vows of wedding, but her original Vow, the one she'd made to Sharess, was scarcely to be thought less sacred. Did Perriad sense the implied reproach? she wondered. It was impossible to tell, but she felt a ripple of confidence as she went on, retrieving words she had carefully considered beforehand. "Of course what you say is true, and I may serve Delven in other ways than by remaining there as its Dawnsinger. Nevertheless my home has a special claim, and I felt I must satisfy myself it would suffer in no way. I could not devote myself to other things unless my mind was at rest on that score."

Then she had to pause, for her mouth had gone dry.

"I quite understand," said Perriad. "Your attitude does you nothing but credit." Praise from Perriad was usually something to be coveted, but Jerya was wary. Those words might seem kind, but the Tutor had again reminded them of her superior position.

Doggedly, Jerya continued, "It was beyond me to decide alone, but who else could I talk to who knew Delven? Only he who escorted me here, and remains to escort me—or whoever it may be—on the return. I... went out into the City to talk to him."

"I trust you disguised yourself," Perriad said simply, in a mild tone almost more disconcerting than open anger. "Of course it is a breach of rules to leave the Precincts without permission. Permission which *can* be granted in exceptional circumstances... but no matter. You are still new among us, probably unaware that rules can be interpreted flexibly if the occasion demands it. And no harm has been done, has it? Rather, 'tis good news if your discussion has had a satisfactory outcome."

I'm sure you'd *think it satisfactory*, she thought, but dare not say. Carefully, she said, "He bore out what I thought. The people of Delven would see little difference between one Singer and another."

"Indeed," said Perriad, with a covert but revealing glance at the silent Railu.

She said nothing more, leaving a silence which Jerya felt almost obliged to fill. But fluency had deserted her. "Well... at least, so long as whoever is sent is... able to meet the needs of my people.. They don't ask much of their Singer.... but that means the Singer has little to do, little contact with folk. It's not a life everyone could take to."

Perriad's eyes fixed on Jerya. She felt an almost irresistible urge to look at Railu. but dared not do so.

"Service to the Guild is not always rewarded with a merry life," the Senior Tutor began. "Primarily it is its own reward. We cannot expect, as of right, fine meals and wines and a congenial bedmate."

This time Jerya could not stop herself glancing at Railu; was there anything Perriad did not know? Hastily, she looked forward again, hoping she had wiped any giveaway expression from her face.

"The true rewards are the deeper ones," Perriad added. "The knowledge that we serve our Guild and the Sung Lands in the keeping of a fruitful peace. Our soul-sharing of the daily resurrection of the Sun... a fuller contemplation than any others can know of the wonders and mysteries of this world... Your Sharess, Jerya; did she strike you as unhappy?"

"No, not at all." That was true, but it troubled her to admit it. Then again, how much time had she spent with Sharess? How could she be sure whether the old Singer had been content with her lot?

"Yet she spent eight years here; and she was young, just as you are, when she was sent out to Delven. I doubt very much she had any selfish pleasure in the assignment. Yet the life she found is, I think, in many ways to be envied."

You take her place, then! Jerya wanted to cry, but that would have been fatal. "*I* can bear the thought of it," she said instead. "That was what I expected to return to. It would not be greatly different from my previous life. Books, and beehives, and solitary walks... I've been somewhat solitary for... well, all my life, really. And if I returned as Dawnsinger my solitude would have meaning. I could live that life. But to send someone who's never known what it's like to be lonely... that would be cruel."

Perriad lifted her brows, a small sign of what was surely considerable displeasure. "You say you have been solitary all your life. Nonetheless, since coming here, you haven't been solitary, have you? Quite the opposite; you've shown no mean aptitude for making friendships, forming attachments..." Jerya felt again the urge, the almost-command, to glance at Railu, but this time she resisted. "If you can adapt so quickly, why should not others make a converse adjustment?"

"Why should anyone have to? Surely there are those who are suited by temperament..."

"I do not need you to tell me that," Perriad responded with the first signs of real irritation. "Rest assured we will consider all the possibilities. Be equally sure we will *not* be swayed by wild demands from Postulants who have no idea of the many factors we must consider...

She leaned forward, hands now forming a 'V' aimed at Jerya. "Now listen to me, Postulant. The Guild does not seek to interfere in personal attachments. I must, however, counsel you against being overly influenced by one whose attitude is known to be... questionable."

Jerya's first thought was that it was about time somebody had the decency to mention Railu by name. The second: *is questioning the same as questionable?*

"Someday, Jerya, with your unique background—and your evident talents—you may rise to high standing in the Guild. If and when that day comes, you will have learned a great many things you do not know now—many of which I could not explain to you now even if we had all day. Several times I have told you that you have much to teach us. The converse is at least equally true. Never forget that. I think there is no more to be said."

Silently, not quite looking at each other, Jerya and Railu rose and turned away.

Perriad halted them at the door with a sharp call: "Novice Jerya! I remind you of your own words... '*A Vow is a Vow for life.*' You had better keep your mind on that track. And you had better accustom yourself to this notion:, no firm decision has yet been made as to who will be assigned as Dawnsinger to Delven. But it will not, under any circumstances, be you. Is that clear?"

Jerya did not trust herself to speak; she could only nod.

They left without another word, went quickly and silently down the stairs, through the court past the grey pool, down the passage between Hall and Kitchens, where the smell of beeswax almost masked the smells of cooking. Emerging onto the path to the hill, they did not stop or speak until they came to the wide lawn of the songstead. At its back a sycamore had grown triple-trunked, one limb sprawling almost horizontally near the ground, forming a natural seat. Here, on bark worn smooth by generations of use, they perched. For a moment there was stillness, then Railu slumped sobbing on Jerya's shoulder. Jerya wrapped her in an embrace and murmured consolation in meaningless sounds because she had no comforting words to offer. Railu's weeping slowly subsided, but it was minutes more before she sat up and tried to smile.

"Thank you," she said. "You tried your best. It's just Perriad...."

"Perriad is a bitch," said Jerya, shocking both of them. The words seemed to come from nowhere, but as soon as they were spoken she knew them for the truth. "That's what we'd call her in Delven, anyway. Not that Delven's ever seen such cleverness, but in our own small way we have one or two with the same way of putting themselves in the right whatever the true ins and outs of a matter."

"But still, to call her... Do you really think that?"

"Aye, I do. She has a dirty cunning... and she's *cruel*. I knew she was cold, but I never saw the cruelty till today. It must have been dreadful for you, all that time and she'd never use your name—and seemed to defy me to do it, so I'd have felt defeated if I had." Anger seethed within her. She bowed her head to hide sudden acid tears and beat her fist on the tree-trunk beside her, almost welcoming the pain.

"It's not the first time I've taken my feelings out on a tree," she said. "You can get a younger one and shake it like fury, like a gale, and maybe a few leaves will drop off—you can't really harm it—or an old one like this; you can beat your fists on it and never leave a mark, yet somehow you feel it knows you're there; it isn't quite indifferent, like stone."

"I must remember that when I'm in Delven."

"You are not going to Delven."

"What? Jerya... Perriad intends.... I know she said *no firm decision*... but she left me in no doubt."

"I know what Perriad intends. And I know it's *wrong*."

"But what can we do about it? What are you going to do... go back and march in and tell her she's wrong? We're only Novices, you know. She made sure to remind us of that."

"Hear me out. Ways and means are not the first question; the first question is whether it's right or wrong. And... Novice or not, fresh from the Backlands or not, I know some things are right and some are wrong. Not in the way my Aunts in Delven might have it: that 'right' is to wear a headcloth wrapped just so, do such-and-such duties, behave just so... Follow the rules, do as you're told, never ask *why*. How many times did I get a tongue-lashing, or even a cuffing, for asking just that? It took me most of my life to realise the reason my asking ired them so much... because they *did not know the answers*.

"Same for Perriad: 'right' is to obey, and never ask for reasons, 'wrong' is to defy her.... but there's a right and wrong deeper than any of that... the same way that three threes are nine is right and three threes are ten is wrong. Or wishing that pi equalled three, not three and a fiddly fraction. It would be convenient if it were three, make calculations so much easier, but it's not so, and there's an end of it. And I love the necessity of its rightness, love having a name for it... Still. Sending you to Delven is wrong. It may be convenient; it may make Perriad's calculations easier—and mine!—but it's wrong." She drew a quick breath. "Never to even ask you what you would prefer..."

"We go where we are sent."

"Aye, but do they know, better than we know ourselves, what we are fitted for? Maybe I don't know, because I'm still too new to most of it, but I've thought several times about what it might be like to be a Peripatetic... but you, Rai, surely anyone can see you should be a Healer. You'd be wasted in Delven."

Railu was silent for a moment. Jerya saw her hands bunching and open-ing on her lap. Then she spoke with a voice which held steady only with an overtone of strain. "Jerya... tell me more about the old Singer who Chose you—Shaless?"

Jerya wondered at the request, but answered plainly. "*Sharess*... All my life she'd been there. I'd hear her in the mornings. My sleeping cell wasn't too deep, else I could never have heard, and still I only could if I was awake and listening for it, and all else was silent. Sometimes I'd be up to see her Sing; I'd stay inside one of the entrances, in the shadows, so she wouldn't see me... And I'd see her in the days sometimes, walking forth: going to mind her hives, I suppose, or simply walking off into the high country; I never knew.

"I only spoke with her for... I don't know, I couldn't mensurate time then—I'm still learning! Inside an hour, I reckon.

"She was infirm; frail, you might say. Yet very much... *alive.* The way she looked at me, listened to me. I felt in some ways she was... that we were alike, somehow. I can't say *how*, but I felt it. I thought I would be proud to take her place. That I could live as she did. It terrified me, but I thought I could do it."

"Then why d'you think I can't?" Railu demanded, mettlesome.

"Oh, love, don't think I'm finding fault. Not unless you think Perriad's standards are the only... I saw your face when Rodal... well, he was acting strangely, as well he might if he'd taken strong drink on top of a blow to the head. But what he said was true enough. You'd be nothing to those people... Sharess was nothing to them; a voice, a passing presence they didn't look at; she was nothing *to me* until that day. Listen, Rai, I know I've said this before, but I still don't know if you truly grasp it... imagine if somehow you were sent to Delven—and I'd never left it. You and I—how close we are now—we would have spent the rest of our lives living only a few steps apart and never so much as speaking to each other."

"Surely... well, not in the village. But you used to go walking in the forests, and so did Sharess, you said. In the forests we could have..."

"No, Rai, I am not the person I would have been had I remained there. I would have seen you coming and... I would have run a mile." She'd said it before, but still Railu's face was stricken as if this was the first time she'd heard it. Jerya hated to see it, but she had to persist. She hated the cruelty, but felt certain it was needful. "I would have fled from you. That's what it means. That's why it's wrong. Believe me.

"I never told you about Marit, the Singer at Thrushgill. The first village on my journey, the first Dawnsinger I'd ever met after Sharess. She wasn't content, like Sharess was—or seemed to be, so far as I could tell. I don't really know. But Marit was unhappy, I'm in no doubt about that. Said she hadn't had a real conversation for eighteen months—and then she just talked at me, hardly gave me a chance to say anything for myself. And she drank... I think she drank too much, not just that night but every night.

"I can't bear the thought of you ending up like her, or worse.... Believe me! Don't I know Delven better than Perriad does? Don't I know *you* better than she does?"

"But what good does it do?" Railu cried despairingly. "You've tried to persuade her, and I'm grateful. You're a true friend, and brave, but it didn't work. Raking over the ground now only makes it harder for me to accept my fate."

"No!" Jerya seized Railu's hands. "*I* can't accept it. Maybe you're the brave one to sit there and speak of acceptance. Or maybe I'm still the only one who sees what it means. Anyway... I love you too dearly to permit it."

"But what else can you do?"

"I don't know... maybe nothing except get you out of here."

Jerya watched Railu's teary grimace slowly sag into open-mouthed disbelief. She felt something of the same shock herself.

"Jerya, Jerya... do you really know what you're suggesting?"

"No. It's but the beginning..." Of what, she scarcely knew. There was no plan in her head, not even an idea, but perhaps there was the first seed of one.

"Jerya, surely... half an hour ago you challenged Perriad as if she'd suggested breaking your Vow. But she hadn't suggested that at all. You recall how she threw your words back at you. But now... now *you* are suggesting it."

"I suppose I am," Jerya agreed. After the shock, a strange calm seemed to be settling upon her.

"But Jerya... how can you say that? 'A Vow is a Vow for life.' You said that yourself."

"I know." She answered slowly: things were still working themselves out in her head. "And surely it is a terrible thing to do—even to consider. But maybe there are worse things. To move people around like... what do you call them? In that game you like?"

"Pawns," said Railu with a faint smile.

"Pawns, aye. To move people like pawns. That's wrong. As wrong as saying pi equals three."

"But still..."

"What else am I to do? Sit quietly and let them send you there? I'd never be able to live with myself—how could I ever be happy, knowing it was at your expense?"

"Jerya! What happiness are you ever likely to have as a renegade—a betrayer of your Vow? Don't do that for me. I'm not that important."

Jerya raised one hand to grasp Railu's jaw and slowly turn her friend's face to her own. "Rai... you're wrong. You're exactly wrong. Nothing is more important than you."

"You only say that because you love me."

"No." Jerya shook her head strongly. "Not so. The truth is—you are that important, whoever you are... No, don't speak. I need to get this clear." She bowed her head. Her thoughts seemed to demand a definite physical effort. Perhaps they always did, but it was too slight to be noticed, just as the effort of walking went unnoticed till you were faced with a gale or a steep incline. She ran her hands over her scalp, and again, and once more, feeling the slight shift of skin over unmoving bone. She'd learned that it seemed to help her thoughts to flow.

"Perhaps it's because I'm a simple country girl. At the last, I can't altogether believe in something I can't see or touch—I can't quite believe in something like a Vow. Or not in the same way... It is not as real as you are."

Railu gave a little spluttering sound—a stillborn laugh, perhaps. "Not real? That doesn't seem to worry you when it comes to algebra. You're not worried about your x's and y's and z's being real."

"But they are. As real as one and two and three."

"That's the difference between a mathematical mind and a non-mathematical one, I suppose. I can do basic algebra—I can manipulate the symbols, follow the rules—but I can't see them as real."

"Even when they give real results? If algebra tells you where to look for Mars tonight, how can you say it isn't real? Or—listen, this is better—if I throw a ball and you catch it—you've calculated without even knowing it. But the ball is caught." *Calculated without even knowing; that's what Yanil meant by 'idiot-savant'*, she thought suddenly.

Railu shook her head. "It *describes* something real, maybe. But algebra is not real itself. Just as a tree is real, and the word 'tree' is not."

"No, no. It's not the same at all. I don't know about words... words are harder... words can seem to be things they are not. But mathematics... I can't see it with my open eyes; I can't touch it with my hands. But I can see it and touch it just as truly... somewhere else. Before I even had any of the words for it, I knew it, I think." She thumped the tree-trunk again. "And it's every bit as real as this tree."

Then she turned her face to Railu once more. "And what are we doing arguing about mathematics?"

"I think you love mathematics more than you love me. Could you really give it up? That's what it would mean."

"I know. Or—maybe they could send me textbooks..."

Railu did not let her continue. "Jerya, let me do the talking for a minute. Everything you say about Delven... aye, it frightens me. Terrifies me." She wasn't looking at Jerya now, but out across the songstead, her gaze reaching out to the distant hills or the clouds that piled high above them. "But, recall, Perriad said Sharess was eight years here, just like me. How do you know she wasn't terrified too, when she was sent?"

"I don't, but—"

"Let me finish, please. Jerya, I..." She pressed Jerya's hand, lying between them on the smooth grey bark. "I sometimes forget you haven't been here that long, that it's still barely three months. But then I remember that first evening, in Refec, the first time I saw you. And you... I could tell you were almost overwhelmed. You covered it pretty well, but I knew. I'm sure you were terrified, when Sharess first Chose you, set you on this path. But you... You've adapted. You've *grown*. It's been wonderful to see, to be in some small way a part of it."

"Nothing *small* about it."

"Thank you... well, anyway, you have. And the thing is, well, I... I agree with Perriad." A soft chuckle. "About one thing, anyway. You belong here. Not in Delven, or any other faraway place. Here, at the heart of things."

At the heart of things... The words called to Jerya, plucked at something in her own heart. But Railu hadn't finished. "In fact... maybe you're exactly what the Guild needs. A fresh way of looking at things."

"You think that's why Perriad wants to keep me here?" It made sense, she supposed. She might have an unexpected aptitude for mathematics but, with all that ground to make up, could she really ever be expected to rank with the best? There had to be something else.

Railu shrugged. "Who knows what Perriad's thinking? And even if she has plans for you, doesn't mean you have to follow along meekly. She might find she's getting more than she bargained for."

Plans for you. Again Railu's phrase resounded in Jerya's mind. "Perriad has plans for everybody, doesn't she? She stands to rise to Mastership within a few years—that's what people say. And she'd be one of the youngest on the Council; in time she might well become Master Prime... She believes it. She wants it. She sees that more clearly than she can see service to the Guild, to the Sung Lands, to you and to me."

"Jerya, that's quite a notion, but how can you sound so sure? It's just speculation."

"Speculation? No......" She summoned one of her favourite new words. "It's *deduction*."

"You're building a lot of deduction on not much evidence, aren't you? Jerya, you're audacious. "

"Evidence enough, I think... and she's a liar."

"Jerya! Can you prove that?"

"Can you *prove* that the sun will rise tomorrow morning? But you *know* it will. Just as I *know* that she was lying. Just as I know the reason—or one of the reasons—she wants to pack you off to Delven is because in a place like Delven you will never be able to do anything whatever with your dangerous ideas about educating women outside the Guild."

"Well, perhaps she's right. Perhaps I'm naive. Perhaps my ideas are dangerous. Perhaps it is necessary, in the interests of the Guild as a whole."

"But that's not what she's thinking of. Not service to the Guild, the Knowledge, the people of this land—it's the power of the Tutors and the Masters. Of *herself*. That's what she cares about."

Railu stared into the distance again, shaking her head a little. "You could be right. But still, what's the use of all this? Even if... never mind whether I should break my Vow or not. I'd never have the courage..."

"Aye, you will," said Jerya, squeezing her hand again. "You've plenty of courage. You've been standing up to Perriad for years. Why, if service means obedience, she might say you've been breaking the Vow all along... To her, the slightest challenge is a transgression of your Vow. After that it's only a question of how big."

Railu said nothing. Perhaps, thought Jerya, she had pushed her friend far enough for one day. And there were many new thoughts for her to absorb and consider too. "Do nothing now. It may never come to the worst. Perriad isn't the only one who decides, though I'm sure she'd like to be... Master your Catechisms and say nothing troublesome. Let Ordination pass... And keep your eyes open and see if you don't think I may be right. I hope I'm wrong, but I'm sure I'm not. Anyway, wait... wait, and let them order you to Delven if they will. Then we'll know."

CHAPTER 25

JERYA

"**N**o doubt it will be a few weeks after Ordination before any Peripatetics are available," said Perriad.

"Peripatetics?" blurted Jerya.

"You can hardly think we would send Railu all that way on her own. Still less ask Sharess, who has been infirm, to travel back here alone."

Jerya's mind raced. She had reckoned with its being early autumn, but even then who knew what they might face? A delay of 'a few weeks' could easily turn into a month or more, and that might be disastrous. Well, there was no knowing whether the thing was actually possible at all, but delays would surely make the odds against them much steeper.

Perriad was watching her closely. Jerya gathered her thoughts. "Railu would not be required to travel there alone, Senior Tutor. I had an escort when I came here, and he has remained in the City, thinking he would be needed for my return. And... if I may make a request?" Perriad looked dubious, then nodded. "Thank you, Senior Tutor. I have heard that Novices are allowed to make a visit home just before or after Ordination."

Perriad merely raised one eyebrow. "That is partly true. It is—*sometimes*—permitted for Novices to take one short trip home at that time... but, however precocious you may be, your Ordination is still some distance off. Furthermore... by no means do all choose to avail themselves of the opportunity, and those who do must make their case before permission is granted."

"I have no family," said Jerya. "I was an orphan; I don't even know who my mother and father were. Half the women in the village had a share in raising me; I called them all 'Aunt'. But I—in later years I was not particularly close to any of them."

"Then I am bound to ask why you have any desire to return."

Jerya took a breath. She had tried to plan what she wanted to say, but plans never seemed to hold together under Perriad's steely gaze. "There is an opportunity. As I said, R—the Escort who accompanied me from Delven... he remained in the city, expecting to Escort me again. Presumably he will be Escorting Railu instead."

Perriad nodded slowly. "Granting that... it does not answer my question."

"I... I have two reasons. One; for Railu's sake. You already know that we went out into the city together. I saw how... unnerved she was. And he—the Escort who'll take her to Delven... She couldn't even speak to him."

"She will need to overcome that. She will need to speak to men—at least to the headman... I am right, am I not? Delven has a single headman, not a council or any other such arrangement."

"Aye, a headman. And that's another—when we get to Delven, I can help her, prepare the ground."

"I suppose there might be something in that; we shall give it due consideration. But you said 'two reasons'?"

"Aye." *Be polite. Grovel, if you have to.* "If you please, Senior Tutor, there is one person there I would wish to see again."

"And who might that be?"

"Sharess. *Dawnsinger* Sharess."

Perriad said nothing. She wielded silence like a weapon, thought Jerya; and if silence was the battleground, Perriad would win. Words were hard, but they gave her a chance. "Well... I never knew her before the day she Chose me; she'd never spoken to me. And then we had such a short time, because she wanted to get me on my way. Less than an hour, I am sure. But there was so much more I wanted to say, to ask her."

This at least was undiluted truth. It wasn't the entirety of the truth, but that was the line she had to tread now.

"You say she never spoke to you before?" Perriad's tone suggested surprise, though as far as Jerya knew this was perfectly normal, not only in Delven but up and down the the Sung Lands. *The Principle of Detachment...*

"No, Senior Tutor." *I think I would remember...* "I suppose she had reports of me via the headman."

"I had wondered why you weren't Chosen sooner... You still recall no Visitation when you were younger?"

"I'm sure I never saw other Dawnsingers at Delven, and I surely would have noticed. So there can't have been a Visitation since I was old enough to understand. Must be fifteen years at least."

"That will be rectified soon. In any case it is common practice for a newly-installed Dawnsinger to receive a Visitation within her first year. That should further reassure Railu—does she know you have asked to see me, by the way?"

If the question, so casually slipped into the conversation, was meant to catch Jerya off guard, it failed. She had anticipated it, had her answer ready. "She knows I am here, Senior Tutor, but she doesn't know exactly what I wanted to ask you."

Quickly she continued, returning to Visitations. "Singer Marit, at Thrushgill, also gave me the impression she hadn't seen anyone for some time."

"No doubt she too would welcome the company of a Peripatetic or two...?"

"I can't speak for her," Jerya said carefully. Marit had certainly expressed some sense of grievance at her 'neglect', but would she be happy for the Peripatetics to discover how much she drank? Ale and wine were freely available in the College, but anyone who appeared to be drinking to excess would soon find herself receiving friendly warnings from her classmates; better that, than it come to the notice of the Tutors.

Well, if things worked out as she hoped, she would have the opportunity to give Marit a discreet warning when they passed through Thrushgill.

"The schedule of Visitations is not my responsibility, of course," Perriad was saying, "But I shall have a word with Master Evisyn... Well, Novice, you make an interesting case, but I see one problem. You will have an Escort to Delven, but then how do you propose to return from there? We can't have you travelling alone, can we?"

"I thought Peripatetics..."

"Peripatetics are specially trained, Novice, and in any case they travel at least in pairs, more usually as a troika."

Jerya felt she would be perfectly capable of making the journey on her own. Compared to the half-formed prospect in her mind, it would be simplicity itself. But she could hardly say that. "I understand that my Escort intends to return here when his duty in Delven is done."

"You're very well informed about the doings of the young man. He wants to settle here, does he?"

"I believe so. I believe..."

"There is some young woman in the case, no doubt." Perriad barely waited for her nod. "Men are so predictable, are they not?"

Jerya wasn't sure about the truth of this, but it seemed politic to murmur something that sounded like assent. "There is a young woman to whom he has grown... attached. And I believe they have it in mind that she would also accompany him—all of us—to Delven. And to return with him to the City." She flinched away from saying 'return with us', because... well, Railu would not be returning in any case, and to suggest that she herself intended to do so would be too close to an outright lie.

And yet... though she had spoken no word of falsehood, she had left things unsaid. That could give a false impression, too; and how was that different from the deception the Guild practised? *We do not preach or proclaim this; we simply allow them to believe it.* Perriad herself had said that to her, and Jerya had recoiled. Why else was she planning to remove herself from this place, this life, that had already given her so much and promised so much more? Not solely for Railu's sake, she knew.

She thought more about it, a few minutes later, as she made her way down the stairs and out into the Court.

There were many reasons to wish to remain in the College. *Books and telescopes and incunabula...* But not everything was so pure. The whole encounter with Perriad had been like crossing a torrent on slippery rocks. Being polite, being *politic*. She had, if she faced up to it, been leading the Senior Tutor astray almost the entire time, however careful she had been to avoid outright untruths. Because she could see no alternative... but perhaps the wise ones of the Guild felt just the same. Perhaps to them too, the deception was a sad necessity.

There was one difference, she told herself, between her deception and that of the Guild: scale. The deceit of the Guild encompassed the entirety of the Sung Lands and had lasted for generations. Hers was small, localised, and would be revealed almost immediately. She wondered if that really made a difference, or whether a small lie was just as much of a lie as a great one.

She found no answer as she hurried across flagstones shiny with rain. She could only think that, right or wrong, she had played her hand. And she thought she had got away with it. But you never entirely knew. She wouldn't really know until Perriad gave her answer.

Chapter 26

Rodal

Part Three: The Edge of The World

A high haze across the sky kept the heat within bounds, made the walking much less arduous than it had been the first time, yet the Scorched Plains still seemed limitless.

Rodal's eyes kept roving into the distance ahead in search of the hills; yet, when the blue-grey outline finally separated from the sky his elation was muted, ambiguous. Home was there—but was it, really, still home? He had lived among those hills all his life, wandered all their ways, loved them in the easy way you can love things which never change. Yet now he could as readily picture the rocks and wild broken seas of the coast as the crags of his youth.

Well, he supposed, it was good to be looking to the future, not to the past. Although the more immediate future, the next few days, in Delven, might present their own difficulties. Would his family—would anyone?—understand his resolve to return to the city, with Annyt, to make his life there?

That wasn't the only thing preying on his mind as he traced the faint dusty trail. He still wasn't sure how Jerya had persuaded him to break the march at the desolate settlement in the middle of the Plains. Oh, her arguments had been sound enough; it would make two easy stages of the crossing that had been so hard before, reducing the stress on Annyt and Railu, neither of whom were accustomed to walking long distances. Not wanting to seem callous, Rodal had found that hard to counter, for it was true that he and Jerya, both far more seasoned wanderers, had suffered terribly there. But Jerya had been so insistent on her plan that he felt sure that some other, unspoken, reason lay behind it.

He wondered if he was being unduly harsh in his suspicions. Jerya and Railu had woken him with their Singing that dawn. Rousing quickly, he had stumbled to the door of the old cottage where he had slept, to see them on the Eastern slope, silhouetted figures hand-in-hand. Never, he thought, had he heard the Song more lovingly delivered. Their voices harmonised comfortably, yet the effect was electrifying.

For that brief span, the old settlement had lived again. For the first time, he had wondered what its name had been.

It must have been the first time they had Sung the Dawn alone, he realised. He could well imagine them wanting no audience but their own friends. Had that been Jerya's reason? But if so, why had she not admitted it? There was nothing shameful about it, surely. Railu, per-haps—full-fledged Dawnsinger as she now was (Ordained, as they called it)—ought not to lack in confidence; but he sensed, somehow, that the argument had not been to do with Railu.

Though how could he be sure? He could learn nothing from Railu. She barely spoke to him. It was correct behaviour for a Dawnsinger, of course, but, generally speaking, that etiquette had been tacitly abandoned as soon as they were out of sight of Stainscomb. Railu did not hold aloof with Annyt, and Jerya was the same with all of them. Railu just seemed to be... suspicious of him; maybe even afraid, though he did not believe he had ever given her cause. She had just been that way, right from the start.

He was not even sure why it bothered him. She would have to be aloof with everyone once they reached Delven; and after that he never expected to see her again. Nonetheless, he had grasped that Jerya wished that while they were alone they should be just four young people travelling together. And... where once he would simply have seen a Dawnsinger, he now saw Railu. She had a name, a face, a blister on her heel.

Often Jerya and Railu would walk together, close as himself and Annyt. Seizing the time together while they had it, he supposed. He didn't know about Railu, but Jerya had shown herself very good at making the best of rough changes. She was—the word came to him—adaptable. She seemed quite comfortable, now, treating him as a friend. A trusted friend, but never anything more. For a few brief, bright, moments they had sensed the possibility of a deeper closeness, but even then it had been out of reach; now it was entirely past and gone. It seemed an age ago, but in truth it was little more than a quarter of a year, and at the time feelings had been very deep and real and painful. On his side and, he thought, on hers.

So, now they were friends—but that, too, would have to end. Physically, he supposed, it might still be possible; perhaps Jerya could still make occasional incognito visits to the Tavern, as she had done before. But for what reason would she come? What would they have to say to each other in a year or two? Himself, he hoped, wedded to Annyt, mastering the trade of the innkeeper, perhaps playing with his children; Jerya drawing deeper and deeper into the mysteries. In time, surely, she would be utterly beyond him.

In which case, to walk alone and brooding was a sad waste of what must be one of the last clear days which remained to them.

He saw, glancing back, that Railu was deep in conversation with Annyt. Jerya was a pace or two in front of them, apparently half-listening; but when she saw him turn, she quickened her stride to bring herself to his side. "That's better," she said. "I wondered how long you'd go on like that."

"Like what?"

"Stomping along with your head down as if you had all the world's cares in your pack. I've been watching you for—for a good while—and I swear you only gave those hills one quick glance. Aren't you a little excited to be going home?"

"A little. Not too much. I s'pose it's better not to think of it as home any more."

"I know," she said. "Had you not thought that it's the same for me?" She touched his arm, just a glancing touch, but he felt eyes on his back. Oddly, it was not Annyt's reaction which concerned him—she would understand. At least he hoped she would.

"You don't want Railu thinking there's any familiarity between Singer and common folk in Delven," he remarked.

"Don't worry about that. I made sure Rai was in no doubt, just as soon as we first saw the possibility of her coming here."

"And what did she think of it?"

"She thought very little of it! She's a sociable lass."

"Not with me."

She gave one of those quick glances which seemed to see more than a long examination from most people. "It rankles, does it? Listen, Rodal, don't fret over it. It's nothing against you. For eight years she hasn't even spoken to a man. And she's taken in some... distorted notions.

"It amazes me, thinking of it. When I first met her, all of them, I felt terribly ignorant; a rough Backland girl suddenly thrust in among all these wise high women. Of course, I soon saw they weren't—the Novices, I mean, like Railu—weren't as different as all that. But still they seemed—they *did* know so much more than I did. All of them, but Railu seemed so... so sure of herself. Then she was the one who advised me how to get out of the College... unofficially. I thought she must have been out into the City herself dozens of times.

"And then I found out she'd barely done it at all, and never alone... Can you imagine what it's like, up there on that hill, in the heart of the City, yet utterly disconnected from it? Who could live like that and not be consumed with curiosity? But some never dare to venture out at all. It's forbidden, of course, but they'd only get a reprimand. The real reason is just that they're scared—and for the same reason they're curious. Because the City's so much unknown.

"They're all scared. Even the ones who do venture out don't seem to do much. Just wander the streets, keeping to the side, just gazing at... at life. Well, I felt much that way when I first came to the City. Aye..." She laughed lightly. "Even though I had you with me!

"None of them in the College really know more than that—not from their own lives. What they know—or think they know—comes from lessons taught by Tutors who learned the same things in their day in their own lessons. And even if their lessons were accurate, they'd never really know what life outside was really like, what it feels like, what it tastes like, what makes people laugh or cry. Yet Rai thinks she knows about men. And all of them think they know more about life than the people who are really living it."

Rodal, bereft of words, could only stare at her. Then she laughed quietly. "I've said too much, I think."

"I don't pretend to understand," he replied. "And it's surely not my business anyway."

"Of course it's your business, you lummox. More than I ever realised... Ah, but it proves one thing, letting my tongue run away with me like that: I still trust you.

"And that wounds me, because I've been deceiving you. But now I... I can't do it any longer."

Rodal kept walking mechanically, his eyes and his thoughts entirely on Jerya. He felt a sudden queasy foreboding.

She blew out a hard breath. "I can't—can't let you go on as our escort knowing nothing of our purpose. Not *you*..."

"Your purpose?"

"What I'm going to say may be hard to hear... but, please, give me your promise you'll hear me out before you speak."

He nodded. What else could he do?

Jerya took another deep breath. Whatever she was trying to say, it seemed hard, weighty. But when she did speak, at first it seemed innocuous. "When we left Delven, everything seemed simple, didn't it? You were to escort me to the City, wait as long as required, then escort me back, to spend the rest of my life as Dawnsinger of Delven."

She glanced at him, as if expecting some response, but nothing more than a nod seemed warranted, even if she hadn't just asked him to 'hear me out'. "Already, that's changed, hasn't it? When I was Chosen, sh—our Dawnsinger told me it was Delven's responsibility to provide her replacement, but in the College they say it's very unusual for a girl to be sent back to the same place she originated.

"And you can understand why, can't you? A Dawnsinger is supposed to stand aloof from the community. That would be hard, wouldn't it, even after a space of eight years, if she had parents, sisters, brothers, right there? That's one reason she Chose me, I s'pose, the orphan girl; she thought it would be easier for me, coming back. But imagine if I were Dawnsinger in Delven and you were there too. I know that's not likely, now, but no one knew that when I was Chosen, not even you. You might have become headman, one day..."

He waved a hand, a modest disclaimer without breaking his promise of silence, but she only smiled. "You'd be as suited as any and better than most. But it won't happen now, and I won't be Delven's Dawnsinger anyway. I'm speaking hypothetically." She must have seen that he didn't recognise the word. "Speaking of what might have been. Well, you can see, it would have been cruel. But... it's not out of kindness that they're sending Railu in my stead. If there's one thing I've learned, it's that kindness is not what drives the Guild of Dawnsingers—of course. The Guild serves a higher purpose, doesn't it? Without it..." Her gaze was direct. "Well, what do you think would happen if... if there was no Singer in Delven at all?"

His mind immediately took him back to the dead village where they had spent the night. She smiled as if she knew exactly what he was thinking. "Rodal, it isn't true. *It isn't true.*"

She looked around a moment, at the featureless, colourless land. "Whatever happened here, it isn't that. If we had not Sung this morning, the sun would have risen just the same."

His steps dragged to a halt. He stared at her for a long time. Then he let out a long sigh. "Annyt said something once."

They both glanced round, but Annyt and Railu were still some way behind. "What did she say?" asked Jerya.

"One morning... I'd been awake early. Not used to light comin' in the room. And you know you can hear the Dawnsong from there, specially when the wind's in the East. I said something about it being a fine thing. And then I thought of you being part of it and I said summat like, 'I wonder how it must feel to command all that power.' And she looked back at me and said 'What d'you mean, command?' I wanted to ask what she meant but her Pa came in just then. But when I got alone I found myself thinkin', did she mean she didn't believe Dawnsong makes the sun rise?"

"But you never asked her?"

He looked almost sheepish. "No. Reckon I thought, either she didn't believe it and then I wouldn't know what to think... or she did, like I thought everyone did, and I just hadn't understood what she meant, and then I'd look like a fool... But if you're sayin' now it don't, I guess that's what she meant all along. But if it don't... Then why? Why do you Sing?"

"That's a deep question. The high ones of the Guild would tell you that it is necessary."

"Necessary for what?"

She shrugged. "To preserve the peace and order of the land, they'd say. Maybe they're right; I don't know. I can't go into all of that now. All I know is that it's a deceit, and I doesn't sit right with me to be part of it. Perhaps it's a fault in me. But the Guild of Dawnsingers demanded something of me which I could not give."

Then she paused, as if expecting some response; but what could he have said? Where could he even begin?

There was only silence, and behind them the soft voices of Railu and Annyt fading and returning on the fickle breeze.

In those moments, under Jerya's expectant gaze, Rodal found many feelings rising: above all, strangely, *irritation*. She seemed to be asking for something—his approval?—which he could not give. It was *unreasonable*. How could he, an ordinary man, an ignorant man, make any sense of all this? How could he judge if she was right or wrong?

He had known Jerya all his life, even if they had only drawn close for the briefest span. She had always seemed to go her own way, as if she knew better than anyone else. Now she seemed almost to be saying that she knew better than the high ones of the Guild.

His head seethed. He had no idea what to say, was as surprised as she was by the words which actually emerged: "And what about Railu? What does she think to all this?"

"If you're so concerned... why don't you ask her?"

He looked round; Annyt and Railu had come up close behind. He did not know how much they had overheard, but the blood had drained from Railu's face, leaching the warmth from the brown. Her eyes shied away from him; as the foursome halted in the centre of the featureless plain, she confronted Jerya.

Railu's robe flapped lethargically behind her, a slow banner. "How could you...?" she asked, her voice so soft he took a moment to realise it was grey with despair.

"Because I trust him," Jerya replied. "I have been too close to him to deceive him, any more than I could deceive you."

Railu stared at her, struggling with objections she could not utter. Jerya stepped closer to her, until their robes were whipped into one by the dry wind. The same swelling breeze tugged at his shirt and teased at the roots of his hair.

"Remember why we're doing this," she said. *Doing what?* Rodal's mind demanded. She had said much, but had said nothing of what they actually intended to do. "It's all about deception; deception, and trust. They say no man can be trusted. I say Rodal can."

Railu made a slow turn, faced him as she had never done before. Long moments passed, silent but for the fluttering of their garments.

"I want to believe that," she said. "And if Jerya's told you, it seems like I have to."

"I can't prove it. Not in words. The proof of the pie is in the taste, as they say in Delven." He considered. "If you want to know why Jerya thinks

I deserve her trust—and yours—ask her, not me. But maybe... maybe I can show you I am not so foreign as you seem to think."

"Aye, walk together awhile," said Jerya. "I'll walk with Annyt. We owe her some explanations also."

She took Annyt's arm and drew her forward. Rodal caught a quick strange look from his beloved, full of bewilderment and an appeal of some kind. He had no better answer than a weak smile and a shrug as she turned away. Then he was faced again with Railu.

"Well," he said with a smile as pale as the one he had given Annyt. "How shall we begin? I'm full of questions and so, no doubt, are you."

She was silent for a moment, her gaze unwavering. Then she said, "Hold out your hand. No, palm up, please."

He obeyed, puzzled. Railu slowly stretched her fingers toward him. At first touch she snatched her hand back a little, as if his flesh were ice, then with the faintest sheepish grin, returned it. "I thought it would be... rougher, harder."

"It's usage makes hands hard," he answered. "I dare say Jerya's worked as much with her hands as I have. Afore these last few months, anyroad."

"There's not a great difference, it's true... I thought there would be. But then I know nothing. Only what I have been taught. And it grows ever clearer that I have not always been taught the entire truth."

"But surely... Jerya said you'd been eight years in the College. Surely before then you must have had some dealings with men."

"I suppose I must," she said with a sigh; then, "Come, they're leaving us behind." They began to walk, side-by-side, close enough for easy conversation, far enough to be sure they didn't touch. "But I was only a child then. I had little enough to do with any but boys my own age or younger, and even they had mostly their own games and their own places. Jerya says it's much the same in Delven. Little enough to do with boys, and even less to do with adult men. My father was almost a stranger."

"Where was your home?"

"Far South on the coast. Kermey. I think he was a seaman, but I don't really know; only that he was away for long periods."

"What sort of a place is Kermey?"

"How can I say? Bigger than Delven, from what I can make out, but still just a village. It was on a rocky coast, in a sheltered bay. The streets were all steep and stony. When the gulls fly over the College, I remember them in the streets of Kermey. I remember it being always alive with their racket... And the streets; the cobblestones were slippery after rain. I cut my knee badly once, falling, I still have a scar..."

"I've hardly thought about it for years. We were never encouraged to talk about the times before we were Chosen, and I suppose memories go cold if you don't keep them astir. But then Jerya arrived. We were all curious, bombarded her with questions about where she'd come from; I suppose after that it seemed natural to ask me about my home. I tried to remember, but it was all fragments, fragments that I could never quite put together into one clear picture."

"And in Delven..." Rodal began. Then, at a tangent, "You *are* going there? What then is your plan?"

"Aye, we're coming all the way to Delven. Jerya says we have to. I think she wants to talk to the Dawnsinger—and also it's for your sake."

"My sake?"

"Jerya says you're charged to bring us safely to Delven. So you'll have fulfilled your task... After that, whatever we do, she says no one can blame you. And she says it gives Annyt a chance to see your home before there's any trouble."

"That's thoughtful."

"That's Jerya; she's not doing this for herself. All this is... Well, it began because she couldn't bear... She saw how it frightened me, the loneliness of life as Dawnsinger in Delven. She didn't have to do this, she could have stayed in the College—a comfortable life, work she loved—but she wouldn't do it." Her gaze roamed ahead, following Jerya.

"I'm trying to understand," he said. "Jerya said... she *seemed* to be saying that the Guild of Dawnsingers..."

"That it's all a lie...? I wouldn't say *all*. No, far from it; the work that goes on in the College is all about truth. And the Guild does a vast amount of good. But not in the way people think." She paused, glanced at him. "Tell me, Rodal, did you believe it? Did you truly believe that if there was no Dawnsinger, no Song, the sun wouldn't rise?"

He struggled to put his thoughts into words. "I suppose I never questioned it... It was just the way things are. Never thought much about it, tell you true. And then, that place where we were last night; it seemed exactly what I'd expect from a place that had lost its Singer."

"But the sun still rises there."

"But you Sang this morning."

"True, aye, but..." she laughed unexpectedly. "Ah, that's one for the philosophers. I was about to say, 'but it rises there every day, Song or no Song' and you would no doubt have said, 'how do you know?' because, after all, we did Sing. So how could I really *know* what would have happened if we hadn't? And the answer to that is that I don't. I only believe, because it's what I've learned. But you believe the opposite, because it's what *you've* learned."

"You're making my head spin."

She took another couple of paces, realised he'd stopped, turned to face him. "It suits the Guild very well if people believe that the Song makes the sun rise. But within the Guild they tell a different story. I believed the first one when I was a little girl, until I was Chosen. Then I learned the second version. Now I think I'll never truly know unless I see for myself."

"And how would you do that?"

She glanced away, ahead, to where Annyt and Jerya were walking on. "By going into Unsung Lands."

CHAPTER 27

JERYA

Jerya woke in the ancient darkness of her cave-cell; a pleasurable shock. It was as familiar and comfortable as an old blanket, yet she knew that she had come out of sleep with an expectation of pre-dawn greyness behind a curtained window.

Once awake, she had never been one to linger abed. She swung her legs to the floor, feeling for her sandals. Limbs remembered how to move about in the blackness, though with something less than the unthinking instancy she had once known. Fingers went confidently to the niche, but a fraction too high, knocking the candle. By a miracle, she caught it, saving a blind grovel on the floor.

The candle seemed dimmer than she remembered, but its teasing scent was somehow stronger. In the brown light she read the time; just after six-thirty. Dawn was a few minutes away; as so often, she had been woken by nothing but some secret intuition of her own.

It was very quiet. Sometimes there would be sounds, or just a vague intimation of someone stirring, but not this morning. It was hardly surprising. The men would all be in the thick sleep that followed drinking: few of them would be seen until the sun was on the floor of the court, and then they would come stumbling out, blinking and wincing as if the light were twice as bright as normal, and every sound ten times as loud.

Jerya smiled; only the weight of the silence kept her from laughing. She now knew a little of how they would feel. She had never drunk as much, never been half as intoxicated, as some had been last night, but once or twice she had taken enough to make her rushed the next morning, arriving dishevelled on the songstead, losing the melody here and there. Now that would be a shocking story to the women of Delven!

She pushed through the heavy drape and unhesitatingly threaded the winding passages. In the main tunnel torches still burned, but feebly now, glowering, smoky. In the thick red gloom she moved quickly on the uneven floor, hastening up to the cavehall and the first outriders of daylight. The light from the sunshafts had a pale keen edge.

It was cool in the entryway, and Jerya shrugged her cape around her shoulders as she emerged into the brisk morning. The court was empty, grey and bare. The breeze stirred the dust like a memory of last night's dancing. It was a sour memory for Jerya; she had not enjoyed being obliged to sit like an effigy of herself, unable even to show her appreciation, much less to join in. Dancing had been a rare pleasure to her; one of those occasions when she felt most truly and completely a part of Delven.

But the whole evening had been like that. Everyone, those whom she had called Aunt and Uncle and Cousin; all had turned into dumb, head-hanging strangers. As they entered the court on arrival, she had immediately spotted Kita: Kita, once a playmate, younger than herself, in the shade with her child at her breast. For a moment, Jerya's heart had swelled with a simple joy that made her forget what she was, what was to come, forget everything but the inexhaustible wonder of new life—and the strangeness of seeing Kita, who had been a child with her, suckling her own now... Then Kita had looked up, caught Jerya's eyes upon her, at once effaced her dreamy smile and pulled her shawl to cover the twinned roundness of her breast and the baby's head. Jerya knew that a grimace had warped her own grave expression for a moment, a fleeting betrayal of a fraction of the pain she felt. She was a stranger now; she had become something alien. And she was not even permitted to show her feelings about it.

How little it took, to set one apart. A white robe, a shaved head, a story that wasn't even wholly true.

She had expected most of it, frightened Railu by predicting it. The fulfilment of her prediction brought no satisfaction, because she had never truly foretasted how it would hurt.

Any doubts she might have harboured had been dispelled in that moment. There had always been the possibility of changing their minds on reaching Delven. No more. Now she wanted to be gone from there, gone from the Sung Lands, as soon as possible. However, there was duty to be done first.

She mounted the steps of the tor, halted before the curtained entrance. There was no door to knock upon, but something stopped her from simply calling out. The tor had been forbidden too long, and then the one previous time she had stepped through that portal, her entire life had changed.

She stood on the threshold, dithering. *This is ridiculous,* she insisted to herself. *You have every right to be here.* And there was another thought: *If you can't even do this, what chance do you have in the mountains?*

That broke her paralysis. Finally, she pushed through. The chamber was empty: Railu and Sharess must be already on the songstead. She hastened up the ladder. Even as she arrived, slightly breathless, they broke into Song.

She was too late, too flustered, to join in; and she found she felt no real desire to do so. Instead she perched on one of the upjutting rocks at the edge of the slab and watched them as they Sang.

Sharess had appeared last night, of course, to welcome Jerya and Railu, and briefly to honour the festivities by her presence. Jerya had, however, had little chance to assess the old Singer's condition. Now in the breaking light she seemed healthy: true, she was holding Railu's arm, but it looked more like an expression of companionship than a need for support. Her colour was better and her voice sounded fine, though she had but half Railu's power. There might be some sore heads woken by the Song this morning, thought Jerya wryly, some who weren't used to it and might not be too reverential in their feelings.

As always, the moment following the last note of the Dawnsong seemed to have a special hush, as if the whole world were holding its breath. Then the breeze rushed over them again, and the two singers turned to face her. Railu's expression was strangely blank, but Sharess's seamed face cracked into a wide smile.

"Ah, Jerya." She held out both her hands. "I didn't hear you."

"I'm but a Novice..."

"Still, you're permitted to Sing. You all Sing in the College, still, don't you? I'd hoped to hear you... well, another morning, no doubt." She held Jerya's hands and looked her up and down. "You look well, my dear. I must say you seem to look older—by more than the time you've been away. There was still something of the child in your face before. Ah, but why are we standing here? It's none too warm yet."

Jerya went first down the ladder, then Sharess, moving nimbly enough, still talking. "Will you have some of the coffee you brought me? It's a rare treat for me, and doubly so if I can share it with the pair of you. Here, sit..." She busied herself in an alcove, revealed by sliding back one of the beautiful hangings. Jerya watched closely; her knuckles were still swollen, but she saw no obvious sign of the enfeeblement that been so evident at their first encounter.

Presently Sharess handed out steaming mugs; mugs like those the men carried on long hunts, bowl and handle carved from a single piece of birch-wood. The coffee was hot, black, deliciously bitter, vivid as a stolen kiss.

"I thank you, Singer Sharess," she said. "This is wonderful."

"Just Sharess, my dear," the old one said, folding herself into a chair. "We're all Singers together now. Oh, it's such a rare delight to have company at all. And two of you... And you, Jerya, looking so well on it. You were so scared before—putting on a brave face, of course, but I could see you were frightened."

Jerya could not answer; she was warmed by Sharess's pleasure, pride-filled by her praise, yet all too aware she was taking it under false pretences. She did not know how to break the truth; instead she dipped her head as if shy, blew on her hot coffee, sipped again.

"And Railu…" Sharess continued. "It was almost like being young again, talking into the dark like that." Jerya looked up in sudden hope, but Railu shook her head tightly. Jerya had never understood so clearly how easy it could be to fall into deceitful ways. There was an enormous temptation to leave Sharess in contented ignorance; but it would only be short-lived. And to think of her discovering their sudden absence, unexplained, or perhaps finding some inadequate letter of excuse, after the fact… It would never do. But, oh, how to begin?

She had to try. "You're in much better health, if my eyes do not deceive me."

"Indeed," said Sharess. "I am myself again. I declare I began to improve almost as soon as I'd seen you on your way—once that load was lifted from my mind."

Jerya groaned inwardly. Those blithe words only made the thing harder. "You'll be Dawnsinger in Delven for years yet."

"I hope I will!" Sharess laughed like a girl. "But who knows? I've been well enough through the summer, but whatever it was that laid me low before… it preys on my mind. It seemed but a fever at first, but I realised afterward I'd been delirious. Don't know how I got myself up to the songstead a couple of mornings. Don't know what kind of a hash I made of the Song… Well, I reckon I was still feeling the effects when I summoned you, Jerya. None of it was done right, as I expect you've learned. It's a wonder to me, now I'm in my right mind again, they didn't send you straight back."

She looked at Jerya as if expecting some response to this. Jerya forced a smile. "Yes, it seemed like Senior Tutor Perriad had that in mind, but she decided they'd take a look at me first."

"And then they decided you were worth keeping after all… Well, I'm glad of that, and I hope you are too."

"I am," she said, realising it for truth. Whatever lay ahead, she was not the same girl she had been four months before, and she could not regret that.

Sharess smiled. "And Delven will have a Singer, even if I fall ill again."

Jerya groaned inside, but she had to find a way to the truth. "I dare say Railu told you, there's to be a Visitation soon."

"There's a new Master of Peripatetics, Master Evisyn, and she's shaking things up," added Railu. "Places like Delven have been neglected, but no longer. And quite likely they'll take you back to the College, and the Healers."

Jerya looked again at Sharess as the Singer listened to Railu. She began to wonder if the old Singer were really as old as she had thought. Her hands were gnarled, besure, but they had worked well enough when Sharess was pouring the coffee; and somehow her face did not look as deeply wrinkled as she had thought it. How much, she wondered, had she been seeing the effects of true age, and how much those of a passing illness? Studying her now, she could not think Sharess above sixty, and she might be nearer fifty.

Still, Railu was right: Sharess needed to be seen by the Healers. And if the Peripatetics found no other Singer in Delven, they would have to leave one of their number in place, at least for a time.

Sharess had been speaking as she mused, and now Jerya caught up with her words. "...A mere chill could carry me off, and I fancy we've a hard winter coming."

"I hope not," said Jerya, with more feeling than Sharess could guess. Her concern for the old Singer was real, but only the half of it. There was also the grim fear that Railu and herself might have to face the same winter without even a proper roof over their heads. It was a hard prospect—but what other path was there?

She went on, "But you could—any of us could—die at any time. A slip when walking in the forest—just a simple fall where no one can find you. What happens then? What becomes of Delven without a Dawnsinger?"

Sharess smiled.. "You know as well as I... some temporary distress, but the place will survive. It's a pleasure not to have to pretend; it's many years since I talked to anyone who knew the truth."

"But do we?"

Sharess gave her a hard look, and Jerya remembered the feeling she had known before, that the old one knew all her secrets. Then it was easier, and the whole long tale came spilling forth; her slow, yet shattering realisation that deceit underpinned the very existence of the Guild; Perriad's almost casual string of half-truths and empty promises; her vindictiveness in consigning Railu to backland exile.

"I'm sure you're happy to serve here, and you know I was prepared to follow you. I suppose still would, if they'd let me, but they wouldn't give me that choice..."

"So what do you intend?" Sharess asked, bringing a merciful end to her limping account. At once Jerya felt she knew what she had been going to say, knew perhaps better than she did herself.

"Cross the mountains," she said simply.

Sharess's expression flickered, almost a wince, but then, after a moment, she nodded. "Where else?"

The sudden silence was unnerving, like a step that isn't there. Outside, in the everyday world, dogs scuffled with blustering growls, a woman laughed, the breeze hummed across edges of rock. Jerya felt a pang, as if all that were lost to her now, never to be shared again.

She straightened her back. Better, she assured herself, to be an honest outcast than forever to live a lie. "You've nothing more to say?"

"What do you want to hear me say? This grieves me to my heart. Yet I think I understand. I don't say that you are right or wrong. That is your choice. I—"

"You didn't give me a choice before," said Jerya, the words falling from her without conscious intent, as if they had some life of their own.

"Did I not?" Sharess returned calmly. "Then who did? You have chosen, after all."

Jerya had no answer to that. Sharess smiled. "Could you ever have made such a choice if I had not picked you out and sent you to the city? Would you really prefer it if all that you have discovered—in yourself, too—had remained hidden from you?"

She shook her head. It was all true, but she did not know how to weigh it up. Did she really wish that she had remained as she had been? Where would she be now? Betrothed to Rodal, or still the solitary wanderer? If there was a third alternative, she could not see it.

"Jerya, Railu, hear me. This tale of yours... I say again, it grieves me to my heart. And it shames me... That I have never so squarely faced these questions. I have simply let time pass me by until I'm too old to do anything but carry on...

"But..." She stopped, gazing into her coffee-cup. "You have made your choice, Jerya, and in doing so you confront me with choices too."

"Are you going to say I—we—should not go?"

Sharess sighed. "I don't know, Jerya. Aye, truly, this pains me more than I can say. But is it just my selfish desire to have you here with me, even if it be only for a few days? Or is it more?"

Jerya took a slow breath. "If you told me... what I could not accept from Perriad, I would from you. If you told me that everything else is justified by the good the Guild does; if you told me to do my duty, I believe I would comply."

She felt Railu's eyes on her—and what was she thinking?—but she could not take her own gaze from Sharess.

"Aye, the good the Guild does," the old one repeated. "That is a weighty matter, no doubt about it. And I have always believed in it. But, perhaps you will say, I was taken from my home at ten or eleven—I don't even remember—confined and schooled until I could not see the world any way but the Guild's way. Draff, how can I judge the good the Guild does, how can I weigh it against your lives?"

"It's not comfort I'm looking for, or an easy life."

"No, for you surely won't find that beyond the mountains. As to what you *will* find... Well, that is something none of the wise ones of the Guild know. And it is also part of what the Guild is, or what it should be, to seek answers." Sharess smiled, but not easily. "Tell me truthfully, Jerya, is that not also part of what drives you to this? Simply, you want to *know*."

Jerya could only bow her head. At this moment Sharess almost seemed to know her better than she knew herself.

※

"There is one thing I must ask you," said Jerya a little later. "Why did you not Choose me when I was of the usual age?"

Sharess looked away. "I don't know... If ever I have fallen short, been unworthy of my Vow, it was then... Perhaps it is different in other villages. Most are visited by a Peripatetic, or two or three, every year or two. I could hardly have prevented you being Chosen then, even had I wanted to. But there has been no Visitation for... more than a tenyear. Considerably more." For Marit, down in Thrushgill, the absence of such attention had visibly rankled; Sharess merely stated the fact. "Oh, I was young then, I thought I would live forever, but I cannot deny... it was the obvious thing to do. But something... I could not do it. I let matters ride, thinking I had years to play with, that some other suitable candidate would come along. It was not to be... Age crept up on me sooner than I expected. Perhaps it is that way for everyone. Time betrayed me... and Delven had sent no one, no one had been Chosen, as long as I have been Singer here. Someone had to be sent, and there was only you..." The question had not been answered, Jerya felt; instead Sharess had danced all round it.

The older Singer gave her an odd, almost shy, glance. "Do you wish I had?"

"I don't know..." said Jerya in her turn. "I've wondered sometimes. If I'd come to the College when I was ten... I suppose things would have been different."

"Of course they'd have been different," said Railu. "If you'd been Chosen at ten, you'd never have found the strength to stand up to Perriad. You'd never even have been able to conceive of doing... what we're going to do. I know I could argue about our practices, but I'd never have been capable of real defiance—*enacted* defiance—without you."

Sharess nodded. "Railu speaks the truth, I'm sure. Had you gone to the Guild then, you would hardly be here now. And certainly not doing what you are doing."

"Do you regret it, then?"

"Do you?" Sharess threw the question back. "That's far more to the point."

"Regret? Oh... I regret everything. But I wouldn't do any of it differently. And... how can I say? If I had gone to the Guild at ten I would be a different person now. I can't speak for that person, she's a stranger. Doubtless she would be a loyal and true Dawnsinger, and content... I would like to be content, too, but I can't. Not the way she would be. And... how can I regret being who I am? How could I wish to be someone else? What could be more pointless than that?"

"No," said Sharess, her voice husky as if she were close to tears. "No, never regret who you are. Be proud, Jerya. As I am proud of you."

CHAPTER 28

RODAL

.

"R odal," said a voice behind him.

He turned and his mouth fell open. Habits ingrained in him from earliest age told him to make a swift exit, but his feet seemed rooted to the earth. *And she addressed me by name.*

The Dawnsinger smiled. Was that sympathy in her eyes? "I must speak with you." She gestured towards the narrow path, that twisted, within a few paces, into concealment behind bright-berried rowans. She must have stepped out from there just as he passed.

"Of course, Dawnsinger." His voice cracked on the final word. Why was it so hard? He had learned that it was possible to converse with a Dawnsinger. Indeed, Railu had been more intimidated by him than he by her. But this was not Railu, or Jerya. This was *the Dawnsinger*, the one who had summoned the sun every day of his life. *Or so I believed.* Perhaps it was, as Jerya had declared, a lie; still, he could not shake off the awe instilled in him over almost twenty years.

She turned back onto the branch path, the one she must have stepped out from, and he made himself follow.

The old woman's stride was slow but steady; whatever sickness had afflicted her at the beginning of summer seemed to have left her. *But it was only because she was sick that Jerya was Chosen,* he couldn't help thinking. *If it hadn't been so...* Well, no one could know, so there was no point dwelling on it.

The path climbed easily, slanting to the right and then back left. He heard the glade before he saw it, the murmur of a thousand bees. So the Dawnsinger had her own hives... That raised other questions, but there was no time to think of them. He followed her white robe, observing the creases in the skin at the base of her skull.

At the far end of the glade, ten or fifteen yards past the last of the hives, they stopped under a huge spreading larch. He saw that poles (coppiced hazel, he registered automatically) had been braced against one horizontal branch, creating a little lean-to shelter, open to the noonday sun. There was a rough bench, just room enough for two; the Dawnsinger waved him to it and he sat. She joined him, so close that if they turned toward each other their knees would touch.

"I need to ask you something," she said.

"Of course, Dawnsinger."

"Do you know what Jerya and Railu intend?"

"Not exactly. They said something about going into Unsung Lands—and then, I reckon, not Singing."

Her gaze was intense; even had she not been the Dawnsinger, it would have been disconcerting. But he made himself meet that regard as she went on, "And then?"

"I beg your pardon, Dawnsinger?"

"You make it sound as if they were going merely to conduct an experiment."

"An experiment? I'm sorry, I don't know what that means."

She nodded slightly. "You've hardly had a scientific education, have you? I mean that they were going to put something to the test; the idea that if they didn't Sing, the sun wouldn't rise, or even if it did there would be something wrong with it. Is that what you understood them to mean?"

"Aye... I think so."

"And how does that make you feel?"

He considered his reply. In the background the bees hummed busily. "It goes against everything I've ever... everything I ever thought was true. I'm afraid for them, besure."

She smiled. "If that was all they planned, I'd hope I could set your mind at rest. We may not have ever put it to the test in the strictest sense, but I can assure you there is no good reason to believe that a night or two in Unsung Lands, with or without Song, will do them any harm."

He believed her. It overthrew, as he had said, everything he'd ever thought was true. Now it was the Dawnsinger—*the* Dawnsinger—saying it, and that made no sense. But it was because it was the Dawnsinger saying it that he believed her. He wasn't sure that made sense either. All he knew was that he did believe, and he was reassured.

For a moment. And then his mind fastened on the first words of her speech. "You said *If that was all they planned*...?"

"I did."

"Then..." He gazed at her. A little piece of him said, *I can't believe I'm staring right into the eyes of the Dawnsinger*. But it was only a little piece. The rest was furiously thinking back over what she had just said, and then over what Jerya and Railu had said during the last part of the crossing of the Plains. "You mean... they're not coming back?"

"Exactly so."

"They told you?" He wanted to howl, but kept his voice steady. *Well, almost steady.* He thought furiously. "Happen they—she—did say something. It was there to be heard, and I just didn't hear it. Chose not to hear it, maybe... but did she say where...?"

"Jerya was hardly specific. But you know her. You surely know her better than I do."

"But not as well as I thought, it seems."

"Still, I think you can puzzle it out."

His mind tumbled over for a moment, and then it all came together. "The mountains. They're going into the mountains."

"Aye," the old woman said, "Jerya always loved to look at the mountains, didn't she?"

He didn't ask how she knew that. It still seemed natural to him that Dawnsingers might have ways of knowing that others didn't. "She did."

"But you're not quite right. Not just into the mountains. She wants to cross them."

"But..." His voice failed him. It almost felt as if his heart was failing him. "But there's nothing beyond the mountains. Only..."

"Only the Blistered Lands?" The Singer supplied the words he could not utter. He stared at her in consternation but then, incredibly, she smiled. "That's another of those things you've always believed, isn't it?"

"Aye, I... are you saying that's not true, too?"

"Let me be perfectly honest with you, Rodal: I don't know. Not with absolute certainty. Not even with the same confidence I can tell you a few nights in Unsung Lands won't harm them. The stories are just that; stories, with no foundation. But I can't tell you the Blistered Lands—or whatever *is* there—are safe. No one knows."

He felt like throwing up his hands and stalking away. It seemed as if nothing he'd ever believed was to be relied upon. It was too much. Even Jerya... Jerya had said she wanted to stop deceiving him, but she still hadn't told him half of it. And she certainly hadn't revealed their true purpose.

If... he thought suddenly. *If the old woman's right.* It was just one more touch of strangeness, to be doubting the word, or the judgement, of a Dawnsinger.

How did he know that Dawnsingers weren't always to be trusted? *Because a Dawnsinger told me so.* He wanted to laugh. Then he wanted to cry. Then he wanted to break something. He did none of these things. He looked out over the feathery tops of larches, showing the first hints of autumn gold, and the thought came to him: *There are some things I do know.*

He turned back to the old woman beside him, who was waiting patiently for him to speak. "If the Blistered Lands aren't... well, if they aren't blistered, burnt, what do you think there is, there?"

She shrugged, shoulders bony under white wool. "I simply don't know. No one does. Don't you think that's part of the reason Jerya wants to go?"

"Aye, of course. She would... she'd want to *see*... But even if it isn't immediate death to enter—even supposing they can get across the mountains in the first place—"

"—Aye, I can imagine that will be difficult enough in itself, perhaps dangerous."

"And if they manage it, the best they're likely to find is..." He shrugged helplessly. "Some kind o' wilderness, I reckon."

"It seems most likely, does it not?"

"How does she think they'll manage that? Shelter, food... they can't carry food for more than a few days." He began to think about the prospects, quelling the stirrings of panic, forcing himself to consider it methodically.

There was only one conclusion he could reach. "I have to go after them, don't I?"

The Dawnsinger smiled, almost as if she were proud of him. "Rodal, you have done your given duty by bringing them safely to Delven. What they do now is entirely their own choice; and what you do is yours. I do not advise or counsel you."

He might have wished for her to take the burden from him; but, really, there were no two ways about it. "I can only see it one way."

"Then I will say this." And the old woman—the *Dawnsinger*—reached out and pressed his hand. He stared at bony fingers, swollen knuckles, lying over his own broader hand. "I am easier in my heart knowing you will do this."

"Thank you, Dawnsinger."

"Nothing to thank me for," she said. She patted his hand once, withdrew her arm. "I'm not sending you on an easy path, seems to me. Now... I would imagine you have much to do, Rodal. And I... my bees still need me, whatever else happens."

CHAPTER 29

JERYA

Railu and Jerya left Delven in the stillness before dawn. At the top of the rise, where grey-red rock blended with the long-trodden sand of the path, they turned and looked back. Jerya had a flickering memory of standing in this spot before, when she had come fearful and wondering with Rodal and seen all the faces turn as one to her.

The court was empty now. The ground, unswept, still recorded the comings and goings of the previous day. Behind and above, on the song-stead, Sharess stood motionless. She was looking directly at them, but made neither sign nor sound.

Then the sun's rays caught the highest dewdrops in the trees above them. Sharess's voice swelled so gently Jerya could not locate the exact moment when it become audible.

The sun rose behind them, but their eyes stayed on the suddenly white and glowing figure, on the light flung across the slope of the land beyond. Dawn woke in the ridge-top forests while shadows and mist trapped twilight a little longer in the valleys. Swiftly, following the angle of the land's fall, the morning reached out into the distant plains, while Sharess's voice reached out they knew not where.

The voice fell away as gently as it had risen. Jerya and Railu stood as if paralysed, hand-in-hand, not knowing when their hands had joined. Then Sharess raised a hand. The timepiece on her wrist glinted like dew in the sun. Released, the two returned the salute, then turned quickly to the East.

"We'd better make good time," said Jerya. "Choss knows how long before we're missed, or what they'll do." At least it now seemed clear that Sharess had told no one. She hadn't believed that the old Singer would do so, but at the same time she had never been quite certain.

"Won't they just think we've gone for another walk in the forest?"

"Maybe. It's to be hoped they will. But with all this we've taken...."

She settled the straps of her pack. Some might call it stealing, but Jerya had dismissed that without a second thought. She was a born member of the community, had worked for it long enough; some of the things she had taken she might have stitched herself. Besides, everything she had previously possessed (little enough: a few shifts and undershifts, a woollen shawl, a couple of headcloths, an apron, a second pair of sandals) would surely have found its way back into the common store the day she left.

And then; if Railu had stayed, she would have been another mouth to feed for a long, long time... They would never again be eating Delven produce, beyond the few days' supply in their packs.

She was more concerned that they had not taken enough. From talking with Rodal on the journey—casually, as if it were no more than idle curiosity—she knew that no one had been much further towards the mountains than she had herself. If there were passes, no one could say how high they might be, nor how rough. It had been exactly the answer she expected, and part of her was even glad. It was the same story she had gleaned in the College of the Dawnsingers: no one had crossed the mountains in this Age of the world. Quite likely, no-one had ever even dared to try, because they were outwith the reach of Song.

It meant, of course, that she had to fall back on her own experience, such as it was; make her own estimates of what might be needed; and then to settle for what she could obtain without alerting suspicion. Food had been easy: she could have taken three times as much if they had the means to carry it. The store-chambers were well-filled after a fruitful summer. If anyone had seen her going in or out... It might be a novel thought, but hardly a disturbing one; Dawnsingers too must eat.

Blankets had come from their own beds. Their weight was burdensome, but it was not to be helped. A clear night in the mountains at this time of year might easily see frost. If the weather turned ill, there could be snow. She had longed for a waterproof covering, but if such a thing existed she had been unable to find it.

Their own clothing consisted of whatever she had been able to pick up, creeping dry-mouthed around midnight store-chambers. Everything she'd found was too large for them, boots included. That had been overcome with three pairs of socks each, which made them clumsy but kept their feet warm, and reasonably comfortable. Both were wearing trousers for the first time in their lives, over-large, gathered with belts in which she'd had to punch new holes. They probably looked absurd, but Jerya had not been concerned with appearances. She did not intend anyone else to see them.

Still, the novelty reasserted itself with every stride. She had worn short smocks as a girl, moved into long shifts, more recently accustomed herself to a Dawnsinger's formal robe and the skirt-and-blouse outfits worn within the College. Some Singers wore culottes, but she had never tried them. She had always known air on her legs, the swinging drape of a skirt. Now her legs felt confined, and yet her stride was unconstrained.

While the trail was good, they moved briskly. The land rose evenly, not steep enough to trouble them. Jerya concentrated on settling into her walking and resisted the temptation to look back; when she did she could see nothing of the village but the rock-gate below the thorn-tree and the topmost part of the tor, the up-jutting rocks around the songstead.

Railu followed her trailing gaze. "We've come a fair way."

"Aye, but we must keep moving. It'll get steeper and rougher soon, if I've any memory." It did, and for a while she was absorbed in coaching Railu how to move more economically over uneven ground. For herself, she had little trouble. It was ingrained to watch the ground ahead, pick her footing in advance. The day-long walks of her growing years had been good preparation.

Load-carrying had been another subject for not-so-idle conversation with Rodal on the journey from the City. She reviewed it now, wondering if she had struck the right balance; too much weight on the shoulder-straps perhaps? Not enough on the belt around her hips? The weight seemed bearable so far, though it was more than she had ever borne before, saving for very short distances. Railu, too, seemed to be coping well enough thus far with her (somewhat lighter) load.

The stony track gradually dwindled into a narrow path, too narrow for them to continue side-by-side. Knee-high heather, its summer purple faded, brushed against their legs. Its abundance blanketed the earth, only a few scattered boulders and outcrops protruding. Scattered rowan and a few huddles of juniper were the only trees.

The forward view was confined by the steepening rise of the ground, everywhere the same, right up to the bright skyline. Perhaps it grew a little more rocky, less heathery, as the steepness increased. Just below the crest they met a broken rampart of miniature crags, called Long Knots. They scrambled with some panting and scraping up a narrow cleft to the top, Jerya behind, watching Railu closely, guiding her not to rush, to place hands and feet carefully.

Suddenly there was a vast space before them; first a long fall of the land to a valley whose floor was dappled with the lurid green of bogs and the silvery gleam of open water: Wisket Moss. Beyond, the mountains rose far past their own altitude. Far off in the North was a sense of something high and white, like a pale projection on the curtain of haze. She had never seen it clearer than this, but it was too remote to make out properly. She thought longingly of telescopes.

She guided them to the right, never dipping too close to the treacherous Moss, then rising over a flanking ridge almost parallel to Long Knots. The ground here was liberally scattered with boulders, their sandstone slowly, by centuries, breaking down into coarse greyish sand. The gritty stuff was still morning-damp, firm underfoot. Their footprints would only be visible to someone already right on their trail. Stubborn clumps of heather filled sheltered hollows.

They perched on a boulder a while, to rest and drink, nibble a little honeyed cake, lace their boots a fraction tighter. Then, before their limbs could grow too comfortable, Jerya ordered them on. As they dropped off the ridge-top, angling into a broad combe, the last vestiges of a path faded to nothing. The heather became more continuous, masking the stony ground beneath. It made for an unpredictable footing, and it was near impossible to keep up any semblance of rhythm.

Slowly, laboriously, they worked across the slope. As the sun climbed, already near the zenith, the heat pressed down on the windless combe. The sour-sweet scent of bog-myrtle drifted up from the damper patches. They stopped to remove their heavy woollen pullovers, leaving loose shirts of soft leather. Jerya loosened the laces of hers, letting the air in. Still the sweat soaked her back. She could feel its clammy touch, but there was nothing she could do about it.

The water-bottle was slung on her belt by a hook, so they could drink at will. It was a light weight on her hip by now, and she was concerned that they had found no place to refill it. Once they heard running water, but the sound came from somewhere deep beneath the jumbled rocks of the slope.

As they neared the far side of the combe she selected a course rising obliquely onto the enclosing ridge. There was a short steep climb; she went up slowly, hands on thighs, hardly raising her rate of breathing, but still Railu fell behind. She was trailing by forty or fifty metres when Jerya reached the top. Only once before had she been this far, so she looked eagerly ahead, hoping her memory was accurate.

A great valley ran back to the right, out of sight, deep into the mountains, peaks looming on both sides. The flanking slopes were steep and often craggy. They would have to descend to the valley-floor. Fortunately the way looked, just here, dry and not too rough.

Satisfied enough, she turned back to see how Railu was progressing. She was still a few metres away, head down, moving slowly, her breathing loud on the breeze. Sweat glistened on her scalp, reminding Jerya of the need to cover their heads now the sun was breaking through. She had packed a couple of headcloths—Delven blue, not Dawnsinger white—for just that reason; she would dig them out in a moment.

As Railu reached her she looked ready to collapse on the nearest rock, but Jerya caught her quickly, held her up with an arm around the waist. She looked into her eyes and was about to offer some words of praise and encouragement, though in her heart she was concerned that Railu already looked laboured.

Before she could speak, Railu's face paled and she gave a breathy gasp, halfway to a shriek. Jerya turned sharply, unable to believe the reflection she had seemed to see in Railu's eyes.

CHAPTER 30

RODAL

R odal smiled. In spite of everything, he couldn't help enjoying this moment. It wasn't often you saw Jerya at a loss for words.

But Railu: he felt sorry for her, after a moment. Her eyes were dark with the conviction of betrayal. "What's your worry, my girl?" he asked gently.

She said nothing, stared back, looking flushed and beaten, sweating, shoulders slumped, chest still heaving. Jerya held herself erect, one hand supporting Railu, the other holding together the flaps of her shirt. Even laced, it was hardly a decent garment for a woman, but he found that he cared less than he had cared that day he first saw her without a headcloth. There were many in the city who showed as much or more; asides, there were weightier things at stake than a shadowed half-glimpse of a breast.

"What's *your* worry?" she demanded finally.

"You are," he grinned, still teasing.

"Explain yourself."

"Well... do you really think you can go wandering off through the mountains—just like that?"

"That's our intention."

"You haven't done too well so far, have you? How d'you think I got ahead of you? I've been trailing you all morning. There's not much cover most of the way; half the time I've been in plain view for any with eyes to see... Then while you were floundering in the heather I went round, above the crag. If I hadn't had this pack, I could have run along there."

She started to speak, but he waved a hand and continued. "Well, I've been this far before, perhaps that's cheating. But Railu's half done-in already, and that was the easy part."

"How do you know?"

"I don't. Never been much further than this. And, true, it don't look so bad for a few miles. But beyond the valley's curve, who knows? No one's ever been far past this. Obviously.... you'd be pushed to go many more miles and get back into Sung Lands before the next Dawn."

"You let us worry about the Dawn," growled Jerya.

"Oh, I will. Still leaves plenty of other problems. What d'you do tonight? Ever made a howff from the hole under a boulder? Can you light a fire when everything's wet? Have you a crossbow and the skill to use one?"

Her silence was as good as an answer. "No, no, and no, ain't it? Gossan, Jerya, what have you been thinking? Good thing the Dawnsinger told me you'd gone."

"*Sharess* told you?"

Is that her name? he thought. *Reckon I'd never even thought about her having a name till lately.* "Aye... I was surprised, too. Not that she told me, it makes sense. But that I stopped and listened. l swear if l hadn't learned a few things from you, I'd have stopped my ears and run, before her first word was all out."

"Well, there's a wonder," said Jerya. "How did she know it was you she should tell?"

"That's easy." Railu spoke for the first time. "You said enough about him."

"Did I?" Jerya seemed genuinely surprised.

"Look," he said. "You two know all about time, and such matters; I don't. But I know I'm hungry, and bain't that a measure of time?"

Jerya actually smiled. "As good as any, reckon."

"It's gone noon, anyway," added Railu.

"So why don't we sit? Seeing as we've stopped anyway, and seeing as talk always goes easier with something in the belly... You *did* bring food, didn't you?"

Jerya scowled but said nothing. He was already shrugging off his pack. He had stripped to the waist at the start of the climbing; now he felt the sun on his back, and welcome it was.

He watched in amusement as Jerya disengaged her burden, all the time keeping one hand at the front of her shirt. Then she turned to root in the pack, and he saw the dark saturation of sweat in the leather.

"That's bad," he commented, "It won't dry under your pack, and tonight when it's cool it'll chill you."

She looked at him over her shoulder. "But what can I do?"

"Change your shirt if you've a spare... no? well, next best thing would be to dry it on a warm rock, let the sun dry your back at the same time. If I weren't here you'd do that, wouldn't you? Except that if I weren't here you might not think of it."

He was about to add, "I'll look the other way," but Railu was already unlacing her shirt. "Where would be the best place?" she asked.

This ready response was so unexpected that Rodal simply answered the question. "One of those rocks there—the sunny side—round a bit where it's already been warmed." He tried not to stare, but it was impossible. Railu seemed quite unconcerned, even unaware. He could not make sense of her. Even on the crossing of the Scorched Plains, she had done no more than relent a little in her suspicion of him—and yet, now, there was this.

Jerya still had her back to him. For a moment she was motionless, then with an almost convulsive movement wrenched her shirt over her head. He could hardly breathe. She did not turn, as he had hoped, or feared—which, he could not tell. Instead, she pulled a cloth—a headcloth, it looked like—from her pack and wrapped it round herself, knotting it at the front. She placed her shirt alongside Railu's before she faced him. There was a strange look to her, almost as if she were embarrassed. It was not like her to be embarrassed, thought Rodal, and she was hardly indecent at all, certainly not by comparison with Railu.

He sat down where he was, facing North to put the sun at his back. Jerya took her seat on another boulder a few feet to his side. Railu was beyond her, almost hidden, but Jerya was speaking low to her, and after a moment she, too, extricated a cloth and—though he could not see clearly—it was evident she was also binding it round her chest. Again, Rodal hardly knew whether to be sorry or relieved.

In the City, he had heard, there were places you could go where women displayed their breasts—and more—to anyone who cared to pay the price of admission. Had it not been for Annyt, he supposed he might have been a little tempted... but only a little. Especially at the prices he'd been told they charged...

The lads back in Delven had sometimes drawn crude pictures, or scratched them on the rocks by the swimming-dub. He was no innocent; he had shared the jocularity, but he had always sensed, as some of the others seemed not to, that their sketches were not much like the real thing. They could hardly even be matched with the shape of a woman as seen through her clothes.

Sometimes you could see a good deal through a woman's clothes. Even the white robe of a Dawnsinger... He had heard no comments; perhaps there had not been any. But he had seen glances, back in Delven, and had read the thoughts behind them. He knew how some minds ran.

Jerya was gazing at him, he realised. She could not know what he'd been thinking, but *he* knew, and his face grew hot. He buried himself in his pack, taking longer than strictly necessary to dig out bannock and pale sharp cheese from Delven's goats.

"Reckon you should say your piece," Jerya said after they'd all made a start on their food.

"My piece?"

"It's simple enough, isn't it? Why are you here, Rodal?"

He took another bite of bannock. He could see Jerya fuming, but needed that moment to think. "That day—crossing the Scorched Plains, last day before Delven. When you said you were going into Unsung Lands. I should ha' known right then. And you said half the things I'd always believed weren't truth. *I should ha' known.* But I didn't guess, the Dawnsinger had to rub my nose in it."

"What did she say?"

He screwed up his face, trying to remember the exact words. It was hard to recall clearly; truth of it, those moments, face to face with the old Singer on that hill-ledge with the hives, had been the strangest of any since it all began. "She said a lot. But I remember this... 'The stories are just that; stories. No foundation to them. But I can't tell you the Blistered Lands are safe. No one knows.' And she smiled a little, and she said, 'Don't you think that's part of the reason Jerya wants to go?'"

Jerya said nothing. Beyond her, Railu was leaning forward to see him, watching his face.

"'I can't tell you the Blistered Lands are safe,'" he repeated. "Don't that concern you?"

"Let me tell you what I was told in the College," said Jerya. "The true Blistered Lands were further South. They believe the land beyond these mountains—" Her hand lifted a few inches, half a gesture towards the peaks— "Was uninhabited in the Age Before, and so it wasn't touched by their wars. And besides, it was centuries ago. Even the places that were devastated should be safe now."

"'Should be'?" He flung the words back at her. "No one knows, is what you're saying."

"No one knows," she agreed equably.

"Then—"

"—Did you know what you were going to find in the city when we set out?" She smiled, but the words pierced Rodal with thoughts of Annyt. "Nothing's certain in this life."

He could think of a dozen answers, but he could only voice one at a time. "Nothing's certain, but does that always mean one path's as good as any other?" Before she could answer, he forged on. "Well, suppose it's right what they told you... though how d'you know that's true when you say they lied about other things? Still, suppose it is. Suppose what's on the other side bain't so different from here." He waved an arm about him; rocks and dry heather, and the mountains vast and still. "Just plain wilderness. How d'you think you'll get on? How d'you think you'd get on trying to live *here*?"

"I wouldn't," she said. Apparently calm, she took another bite, chewed, swallowed, then said. "I'd head further down. On this side of the mountains, most people live in the lowlands. I think Delven's higher than most places, and it's not the easiest place to live. Why would we make things hard for ourselves on the other side?"

"But you don't *know*."

"No, and I've never pretended otherways. Look, Rodal, it's simple, really. Ihatever you say, I'm going on." She paused. "Railu can make her own choice. Maybe she sees things differently now she's seen Delven."

"Maybe I see things differently after this morning," said Railu. He saw something flicker across Jerya's face. Well, it had been obvious to any onlooker that Railu was making heavy weather of it; perhaps Jerya was thinking she would get along better on her own. And she might well be right. He wondered if Railu would have more to say, but she remained silent. Was that hope in her eyes, though? Was it, even... *trust*?

"Beside," said Jerya, "If you're so determined to drag us back... What's all that in your pack?"

"Ah, well. Guess I knew I probably wouldn't be able to make you see reason. So I thought I'd better be prepared for the worst."

She ate another contemplative mouthful, then asked abruptly, "Rodal? What about Annyt?"

It was, perhaps, the one question he'd hoped she would not ask. He'd reckoned Jerya—and Railu—had enough to cope with, without the added burden of his private worries. he hated to think of Annyt reading his note, wished he was a better hand at writing... *better not think of that.*

"We are not betrothed, as you know," he said with care. "By the custom of the city, we cannot be until we have known each other for a year. Why should I not be there before that year is ended? I have her promise to wait that long... and I know that with the two of you along I won't lose count of the days."

"A year?" Jerya sounded incredulous.

He shrugged. "If you're really determined to go through with this, I may as well do what I can to give you the best possible chance."

"Does that mean you're coming with us?"

"*If* you're truly bent on going on. Don't see you leave me any choice."

About the Author

Jon Sparks has been writing fiction as long as he can remember, but for many years made his living as an (award-winning) outdoor writer and photographer, specialising in landscape, travel and outdoor pursuits, particularly walking, climbing and cycling. He lives in Garstang, Lancashire, with his partner Bernie and several bikes.

If you enjoyed this book...

There are several more volumes to come. To be the first to hear about these, and to get other news and insights, please consider signing up to my mailing list: go to tinyurl.com/4dvf7pt. There's a free short story as a thank you.

The Shattered Moon website is at https://www.jonsparksauthor.co. I also have a Facebook Page at https://www.facebook.com/profile.php?id=100089266940531. (Sorry, e-book readers, I have to put these links in full for the sake of anyone who's reading the print edition.)

Acknowledgments

I said it in the dedication and I'll say it again here: my partner Bernie is my first, last, and best beta-reader, and a whole lot more.

Thanks are also due to many others who've read and commented on my work, notably Marion Smith and Jago Westaway. I've learned a lot from the many excellent editors I've worked with in my non-fiction career, particularly Ronald Turnbull, Sue Viccars, John Manning, and Seb Rogers. Many other members of the Outdoor Writers and Photographers Guild have helped me too.

I'm also indebted to readers and editors from various SF magazines who've taken the time to offer feedback on short story submissions; and to literary agents who've said nice things about my submissions, especially (on two occasions) Julie Crisp.

Every writer surely starts out as a reader, and I've never stopped. Posthumous thanks go to two writers who particularly inspired me; Arthur Ransome as a formative influence, and Ursula K Le Guin: a legendary writer as well as a writer of legend.

Lightning Source UK Ltd.
Milton Keynes UK
UKHW011824020223
416378UK00001B/1